The Unfriended

The Unfriended

Jane McLoughlin

QUARTET

First published in 2015 by Quartet Books Limited
A member of the Namara Group
27 Goodge Street, London W1T 2LD
Copyright © Jane McLoughlin 2015
The right of Jane McLoughlin to be identified
as the author of this work has been asserted
by her in accordance with the
Copyright, Designs and Patents Act 1988
All rights reserved
No part of this book may be reproduced in
any form or by any means without prior
written permission from the publisher
A catalogue record for this book
is available from the British Library
ISBN 978 0 7043 7394 5
Typeset by Josh Bryson
Printed and bound in Great Britain by
T J International Ltd, Padstow, Cornwall

This book is dedicated to all the special women I did and didn't know at Trinity College, Dublin in the Sixties for whom that time and that place was truly an Age of Enlightenment

The
Unfriended

Part One

(

But they're all boring; as boring as all other young women just starting at university. And they think they know everything.

That's what Ffion Finlay thought as she walked into the bedroom. And the others who would share the room in Trinity Hall, the women's residence for Trinity College, Dublin, seemed to feel the same.

Ffion met three pairs of disappointed eyes reflecting her own shock of anti-climax.

'Yuck!' she said.

Christ, she thought, how will I ever remember which is which? She looked them over, but could find nothing to mark anyone out; just Big, Bigger and Biggest. Here I am, about to take flight on what should be the best time of my life, she told herself, and it's about as exciting as a Church social in Surrey. Whatever did I think I was doing coming here?

The biggest of the big girls smiled and said, 'We'd better make the best of it; we're stuck with each other for the next year at least. My name's Ellie. Ellie Bassett.'

No one had anything to say. Ffion thought, that says it all.

The middling big girl said, 'I'm Hilary Roberts. Perhaps we should get acquainted.'

They all looked as though they'd rather not. Nor share this dull white room with its barrack-like beds covered by rose pink candlewick bedspreads which had long ago given up on making the room look cheerful, as had the faded flowered curtains and the grey Tintawn carpet.

Ellie said, 'We could play the Truth Game. It's a good way to get to know each other.'

Ffion said, 'No one needs the Truth Game to tell us you're the eldest in a large family.'

Ffion, the only one of the four of them who already looked grown up, made it sound as though being part of a big family was something Ellie should be ashamed of. After all, it was the start of the Swinging Sixties; they had come to university in Ireland to forget about being dutiful daughters.

Perhaps they were all a little in awe of Ffion, who was really unfairly beautiful; like a film star with her flowing black hair and her deep blue, almost violet, eyes.

'How can you possibly know that?' Ellie said.

Hilary, brought up to think charitable thoughts, wished Ellie hadn't asked that question. Let it go, Hilary was willing her, you'll only encourage her to make a fool of you. But Ellie, heavily-built, ponderous, beady-eyed behind decidedly cheap-looking NHS spectacles, looked like a girl who wouldn't let a subject drop in a hurry.

Ffion's voice was silk. 'It doesn't take rocket science. It's the way you automatically try to take charge. Typical of the inevitable fascist tendency in big families.'

Hilary wondered if this exotic creature was making a joke. Should I laugh? she asked herself.

Hilary didn't want to play the Truth Game, not now or ever. But she didn't dare say so. Fresh-faced, with pale eyes seeming perpetually wide-open in amazement, she was too obviously a girl without guile. She didn't want to have to tell the truth, it was too boring. But she couldn't lie. She could imagine Ffion's chilling, inscrutable gaze turned on her to deliver what the Rev Dad would call the mot juste; or rather, *les mots justes*: A formless blob who won't stand up for herself, a real daughter of the vicarage longing to be liked. Who gives a damn?

Ffion doesn't have to speak out aloud, Hilary thought, just give one look with those basilisk eyes; and that'll be me put

2

in my place for the rest of my time here, labelled Not Wanted on Voyage.

Then thinking of the Rev Dad brought on a wave of homesickness almost as bad as feeling seasick on the boat coming over from Holyhead. Fighting back tears Hilary thought, I want to go home. I don't belong with these girls, what am I doing here? Oh, God, I wish I'd never come.

'What the feck's that supposed to mean?'

The sudden harsh Northern Irish accent startled them like the crack of a whip. It was the first time Sandra had opened her mouth.

They all stared at her. Sandra looked like one of them, more or less. More was a monumental bosom, less because the rest of her was quite small. They'd assumed she was an ordinary English mouse, she even looked like a rodent; and now the moment she opened her mouth she was suddenly revealed as hostile and incomprehensible; and alien. It was such a shock they didn't even notice that word.

Then Ffion raised an expressive eyebrow. She murmured, 'A revolting peasant?'

Ellie felt guilty at her own immediate judgmental reaction to Sandra's voice. So she made herself sound extra friendly, asking, 'Where do you come from?' As if she cared.

Sandra gave her a pitying look that plainly said that this overweight schoolgirl must be dim-witted. 'Belfast,' she said. 'Can't you tell?'

Ellie forced a smile to hide her alarm. 'Oh,' she said. And then, because that sounded rude, she added, 'No.'

Shut up, Ellie told herself, don't let her see I'm beginning to be afraid she's not housetrained.

She turned to the others, saying, 'Come on, we might as well play, what else is there to do?'

Sandra shrugged. 'What's the point?'

Ellie started to explain. 'The point is it gives us a chance to sort of set out our wares as the people we're going to be over the next year. We can say who we want to be, not who we are, and no one will know.'

Ffion grimaced. She thought, Oh God, that patronising and slightly desperate voice comes from years of trying to reason with children. My God, there's no way I'm going to survive a whole year without killing Ellie Bassett.

She looked around the dreary institutional room, made more depressing by the scattering of framed family groups already set out on the white-painted hospital-like cupboards beside each bed. Like identity cards, explaining everything anyone needed to know about where these unpromising women came from.

On Hilary's personal surface sat a round tin alarm clock with a smiley face. Beside the clock, a shell-encrusted framed photo of a cheery man in a dog collar sitting on a bench beside a woman in a drooping crepe dress, her colourless hair pinned back with schoolgirlish Kirbigrips.

Sandra's bedside space sported a worn leather-bound book stamped with rubbed gold lettering – T E BI LE.

Ffion allowed herself to hope that the girl was a spy for a foreign government working undercover, and this was her code book. That wouldn't be boring. But of course it was a Bible; and next to the Bible, a picture of what looked like a page cut from a newspaper, showing a tall, thin bald man in thick-rimmed spectacles shaking hands with Dr Ian Paisley. The two men stood in front of a small terraced house which looked as though it was waiting in trepidation to be devoured by cranes suspended from a massive gantry which loomed behind the street. That must be the shipyard. Why should I think of Cerberus and the Gates of Hell?

Ellie's reminder of home should have been scarier, a group photo of gurning adolescents – the two fattest and tallest

4

were presumably the parents – taken in what seemed to be a sandpit in a fenced back garden. Team Bassett, going great guns in the suburban Good Citizens League? Ffion's heart went out to a single broken-limbed fruit tree struggling to survive in that barren place.

Ellie was still talking, prepared to repeat herself until she was sure the others understood what she was trying to say. 'Being here, away from home, we're all reinventing ourselves. We're here to give birth to ourselves in new identities. Haven't any of you read Ronnie Laing? You've all got to read him, he makes everything clear. I've seen *Knots* four times.'

There was an awkward silence. They were all afraid they were going to laugh. Ellie seemed so serious, and so, well, weird…

Sandra yawned. In a Northern Irish accent, Ffion noted, who'd have thought that was possible. But then they say garden birds sing in strong regional accents.

Ellie went on, trying to explain but not really quite understanding herself what she wanted to say. 'We've a responsibility to redefine womanhood, don't you think? We're different from all the women who've gone before, thanks to feminism, but now it's up to us to be the first post-feminists.'

Perhaps even Ellie realized she had lost the others' attention. She added quickly, 'We're pioneers, the ones who've got to draw up the terms for what being a woman means for the future.'

Gawd help us, Ffion thought.

And Hilary's eyes were filling with tears. Surely she couldn't be uplifted by Ellie's stirring message? But in truth Ellie's revved-up cadences had reminded her of the Rev Dad's sermons. She felt more homesick than ever. I wish I'd never come here, she told herself, I could be peacefully sitting with Mother in front of a roaring fire, watching *Sunday Night at the London Palladium* and not thinking about anything.

These women here all despise me; I've nothing in common with them.

Sandra sounded puzzled. She interrupted Ellie, 'You mean we can play the game by making up our answers and say we're anything we want? And then whatever we've said will be the truth?'

There didn't seem much point to the Truth Game when they didn't have to tell the truth.

Then Ellie said, 'Oh, come on, we might as well play the game. I'll start by answering Ffion, even if it wasn't a proper question. Yes, I've got seven younger sisters. My Mum goes out to work so I had to take charge of the others after school. Satisfied?'

Sandra blurted out, 'How the hell did you get to come here?'

They all took it that Sandra meant how could Ellie's parents afford to send her to university and how did Ellie manage to pass the necessary exams to qualify to come to Trinity with all those siblings holding her back?

Ellie said, 'That's easy, I got a County grant, just like most of the rest of us English students here.'

But Sandra told herself, that's not what I meant. What I want to know is what motivated her so she dared to break away from those family obligations and strike out on her own. How come she dared do something so self-centred?

There was a brief silence.

My God, Ellie asked herself, is Sandra so foreign she doesn't know we get grants? Don't people from Northern Ireland count as fully-fledged English?

They all looked at Sandra but no one dared to come out with the question. Was Northern Ireland the same as England? Presumably Wales was. Holyhead was in Wales, going back to England they'd go straight through Wales without stopping, so it was a fair guess it would be the same as England. But

6

what about Scotland, that had a border, didn't it? And Belfast could be like Dublin and you needed a passport to go there.

Another silence.

'OK, it's my turn.' Ffion's eyes narrowed as she looked at Hilary. 'Are you still a virgin? Have you ever had a boyfriend?'

Sandra gasped. 'What kind of vindictive cow are you, asking her that?'

Hilary's earliest memory, when she was about two, was of a German V-1 rocket falling on her house. Not that she even knew there was a war on at that age, but Ffion's question made her feel a bit the same way as she felt then, as though the world had come to an end with a huge explosion she didn't hear because it had already deafened her. Then the front of the house disappeared and her clothes were blown off in the hot blast as though she'd been skinned. All the air was sucked out of the world, replaced with thick dust not falling, but thrusting upwards to fill the empty sky where the roof had been.

Now the impact of Ffion's question felt as bad as that; something about the rudeness of it, the unexpected brutality, the ripping away of her protective covering.

And Hilary reacted as she now realized she'd reacted then, because she remembered the feeling of being helpless; except now she wasn't a baby any more, she could say what she felt. She was angry.

'I don't want to play this stupid game,' she said. 'You're asking the wrong person; ask the men who haven't tried to make love to me.'

They all stared at her in amazement. Even Ffion.

Sandra said, doubting, 'What, never?'

Ellie said, 'But someone must've tried it on. When they were drunk at least... Hasn't anyone ever even tried to kiss you?'

'We're not that kind of a family,' Hilary said stiffly.

7

No one could think of anything to say to that.

Ffion smiled at Sandra. 'You want to know what kind of cow I am?' she said. 'Fair question, you're not the first to wonder. All I can say, it must be in the genes; I'm my mother's daughter. She really is a fucking cow.'

Hilary said, 'What about your dad?'

'He varies.'

'What do you mean, varies?'

'There's a succession of them. As Beverly – she doesn't like me to call her Mum – gets older, they get younger. These days she keeps me out of their way. She tells everyone we're sisters.'

Ellie said, 'She must feel guilty? Perhaps there's something wrong with her; you know, some psychological disorder … or TB. That's supposed to make women into nymphomaniacs?'

'No, she's afraid I'll steal them, it's that simple. Suits me, she pays me to make myself scarce.' Ffion laughed. No one else did.

Ellie asked her, 'Have you ever been in love?'

'No, thank God. I'd rather have a terminal illness. Except of course love is a terminal illness, in the end it kills almost everything worth living for.'

Ellie didn't like that; she didn't think disease was a subject to make flip jokes about. Sounding indignant, she said, 'How can you say that? You've just told us you've never been in love; you don't know anything about it.'

'Do you?'

Hilary interrupted, 'You don't mean that, Ffion, not seriously. Surely that's something we can all agree on, it's the whole point of a woman's life to marry the man she loves and bear his children? Isn't it?'

'Yuck!' Ffion said.

Sandra had never before doubted that she thought much the same as Hilary about a woman's role, but hearing it said out loud like that, in Hilary's slightly churchy tones, she felt suddenly downcast by womanhood. 'At least as university graduates we'll have something that can benefit our children...'

'Thus significantly advancing the calibre of the human stockpile, you think?' Ffion mocked her. 'Dream on.'

Ellie smiled as though with superior knowledge. Perhaps, having all those siblings, she knew what she was talking about. 'It's the 1960s,' she said, 'we don't have to choose. We can have it all – wife and mother, and a career. That's what I was trying to say earlier about new beginnings. It's up to us now. We decide for ourselves. Being a woman can cover anything we like.'

Ffion lit a cigarette and blew smoke rings which twisted out of shape in a draught from the window. One day, she thought, there will be women at the top running countries and institutions, but their power will come from dissociating themselves from women like Ellie Bassett.

She stubbed out her cigarette. Ellie's face flinched with disapproval. She reached into a drawer and held up an atomizer to spray toilet water towards the stub.

'All I want is to have a child of my own,' Hilary said. 'I'm not looking for anything more than that.'

'Then why are you here?' Sandra's accent made her sound harsh.

'I need to find a man to marry me first. I hoped to meet someone here.'

No one dared ask why she used the past tense. Had she given up hope already?

'There's nothing wrong with that,' Ellie said.

Ffion smiled at Ellie, then lit another cigarette, inhaled deeply and blew out a long, slow stream of smoke. It's a declaration of war, Ffion told herself.

Then she thought, Perhaps there's hope for the other two; they may not be as boring as they look. But Ellie Bassett?

Being boring is in her genes, she won't change. But it could be fun trying.

Ffion put a framed picture of Jean-Paul Belmondo, signed 'To the gorgeous Ffion with love and kisses from Cheri' beside the ashtray on the top of her bedside cupboard. 'Well,' she said, 'let the game begin!'

2

Ellie Bassett, Ffion Finlay, Sandra Redmond and (always the afterthought) Hilary Roberts, spent the next week or so finding their feet in their new lives. Under the spell of Trinity College, they were. Entranced by the physical beauty of the college buildings. Awed by the subtle strangeness of Dublin.

Each responded in her own way to the difference of the place from anything she'd known before.

Years of children's bedtimes telling tales of passion and betrayal among ancient Celtic kings in crumbling strongholds shrouded in mist and mystical gloom filled Ellie's head with dreams. Mythic figures like Brian Boru and Finn McCool and Hugh the O'Neill made her heart sing with romantic yearning.

So when Ellie stepped off the teeming pavement in College Green and walked in through the front gate of Trinity, she was transported to a calm, fortified sanctuary where she took it for granted that a diminishing band of high-minded scholars and poets gallantly defended her anglicized vision of Ireland against barbaric hordes outside the gate in 20th century Dublin. 'Twas ever so, she thought, *Baile Atha Cliath*, named for the stockade the early English settlers built to keep marauding natives out.

Once inside, Ellie was transported back to an imagined era of enlightenment; but Trinity was real, and in the present. Here were real people with real things to do on every side, making their way across the dappled grey cobbles of Front Square; on the way to lectures they propped bicycles against the chains keeping students off the grass around the

Campanile; undergraduates in dusty black gowns hurried past the magisterial Graduates' Memorial Building to a tutorial in some don's rooms behind the glowing redbrick walls of the old rose-red brick Rubrics with their numerous and elongated chimneys.

This morning Ellie stopped to listen to a short, fat, tousled leprechaun who had taken up a position on the rain-glistening steps of the Chapel to proclaim poetry. At least, it sounded like poetry. He sounded like Dylan Thomas. So magical was the music of his voice that for a fleeting moment Ellie believed that she, not Dylan, had died and gone to Heaven. Stupid, she thought, I don't understand a word this man says.

She moved closer to the poet and laid a coin on the step in front of him.

He looked at her; and, meeting his vivid blue eyes, she felt as though he had siphoned all the thoughts from her brain before he threw back his head and laughed.

She felt shaken and moved across to a pillar she could lean against.

'Did you hear that?' she asked someone also standing around.

The answer made it impossible to acknowledge that something amazing had happened to her. The man seemed unaware. He said, 'Brendan? Our resident poet. He's a junior lecturer in the English department.' And that was it.

But the poet's sapphire eyes were so cold. She thought, I didn't exist to him. He had nothing to share with me. Did he think I was making fun of him? Or that I assumed he was a beggar? No, he didn't think of me at all, not even as an insect he would step on. He seemed to want to exclude me. And yet to me he was a revelation.

She walked across Front Square, not sure where she was going, but wanting to take in the aura of the place. A distillation, rather; her own unique essence she would wear like perfume for life. This, Ellie thought, is where I belong. For the rest of my life this place will always be a part of me. I shall never be as happy as I am now.

Two old men sweeping up leaves around the Campanile leaned on their rakes to watch her pass. They were talking about the Tans. She had only a vague idea. Her instinct was to turn round and shout at them, 'Don't stare at me like that, don't you know it's disrespectful?'

A sheet of paper only half-glued to a wall advertised *The Playboy of The Western World* this week at the Abbey; And *The Plough and The Stars* in two weeks' time.

The autumn morning air was wonderful, with the scent of wet leaves; and the unstained blue sky. How perfect, and she was young.

She saw Sandra approaching and turned aside to avoid her. That voice, after the poet's, she couldn't bear it. It's all right, she hasn't seen me.

But Sandra did see Ellie, and was glad not to have to talk to her. Sandra's first reaction to Trinity was defensive. She couldn't find words for what she felt, even in her thoughts she simply used obscenities more often and more vehemently.

Sandra was daunted by the elitism she detected from the elegant 18th century aura of Trinity's inward-looking squares, as though the university had turned its back on the living city. She felt excluded because of the oppressive weight of tradition here, resenting what she saw as an absence of intellectual practicality in everything Trinity seemed to stand for.

It made her conscious that, coming from a city fathered by the Industrial Revolution, she and her Caledonian tribe had no part in the legendary nature of Hibernia.

She spent her time finding her way around, looking for what she wanted to see; the shabbiness of the buildings, the obsolete facilities that, she thought, were not fit for purpose in

13

a ground-breaking modern factory manufacturing graduates for a modern technical age. It seemed to her that even in their own minds the students were accidental to the structure and appearance and the past of this place of learning.

By the end of the second week she thanked her Protestant God that this was how it was; she was leaning on a lamppost outside No.6, Front Square, the preserve of women students. She was wishing. Not wishing anything in particular, just a general undirected yearning which often occupied her mind since she'd come to Dublin. And then Sandra felt her brain suddenly able to breathe as though a cast-iron skull-lining had cracked open in her head and she was released from a great weight of accumulated preconceptions. She had discovered the great gift Trinity offered, the space and freedom to think her own thoughts. She had suddenly, hardly thinking of it, let go of the Hand of God. She told herself, glad and a little ashamed at the thought; I never, ever, want to go back to Belfast.

Sandra tried to explain some of this to Hilary one evening when they were drying their hair in their room at Trinity Hall. But it was pointless. Hilary could not understand.

She wasn't unsympathetic; she was struggling to make sense of her own reactions. Hilary knew before she came that the majority of Trinity's two thousand or so students came from England. It hadn't even dawned on her that the university could be Irish. She chose TCD because she was afraid to try for Oxford. If she failed to get into Oxford, her shame at letting down the Rev Dad, once a scholar at St John's, would be dreadful. Everyone would know. Among her parents' friends no one knew enough about Trinity to hold opinions about what going there might say about Hilary.

And Dublin was a beautiful place, and many great men had graduated from Trinity; men like Jonathan Swift and Edmund Burke, Samuel Beckett and Oscar Wilde – though

Hilary didn't mention that last name to Rev Dad. Also it was an Anglican university, a bastion of the Protestant Ascendancy; Irish Catholics were actually forbidden to go there unless they got a special dispensation from their bishop. So any Catholics would be English, which was surely more than half-way to being Protestant. The Rev Dad would approve.

So Hilary had not expected, as she disembarked from the ferry in Ireland, to find herself in a foreign country. The air itself didn't smell like English air, carrying as it did the whiff of the Guinness brewery with a smell of decay from the Liffey mud. Even familiar everyday things had un-English names. Hilary blushed every time she thought of how she'd walked into the men's WC at the *Busaras* because, given a choice of *fir* and *mna*, she'd thought than *mna* must mean Men.

Fortunately an old Irish woman had stopped her and put her right. Then the cab driver insisted on carrying her heavy case to the door of Trinity Hall, which embarrassed her because he was quite elderly and half her size.

She remembered the old woman and the taxi driver her first day in college as she tried to find her way to her lecture, on Anglo-Irish Literature. None of the English students, nor anyone else, tried to help her out.

Hilary didn't need to be told why. Simply they didn't even register her existence. People didn't, they never had. English people didn't. It occurred to Hilary that those foreign Irish people had.

Even coming over on the boat – it was an Irish ferry – Hilary had started to worry about the way the English treated the Irish in their own country. They ordered them about, practically saying 'My man' and giving them tips as though there had been no 1916 and no 1922, and they thought Ireland were part of the Raj.

She asked herself, Why are they so arrogant, so sure of themselves? I'd understand if I thought they knew why people

15

from other countries don't like them, but they don't. Then it would be bravado. They've never known what it's like to be a defeated people. Except for the Normans, who came from France, had French names and spoke French but somehow were not French. The Dutch also. The Glorious Revolution, with drunken Dutch soldiery kicking Englishmen out of their way in the streets of London. They also ignored that.

She thought, is it because they're so self-absorbed? It seems to me that all the English are, with those public school accents of theirs, and that air of having an automatic right to anything they want. What do real Irish people think of their insouciant air of triumphalism in a defeated country?

And she thought, I don't want to be seen as one of them. On the bus into town in the morning, in the Cafolla coffee bar in O'Connell Street drinking too-milky coffee from a Pyrex cup, or simply walking the streets, it was the same; I'm sorry, she wanted to tell the Irish people outside Trinity's walls, I'm sorry for what we did to you.

But her silent cry was drowned by the screeching of seagulls gathered on the statues of Burke and Oliver Goldsmith outside Front Gate.

And Ffion?

Whereas each of the other three was experiencing Trinity in her own, wholly subjective, way, Ffion was bent on using the university to pursue a personal agenda.

She appreciated the beauty of the college and the intellectual freedom outside the English education system as much as the others, but she saw it as something she could harness solely to her own interests. Before she suggested to her mother, Beverly, that it might be to the advantage of them both if she went to university outside England, Ffion had done her homework.

She flirted with the idea of the Sorbonne, but her schoolgirl French was not good enough. She liked the idea of America, but knew Beverly would balk at paying for a university education.

Ffion decided that Trinity would be the perfect career move. She knew her strengths and if they weren't exactly catered for on the TCD syllabus, this old trollop of a place wouldn't let her down.

A good proportion of the male students were the sons of rich or influential men happy to get the layabouts off their hands for four years. That meant, Ffion thought, there'd be a supply of young men who were rich and stupid and bent on having a good time. Meat and drink it was to Ffion.

The beautiful Trinity buildings looked like a ready-made film set for historical drama, convincing as ancient Rome or 18th century London, or even among the buildings round Botany Bay, as grey Dickensian grim Victorian tenements. Anyway, the new film studios at Ardmore, not far away, promised the chance for someone with Ffion's looks and self-confidence to get work as an extra at least.

And Ardmore offered access to film stars and movie moguls who would stay in the fashionable Dublin hotels and eat and drink out in Dublin restaurants and bars. Ffion was in her element.

Already, before the end of the first week, they had all discovered that they had almost nothing in common. Except, Hilary told herself, that they didn't like Ffion. She said to the other two, one evening when they'd watched this exotic cuckoo in their nest getting ready to go out, 'What is it about her?'

It was a rhetorical question, of course. Each thought they knew the answer but they wouldn't want to admit it. Sandra hated the way being near Ffion's stellar beauty made her feel awkward and ugly in comparison. Worse still was being aware that even if she didn't feel awkward and ugly, no one would notice her when Ffion was around anyway. It wasn't just looks, either; everything about Sandra that people judged her by – what she said, her personality, her wit – paled to insignificance beside Ffion. Indeed, at the mere *thought* of Ffion. She stunts me, Sandra told herself. Who wants a constant reminder that one is ordinary?

She looked at Hilary sprawled on her bed eating fistfuls of crisps from a family pack. She'd make a great cartoon character for a child's book – Hilly the Hungry Hippo. How would she have answered her own question? That fecking Rev Dad must've brought her up not ever to ask a question she didn't know the answer to.

Ffion's looks won't be what bothers *her*, Sandra thought. Look at her, no one who gives a damn what people think of her would let herself be seen in public like that; and we *share* this bedroom, it is a public place. She doesn't even bother to brush her hair most days, just cleans her teeth, scrubs her face till it shines, pulls on jeans and a sloppy joe and that's it.

Hilary looked up and caught Sandra watching her. What's she thinking, she wondered, she looks miserable. Poor Sandra, she's so bitter about everything. Talk about an inferiority complex. She's eaten up with jealousy of Ffion. Of course, now that Ellie's learning all that social psychology guff, she'd probably say that Sandra's suppressing lesbian tendencies towards Ffion, which seems to me a pretentious way of saying she's fascinated by her. We all are.

Hilary didn't like Ffion; she thought her hard and arrogant, even cruel. There was one guy who was positively besotted by her. He waited outside their bedroom window at Trinity Hall, the one which looked out on the street, begging her to come out to him. He howled like a wolf. 'If you don't, I'll kill myself,' he wailed. Ffion threw up the window and flung out a bottle of aspirin. 'Have a nice death on me,' she shouted, 'now for God's sake go away and get on with it.'

What happened to him? Hilary worried for days that he had killed himself, but she never heard of him again. I'd have heard if he had, she thought; but would she? Ffion wouldn't bother mentioning it.

At least the woman gives us something to talk about among ourselves, Hilary thought. And it was true; they wouldn't have much to say to each other if they couldn't disapprove of Ffion. It was friendship of a kind. Better than the Truth Game as a way of getting to know each other.

But what did Ellie think? Ellie lay awake in the dark asking herself that question. The sound of the others' breathing in their sleep was as distinctive as language. Except Ffion. She made no sound. Sleeping, we revert to animals, Ellie thought, but not Ffion. Ellie didn't know why, but Ffion made her afraid. I can't control her, she thought, she threatens me. But with what; and why?

Ffion won't play her part as a woman, Ellie thought; she refuses to be one of us. Women have to stick together, but Ffion is indifferent to us all. She's outside our control; and she won't take responsibility for being a woman. But responsibility for what, or whom?

Ellie listened to her room-mates' breathing and she thought she understood. Sociological studies showed that women living together menstruated at the same time, as though they were atoms of one immense physical presence. Ellie imagined that in student cold water bedsits in crumbling Georgian houses in Merrion Square; in prim terrace houses in Rathgar and Rathmines and in the spare bedrooms of family homes in Foxrock and Blackrock; all over Dublin and England, Europe and America, young women slept, inhaling the empowering oxygen of emancipation.

Ellie started up in the dark. She wanted to shout out, 'Our time is near'. Women who cherish the weak, the old, the sick, the young; the sad, and the maimed, the mad and the lonely; women who understand what is needed of them, not men. Men can make speeches and policy and money, they play power games and they start wars, but it is love and the demand for care which will take over the world.

What all of us could do if we believed it, Ellie told herself. She shook her head, she wasn't even sure she believed it herself.

Sandra sat up in bed and turned on her beside light. 'What the feck's the matter?' she said. 'What the hell do you think you're doing, it's two o'clock in the morning?'

'Don't you see,' Ellie said, 'it's happening around us and we're part of it.'

Sandra groaned and turned off the light. 'Oh, go back to sleep,' she said. 'You've had a nightmare, that's all.'

'Women's priorities are what will count,' Ellie said, smiling to herself as she lay down and pulled up the bed covers. In her head she added to Ffion, You can't win.

'Oh, go to fecking sleep,' Sandra muttered in the darkness.

3

And then Ellie met Matt.

Hilary and Sandra, getting ready for their first college dance, a semi-formal 'do' where Freshers could meet other first-years and more battle weary students could check out the new talent, persuaded Ellie to go with them. She'd planned a night in.

'Oh come on, you might meet someone,' Sandra said.

Hilary said, 'What's to lose? Best to attack in force.'

They were shy with each other that night. In their best clothes, their hair carefully done, they looked at each other through highly-decorated eyes and it was as though they had turned into Picasso images of their daytime selves. Painted to look what they ain't, as the song went. Faintly ridiculous. But there was magic in the air. Anything could happen.

The chairs lining the walls of the Exam Hall were already mostly occupied by groups of self-conscious, war-painted girls talking animatedly together trying to give the impression they were having a good time. A few men gathered at the far end of the room behind the dance floor appeared not to notice them.

Trust me to get here much too early, Hilary thought, at heart I'm still the daughter of the vicarage. However much I don't want to be.

Ellie said, 'It'll get better when the pubs close, that's when the men will start to stagger in.' They all smiled.

Sandra put her hand into her handbag and pulled out a flask. 'This'll help,' she said, and took a swig. She coughed and spluttered. 'Fecking hell,' she said.

Ellie took the flask and drank. She caught a look of panic in Sandra's painted eyes. The flask was empty. Ellie understood. It was an act of bravado, Sandra's attempt to fool them and herself that she was something other than she was.

Ellie handed Hilary the flask. 'Sorry,' she said, 'I think I've drunk the lot.'

Hilary wouldn't have drunk anyway, there might be germs on the rim of the flask, but wasn't that typical of greedy Ellie? Hilary thought, that must be what it's like in big families, she has to grab what she can to survive, like litters of animals have to. And Ellie is no runt, she must've got good at it. And yet she's always on about bringing about a caring, sharing society, she's not consistent.

Sandra said to Ellie, 'I don't think I left much for you anyway.' She hoped Ellie could tell she was grateful to her for not giving her away.

Ellie, Sandra and Hilary found three wallflower seats together and, with fixed smiles, sat down to take stock. Sandra took a vanity mirror out of her handbag to check the false eyelashes she was wearing for the first time. One had come adrift and made it look as though she was winking.

'Oh, God, look who's here,' Ellie said.

Ffion stood alone at one end of the dance floor. She was wearing a short black velvet dress and leaning in a languid pose against one of the white pillars at the far end of the room in the beam of a spotlight which highlighted the crimson rose pinned in her dark hair.

Still she looked profoundly bored, lighting one cigarette from the stub of another.

'She didn't say she was feckin coming,' Sandra said, put out at what she saw as unfair competition. Which, of course, it was.

Hilary's clenched her fists to stop her hands shaking. Tonight was the first when men she'd never met before might be on the prowl.

'Sandra,' she said, 'just for tonight do you think you could try not to use that sort of language? It sounds so... it gives the wrong impression.'

Hilary expected a feck-filled string of abuse, but Sandra seemed not to mind. Instead she glared at Ffion and muttered, 'Fecking patronising cow.'

Hilary said, 'She looks like a painting of Frida Kahlo, don't you think?' Hilary was thinking if Ffion were a painter, she'd do self-portraits all the time. That's what made me think of Frida Kahlo.

Ellie shrugged. 'She's on the prowl, I suppose. Thinks there's a chance some of the junior lecturers might come by to look over what's on offer.'

The sight of Ffion made Ellie feel suddenly embarrassed, as though she'd just realized she'd been walking in the street with her skirt caught up in her knickers. She was surprised when Hilary voiced her own thoughts, 'Oh, I hope she doesn't see us. She'll think we haven't got anything better to do.' Ellie thought, Perhaps there's more to Hilary than I thought.

Sandra said, 'Well, Ffion's here, what's the difference?'

But there was a difference, and they all knew it. Ffion was alone and her disdainful expression made it clear she preferred it that way. The others wouldn't have come here alone. To put themselves on show to men like this, they needed each other's support. Ffion, unselfconscious, came to pick; they came to be picked and if they weren't picked, they needed friends around them.

They all looked hopefully towards the small knot of men who seemed to be trying to overlook the presence of women.

And then a slight, sun-burned man in a leather jacket and jeans – young but not as young as the rest – came in through the door like a gust of wind and brought the room to life.

This was a man like none of them had ever known, not anywhere near their own age anyway. A man, not a boy. He was older than the others in freshman year, and so must have earned his own living. He had already learned how to survive in the outside world and he wore that knowledge like sheen, setting him apart from the rest.

To the now expectant young women around the room, he brought a frisson of excitement and danger, the peril of a feral animal loose among the domestic flock.

He approached Ffion first and asked, 'Do you paso doble?'

She stared at him, considering. She knew she was not a good dancer, too stiff and self-conscious. Instinctively she feared that this man would show up her terpsichorean flaws, make her mundane. Or, worse, absurd. Every woman in the room would watch them together and see only him. Ffion didn't like the thought.

She shook her head. 'No,' she said.

The man shrugged, smiled and moved away towards the line of waiting girls.

He stopped when he came to Ellie and held out his hand to her. 'Can you paso doble?'

Without a word she stood up and followed him out onto the floor. 'My name's Matt,' he said.

Hilary and Sandra stared. They doubted that Ellie had ever heard of the paso doble – they hadn't.

But something was happening to Ellie, anyone could see that. It's as though she doesn't care about anything else, Hilary thought, it's as though she isn't fat and flabby, she's melted away.

Hilary had to look away for a moment. There were tears in her eyes. Envy, yes, but more self-pity that what was happening to Ellie would never happen to her.

Sandra said, 'It's fecking disgusting.'

But they could not stop watching. Ellie moved as though transported. Watching her, they were a little frightened.

'Is she all right?' Hilary said.

Sandra sounded sullen.

'Of course she is, it's just sex.' She was filled with envy, hugging herself. 'Oh, God,' she said under her breath.

Hilary's memory stirred. A blustery day, years ago. She was in London. In the Kings Road, for some reason she couldn't remember, but it must have been extraordinary. She had walked away from the crowds round Sloane Square and Peter Jones. Perhaps that was why she was there: her mother might have wanted her to buy something there, it was her favourite store?

If she did I didn't buy it, I didn't go in, Hilary thought. Funny how her memories were so often of what she didn't do. But she'd been walking down Kings Road playing a game with the wind, side-stepping to avoid skittering cigarette packets and loose flapping pages of the *Evening Standard* as she went.

And then, on the other side of the street – the sunny side, it was that day – she caught sight of this man. Beautiful, he was. The most beautiful man she had ever seen. Tall, dark – beyond description, really.

She stopped, she couldn't move her feet, just stared. It was like suddenly being turned to stone by one of the gods from Olympus. The traffic moved forward as the lights changed, and a crowded bus went by, cutting off her view. She couldn't stop herself, she ran across the road. There was the man ahead of her. He was walking – he seemed to be half-dancing. He wore a cape. How odd.

Hilary turned back the way she had come and followed him up the street. She'd never done anything like this in her life, not even as a child. Perhaps he'll look behind him and see me, she thought, he'll hold out his hand to draw me to him under the cape. If only! She really believed he would. That's what she told herself. He didn't, of course. He was joined by three gorgeous blonde girls She followed the group until suddenly they turned all at once like a circus troupe off the pavement and through a high wrought-iron gate. They climbed as one up a flight of steps to go through the front door, which opened in front of them, into a great house like an illustration in a book.

I wept all the way home, Hilary thought, I remember that. Even now I sometimes dream about him.

Now the group of hesitant young men had broken up and approached the girls. An overgrown pale schoolboy with dark-rimmed spectacles and prominent pink ears asked Sandra to dance.

'Yes,' she said, 'OK.'

She clamped her body against his and began to move in time to the music. Hilary saw his face, puzzled, as he tried to hold her away from him. She almost laughed.

'My name's William,' she heard him say. He had an Ulster accent as strong as Sandra's own. 'I'm doing theology,' he went on, 'I'm going to be a clergyman.'

Sandra, in the throes of carnal frottage, ignored him.

The music changed. The Shirelles began to sing *Will You Still Love Me Tomorrow?*

Matt swung Ellie off the dance floor.

'Let's get out of here,' he said.

She followed him out of the hall onto the gas-lit 18th century College Square. Transported by romance to God knows where; she didn't care.

Anything seemed possible. She told herself, I should tell the others, they'll worry about me. I've left my coat. I don't know anything about this man. He may not even be at Trinity, he could be anyone. He's got a Cockney accent; he's probably a crook… A wide boy.

But she didn't care. At that moment all she wanted was to spend a few more hours with him.

He put his arm round her. 'Come on,' he said, 'I've got a car.'

It was an ancient Morris Minor. He must be all right, Ellie told herself, his car's parked in college, he must be a lecturer or something.

'Get in,' he said, 'there's a rug in the back. You can wrap that round you.'

He took a grey herringbone tweed overcoat and a brown felt trilby from the back seat and put them on.

'Where are we going?' she asked.

'Home.'

'I live in Trinity Hall.'

'That's no one's idea of home,' he said.

They seemed to drive for miles, way out of the city and through endless suburbs until there were no longer street lamps and bus stops at the side of the road. Am I being abducted, Ellie thought, he may be a white slave trader.

'You do this trip into college every day?' she said.

'No, I bunk on a friend's sofa most nights in the week and come down here for the weekends.'

He's laughing at me, he knew what I was thinking, Ellie thought.

Matt began to sing as he drove. The same song that had been playing as they left the dance. She asked herself, Will He Still Love Me Tomorrow? To avoid answering her own question, she started to sing with him.

Then she could smell the sea. When he stopped the car she heard waves breaking on sand.

'Where are we?'

'Brittas Bay, behind the dunes. Come on, it's this way.'

The moon was almost full. Pockmarked sand and the reeds; a lunar surface. The wind off the sea felt cold here. She took the rug out of the car and wrapped it tight around her. She floundered on her high-heeled party shoes. She slipped them off. The sand felt clammy between her toes as, barefoot, she followed him up a track towards far-off hills.

27

They reached a corrugated iron shack beside the path.

'This is it,' he said, holding her arm as he unlocked the door.

'Where do you think I could run to?' she asked, laughing.

'I wasn't thinking. Most of the people I bring back here are drunk. I suppose I thought you might fall down.'

Before he opened the door he pulled her towards him and kissed her. His mouth felt hard, pressing her lips apart. She didn't expect his tongue. It was pointed and sinuous with a life of its own meeting hers. Like a hungry fledgling bird demanding sustenance.

He said, 'Let's at least get inside.'

Ellie didn't know what she should do. He didn't seem roused.

'Let's have a drink,' he said. 'There's a case of white wine outside the back door keeping cool.

'No,' she said, 'I don't want a drink. I'm cold.' And indeed she started to shiver, but it wasn't altogether from cold.

He came to her and put his arms around her to pull down the zip of her dress.

'Here,' he said, 'here's a hanger.'

She took the dress off and he hung it up behind the door. He took off her bra and his hands brushed her nipples. She gasped and fell backwards on the bed, dragging him down on top of her. My God, she thought, can you die of sex?

Back in the Exam Hall at Trinity, the Campanile clock tolled once and was silent. Hilary and Sandra, shivering with cold, walked together up a deserted Grafton Street.

'There may be a taxi stand outside the Shelbourne Hotel,' Hilary said. 'We can't walk back to Trinity Hall.'

Sandra scowled, grumpy as a baby. She said, 'The way I feel, I'll just jump out in front of a car and make the driver take us back. Promise him anything, he won't dare make a fuss when he realizes he's outside Trinity Hall.'

Hilary said nothing. She was thinking, Oh, God, what's Ellie doing now? Why did that man pick her and never glanced at me? When will a man ever sweep me off my feet and carry me away to make love to me? Ellie's not pretty; she doesn't even try to be. She's not fascinating in any way, unless you're interested in Emile Durkheim or rights for women. Neither of them subjects conducive to flirtation. That man didn't look the sort who'd want to know what Freud would've made of his performance.

Ellie woke up in the morning to the sound of the sea and the sigh of wind in the reeds. And she was in love.

Matt was still asleep. She propped herself on an elbow and watched his face in wonder. I love him, I love him, she told herself; she thought she must burst, she was so happy.

She swung her legs out of the bed and sat up. She was impatient for him to wake, wanting to hurry forward into her new life. I wonder where he keeps his household stuff? she thought. This room could do with a good cleaning. I never thought I'd end up with a man living in the wilds like this. I wonder where I'll have to go to do the shopping?

She got up and went to the kitchen. First things first, and they could both do with some coffee.

There was a tap over the sink but when she turned it on, there was no water. She looked for a fridge. No fridge.

Matt was awake when she went back to the bed.

'The privy's outside,' he said. No romance there.

'There's no water. I was going to make coffee.'

'There's wine.'

She said nothing. She told herself, Things are going to have to change around here.

Matt reached up and pulled her back down onto the bed. 'What's the hurry? Come back to bed.'

Well, she told herself, I can deal with everything later.

Visitors started to arrive in the late afternoon.

'Did you know they were coming?' Ellie asked, her expression venomous as she watched a group of strangers struggling up the track from the dunes with a crate of beer.'

'People drop in at weekends.'

'But what about food?'

'They bring supplies.'

'But what should I do?'

'Whatever you like. Everyone does their own thing.'

But why do you need other people when I'm here? Ellie almost asked but stopped herself just in time. She knew she was going to have to tread carefully. It's a good sign, she told herself, it means he's not involved with anyone else. No couple committed to each other could put up with all these other people dropping in.

Ellie tried not to protest as people walked in, giving her a smile in passing, and made themselves at home. They were all strangers to her, but they didn't introduce themselves. Or defer to her in any way.

And then most of them stayed the night. They'd brought sleeping bags and they bedded down where they could. Someone found a guitar and began to strum along as a group of them sang.

'What's that they're singing?' Ellie asked Matt. The song moved her so much she was afraid she was going to cry.

'*The Auld Triangle*. It's from Brendan Behan's play, *The Quare Fellow*. Don't you know it?'

Ellie was doing Social Studies. She could have carried on a passable conversation on Durkheim or even Ronnie Laing. She'd come to TCD expecting an English university on Irish turf. Till she'd actually arrived in the Republic and saw the traffic signs written in the quaint language, she'd assumed that Dublin was in Northern Ireland. She hadn't been the only one, either, she told herself with defiance.

But she did know better than to say, 'Who's Brendan Behan?'

She got to her feet and started for the door. 'I feel like some fresh air.'

She moved away from the shack, feeling disconsolate and afraid. She was a child of the London suburbs. The night was intensely dark, with a blackness she had never seen in England; and the sky was vast, she had never imagined there could be so many stars.

Matt came quietly up behind her and took her hand. 'OK?' he said.

They stood close, listening, between the breaking waves, to the silence which stretched in front of them forever.

'Come back inside,' he said. 'I want you so much.'

She pulled away. 'We can't. All those people...'

'Come on, for God's sake. I'm bursting. You don't want to give me blue balls.'

Early next morning, Matt drove her back to TCD. He dropped her outside Greene's Bookshop in Nassau Street. Ellie leaned over and kissed him as she got out.

'See you around,' he said, and waved as he drove away.

4

Ffion, seated in the Buttery Bar waiting for some no-mark who was queuing to buy her coffee, caught sight of Matt among a group gathered on the Library steps. Holding court, was he? As usual. It was always the same; he always had a crowd around him. She'd never seen him alone. He was always surrounded by men like minders. And the most lusted-after women in college.

She wondered, what's he got that the others haven't? He was standing with his back to her outside the library, she couldn't see his face, but she'd recognize him anywhere. She thought, He's not particularly good-looking; he's shorter than I am, and if you look carefully his hair's receding. What the hell's so special about him? Nothing... Nada... He's the man who picked Ellie Bassett to screw rather than me, someone of no consequence at all.

Being honest, she told herself, what's really got me going is how, when I refused to dance with him, he didn't care a bit; he picked up Ellie as though, me or her, it was all the same to him. As though dancing the bloody paso doble was what he cared about, not who he did it with.

Ellie herself was now walking across Front Square. She was carrying a shopping bag. There's something about her, Ffion thought, whatever she's carrying is always going to look as though she's humping the ingredients for a nourishing meal.

She watched Ellie catch sight of Matt and turn aside to go to him. So she, too, recognized his back view. Ellie's step had quickened at the sight of him. She wants to catch him before he can escape, Ffion thought, she's in love with him.

But before Ellie got near, the group on the steps broke up, like feeding pigeons disturbed by a gunshot. Matt disappeared inside the library.

I'm not in competition with Ellie, Ffion told herself. Surely not? As if. There's no way anyone who could choose to become Ellie Bassett's lover could conceivably be any use to me. But she thinks she's scored against me. Everyone saw him reject me and choose her. He may not even have noticed what he did, but every woman in that hall saw me publicly humiliated.

There wasn't much point in trying to get her own back on Matt, she knew that. He wouldn't care, he was like Teflon, women's emotions wouldn't stick to him, he didn't take them seriously.

Ffion said to herself, I'll have to make Ellie pay. That's what I'll do.

She stood up to go. The no-mark was at the head of the queue, waiting to pay. He gave her the thumbs up, but she shrugged her shoulders and walked out of the Buttery.

Later that day, seated on the top deck of a bus inching its way through rush-hour traffic on Stephen's Green towards Dartry Road, she considered how she would punish Ellie Bassett. How odd, she thought, that one small incident can put a match to total indifference towards somebody and set fire to absolute enmity.

Actually, Ffion was well aware, indifference was her default attitude towards other people until something happened to change it. All women, anyway. A man she might fancy, or warm towards if she felt she could use him. She saw no use to be gained from women: if they might have something to offer her, she had no skill to hand to exploit them.

But vengeance was something else. And Ellie, unconscious of Ffion's awakened antagonism towards her, made no secret of her vulnerability. She was helplessly in love.

Ffion had started work three nights a week doing the washing up in a small and very exclusive restaurant in a mews behind Kildare Street.

Her room-mates found it incredible that Ffion should take any job involving serving the public, cooking or washing pans. Nor was it easy for them to believe that anyone would pay to eat in a restaurant desperate enough to employ her.

But Ffion always had an ulterior motive. The Soup Bowl had only room for a handful of tables crammed close together; the place was like an intimate club. The menu was limited to superb sirloin steak or lamb chops, both served with jacket potatoes and peas, but accompanied by the finest wine. All Ffion had to do, apart from washing up, was to keep an eye on the meat under the grill while the couple who owned the place turned the dining-room into a kind of discreet salon for some intellectual in-crowd. Even scrubbing the pans wasn't that bad when it was accompanied by wine from the cream of Bordeaux's vineyards and the company of sundry of Dublin's artistic elite who drifted into the minute kitchen to chat on the way to the telephone or the bathroom in the basement.

What was more, the Soup Bowl also had a cosmopolitan clientele: film moguls and international movie stars filming at Ardmore, stage actors from the Abbey, painters and writers, were regular customers. The Soup Bowl was an exclusive club. On her third night at work, setting up tables while the owners were out, Ffion turned away Elizabeth Taylor and Richard Burton because they hadn't booked and the restaurant was full.

She told her boss. He seemed about to sack her on the spot.

She said, 'Oh, they'll be back. It's like Maud Gonne rejecting Yeats' marriage proposals, refusal just makes them keener.'

She was right; they were. She wasn't interested. Two people in love like Taylor and Burton were had nothing to offer her.

Suddenly she jumped up from her seat on the bus and ran down the stairs. Why bother going back to Trinity Hall? She could go straight to work. If she turned over her waistband a couple of times, her skirt would be short enough to give favoured customers a flash of her red lace knickers. Oh la la, it was so ridiculous.

It was midweek, a quiet night. The only customers were four men involved with pre-production discussions on a spy movie based on a book by Ian Fleming.

Waiting in the kitchen after washing up, Ffion's thoughts went back to that night when Ellie became her enemy.

Through a haze of her own cigarette smoke, she'd stayed on to watch Ellie dancing with that Cockney leprechaun. Paso doble my backside, she thought, Ellie hasn't the first idea how to do it. She moves like a big Dutch doll.

But in that man's arms, there wasn't a woman in the room wishing she wasn't in Ellie's place.

In the cramped Soup Bowl Ffion's mind went back to the dance, reliving it. He wouldn't have looked at her if I'd danced with him, she told herself.

She remembered trying not to look at Sandra on the edge of the floor, dancing with an earnest kid who looked like the school swot as he tried to steer her through the other dancers. He looked like a railway porter pushing an old-fashioned sack trolley on a crowded platform.

Men had come up and asked her to dance, but she shook her head; some tried to engage her in conversation, but she avoided their eyes and looked away without smiling.

She lit another cigarette. And another.

'Why did you come if you don't want to dance or talk to people?'

The speaker sounded amused and, she decided, sympathetic. He was a broad-shouldered young man with thick blonde hair which he kept having to flick back from his face. He was extravagantly good-looking. But he's not in the least sexy, she told herself, not like that *jolie laide* little bastard publicly seducing the lumpen Ellie to the sound of some smarmy American ballad.

'Isn't that a typically English scene,' she said, 'a room-full of lubricious virgins bringing themselves to the brink of climax with total strangers? And most of them thinking they've met the love of their lives. Why doesn't someone teach them that sex isn't love?'

'Probably their mothers never knew the difference. Don't mothers teach their daughters that sort of thing?'

Ffion shrugged and threw down her half-smoked cigarette grinding it against the marble floor under her stiletto heel.

He offered her one of his, lighting hers and one for himself. 'Aren't you English?'

'What really makes someone English?' she said.

'Birth? The nationality of your parents? Where you pay taxes? You tell me.'

'How the hell should I know? I was born in Switzerland, where my mother was working as a chalet girl; her passport is British but she's Jewish. My father could've been anything at all, possibly Welsh, hence the name. And I don't pay taxes. What about you?'

'Oh, I'm a true son of the Shires. My name's Howard, by the way. I'm doing fourth year medicine. You didn't answer my first question. Why did you come?'

She dragged on the cigarette then let it fall to the floor.

She smiled. 'I'm beginning not to be sorry I did.'

'You're beautiful when you smile.'

'Aren't I beautiful anyway?'

36

'I suppose most people would say so. But not to me you're not. I've seen too many corpses with blank chilled expressions like yours on their faces.'

Ffion was startled. 'Oh, please, spare my blushes!' Then, intrigued, she went on, 'I suppose people tell you you're beautiful, too, but if you want to know, for me there's something missing...'

He laughed and took out a pack of Sweet Afton and held it out to her.

They stood for a while watching the dancers. But she had eyes for only one couple.

She said, 'Who's that little guy dancing like a hotel gigolo? The one with the mousy fat girl?' Ffion glanced up at Howard as she asked the question. His eyes, too, were watching Ellie's partner.

Howard said, 'His name's Matt. Matt Brewer, I think. He's a First Year, doing English and French Honours. Apparently he left school at sixteen and did other things before he came here.'

'It must be funny for him, being among so many younger people.'

'It's not so different for us medical students, it takes us years to graduate. And there's a woman History student around who's spent something like twelve years getting to the Third Year.'

'Christ! She must be bored out of her mind by now.'

'No worse than working in some dreary office, surely?'

'At least she'd get paid.'

There was a short silence, then Howard asked, 'What are you studying?'

'Law.'

'You want to be a lawyer?' He sounded doubtful.

'No, but law attracts the right kind of people – the ones who might become famous or powerful. Meeting them is a necessary grounding for life.'

'You could say the same thing about medicine.'

'Not me. Medical men may get to be rich, but they've always got this thing about helping sick people; I've no time for that.'

When Ffion turned away from him to look back to the dance floor, Matt and Ellie had gone. Sandra was still hanging apron-like from the neck of the boy who hadn't started to shave yet.

There was nothing to keep Ffion now. 'I'd better go. I'll miss the last bus to Trinity Hall.'

'I've got a flat in Merrion Square, you could stay over. It's four floors up, but that's surely better than walking back to Dublin 6.'

'Yes, OK. Frankly I'd rather spend the night with you than have to listen to my room-mates going on about what might or might not be happening to Ellie Bassett. Ellie being the girl Matt Brewer was dancing with.'

'Glad to be of use. You don't mince your words to spare a fellow's feelings, do you? I'll take your acceptance as some sort of back-handed compliment.'

They walked in silence across College Park and passed the Medical School buildings to go out of Lincoln Gate. Ffion felt relieved she wouldn't have to walk much further in her high heels. It was worth putting up with sex with this Howard to avoid that. When he offered her his hand where the pavement was uneven, she took it. He's nice enough, she told herself.

But she was really thinking about Matt Brewer, and what he might be doing to Ellie. That's how she wanted to be feeling now, the world well lost for love. She'd read books about that feeling, seen plays and films about it, tried to lose herself in sentimental songs about it. But she'd never felt that way herself.

At least with Matt Brewer she could imagine what it was like. I want to feel the way she's feeling now. But it won't last. He won't need Ellie. OK, perhaps he'll tolerate her for a while as a functionary, fetching and carrying and sex; but never as a person in any kind of intellectual or spiritual way.

Ffion wondered how soon Ellie would realize the threat Matt posed to her. She's his absolute opposite. Ellie's whole function in life is to be needed by a man. Matt will never need her. If she's not careful she's going to be like one of those women who fall in love with homosexuals because they think they can 'cure' them.

Watch this space, Ffion told herself, this might get interesting.

As she and Howard got closer to Lincoln Gate, past the Medical School building, a dog started to bark.

She stopped. 'Wait, we can't leave it, it must be lost. I've never seen any sign of a dog in college.'

'He belongs to the Department,' Howard said. 'We keep him here to do experiments on. Superficial stuff, mostly, but part of our training.'

'That's obscene.'

'In the name of science?'

'Man's best friend.'

'Why's that different from a rat or a frog? We've got to train on something.'

'Right, that's it. I'm going back to Trinity Hall.'

'Don't blame me, take it up with the Professor or someone.'

'Perhaps you'd be kind enough to point me in the right direction from here to Dartry Road?'

'Don't be stupid, Ffion, it's miles.'

'The dog's probably even got a name.'

'You're being ridiculous.'

She turned and started to walk, tottering on her high heels.

She heard him call something after her but she took no notice. Nothing would make her look back at him, it would be a sign of weakness.

She was crying with pain and frustration, full of disgust at the inhumanity of Man. A taxi drew up beside her. The driver leaned across and wound down his window.

She snapped at him, 'I haven't any money.'

'The gentleman paid already. He said to take you to Trinity Hall. Sure, you're going in the wrong direction altogether.'

She looked around in case Howard might be watching. He'll never know whether I took the taxi or not, she told herself. He's a right fool if he doesn't expect the driver to take his money and forget all about me. But not such a fool as the taxi driver, who didn't take the money and run.

She opened the door and got into the back of the car. 'Thanks,' she said.

The coffee percolator keeping warm on the hob suddenly boiled over, bringing Ffion back to the Soup Bowl with a start.

She turned the gas down, cursing her inattention. Now she'd have to clean the hob.

In the restaurant the four men were getting up to leave. She picked up the percolator and hurried to offer them refills. That way they might give her a tip, not just add a percentage to the bill.

But she was too late, they were leaving. She threw away the coffee, then cleared their table and started to wash their cups and side-plates.

That'll learn you, she told herself, wasting time thinking about what can't be mended. And then she thought, Howard Who? He didn't say. He's gorgeous-looking.

She dried her hands. Yes, she said to herself, he is; why am I wasting my time on Matt Brewer when I should be asking myself why I don't find Howard sexy?

And she thought, I'll have to work on that.

5

Another wet and windy evening, and Sandra and Hilary were together in their room at Trinity Hall. It happened quite often. Ffion worked three nights a week at the Soup Bowl, and when she wasn't working, she was out somewhere else, she and her long legs and her sneer. And Ellie spent most evenings now searching the favourite haunts of Trinity students in the city centre looking for Matt.

This particular night, rain was hammering the window panes. The wind howled like a banshee in the chimney, though what a banshee was and why it howled Hilary had no idea. Whatever, there seemed to be a riot going on in the street outside. Sandra went to close the curtains. 'There's dustbins and rubbish flying all over the place,' she said. 'There's a right gale blowing. I'm glad I'm not out tonight.'

But the shared bedroom in Trinity Hall felt like a prison cell even so. They could find nothing to say to each other.

Sandra asked herself, Why does Hilary watch me like that? Even when she's plucking her fecking eyebrows she's keeping an eye on me in the mirror.

And Hilary wondered, Why do I keep thinking I'm going to catch her out doing something underhand? It's crazy, I can't even imagine what I think she might do. But I can't help worrying she's going to invent something to make trouble.

Why can't I trust her? And what do I mean by trust anyway? I don't think she's going to steal money from my purse, nothing like that. It wouldn't occur to me to be wary like this around Ellie or Ffion, though both of them would be more likely to help themselves to my things. Ffion assumes

41

because we share a room what's mine is hers, and Ellie might give my things away to someone who wanted them and think that's all right. I feel I know what I can expect from them, but not

Sandra. Is it because she's Irish?

Hilary was ashamed now. She didn't like to admit it even to herself, but her real problem with Sandra was that she couldn't bring herself to accept her room-mate as truly Irish, actually from this banshee-howling, rainy, not-English island.

Why? What's the matter with me, she thought, I believe in a united Ireland, she was born in Ireland, therefore she must be Irish. But Hilary didn't convince herself. She asked herself, how can an Ulster Loyalist be Irish? Her people are settlers, they're not loyal to Ireland. They want to be British.

Her next thought slipped into her mind as easily as an oyster down her throat from its craggy shell. I don't. I don't want to be British against Ireland. So where does that leave me? I'm English, but I feel myself on Ireland's side against England. But I never can be, not to the Irish.

Hilary gave up on plucking her eyebrows. She turned away from the mirror and met Sandra's eyes. Sandra flushed.

She asked herself, what does Hilary see when she looks at me like that? What does she think of me? Why am I so sure she's judging me and finding me guilty? Guilty of what?

Hilary got up and went to fill the electric kettle.

'Do you want a coffee?'

Sandra nodded. 'Please.'

Hilary made coffee and handed a mug to Sandra. We're both Protestants, she thought, both brought up in religious families; she and I ought to have something in common. Perhaps she's the same as me, we're neither of us sure of where we fit in. She raised her mug to Sandra. 'Cheers,' she said.

A violent gust of wind sounded like an explosion against the window.

'Poor Ellie,' Hilary added, 'I don't fancy her chances of finding Matt on a night like this.'

'More fool her for trying...' Sandra stopped, then said, 'I mean, would you run after someone like that? Think how awful it must be for Matt, having her tagging after him wherever he goes.'

God, she's hard, Hilary thought. She said, 'Ellie's in love.' She asked herself, why's Sandra getting so uptight?

'That's no excuse. If you want my opinion, it's more a case that she'll do anything it takes to get what she wants. I won't be surprised if one day Ellie will find him in bed with someone and she'll stab him to fecking death to make sure that if she can't have him, no one else will.'

Hilary laughed. But something cold-blooded about the way Sandra said it made the hairs rise on the back of her neck. She thought, she's not English after all; there's no trace of sentimentality in her.

Sandra said, 'Sorry, that fecking just slipped out. I know you don't like swearing.'

'It was just that first time in public when I said that. I was out of line. It was because I'm not good at dances and parties, no one ever seems to want to pick me up, and I look for something to blame. I should never've said anything...'

'If you want to know,' Sandra said, 'I never swore at all until I got into Trinity. Then I was so desperate to avoid being seen as some sort of straitlaced Northern Irish prude I went out of my way to become the opposite. They'd excommunicate me at home if they heard me...'

Hilary, flabbergasted, said, 'Really? It sounds as if it comes naturally to you.'

Sandra giggled. That giggle doesn't sound as though it comes naturally to her, Hilary thought.

'I taught myself, like learning a language. I went to local rugby matches. All the RUC games. The RUC's the worst. Policemen's language is really bad.'

She thinks I'm crazy, Sandra thought. She won't know what it's like to throw your lot in with the devil to disassociate yourself from everything your family believes.

'That explains the look on that boy's face – you know, poor Whatsisname, the one you got off with the night Ellie met Matt. He looked terrified.'

Sandra actually flinched; at least, that's what Hilary would swear she did. Hilary had expected her to laugh.

The life had suddenly gone out of Sandra's voice. 'William Carson, that's his name. I don't know why you call him "poor".'

Hilary, gradually realizing that Sandra was close to tears, hesitated. 'You haven't seen him since, have you?'

Words started to gush out of Sandra's mouth. And now she was sobbing, too.

'I see him every day. He turns up everywhere. I'm really scared. It's awful, he won't let me alone. I spend almost all the time when I'm not at lectures holed up in No 6 because men can't go there, and then every evening here in Hall with you and the other dogs who don't get asked out.'

Sandra's voice had been rising hysterically, but then she ran out of breath. On the crest of a sob she added, so quietly that Hilary had to strain to hear, 'I don't know what to do. I'm afraid he'll never let me go. I don't want to go back.'

Hilary kept quiet. This was the sort of thing her mother had to deal with all the time. What did Mother do if a troubled parishioner gets out of control like this? Give her a slap, probably, and then comfort her. I wouldn't mind slapping her for calling me a dog, but no way can I bring myself to hug her. She's too bony; I'd hug her like a stuffed toy if she was fat, but no one hugs a wooden puppet. If only Ellie was here, she'd know how to cope.

'Slow down,' she said, 'you're sounding crazy. Why haven't you told someone what's going on? You don't have to put up with it. Why can't you just ask him to leave you alone and if he won't, you must tell someone.'

'That wouldn't be any good.'

'Sandra, that's what they have a Dean of Women Students for. If he really is stalking you, tell her. She'll deal with it.'

'It's no good, you can't understand.'

'Is he trying to force you…does he molest you?' Hilary didn't want Sandra to know that the first time they'd met, she'd taken her room-mate for a right scrubber, but she had. Now Hilary thought she was beginning to understand. She couldn't really blame William, the way Sandra had thrown herself at him that night; it wasn't surprising if he'd got the wrong idea.'

Sandra looked exasperated. 'For Christ's sake, do you think he wants to sleep with me?'

'Feck you, you mean?'

It was Hilary's little joke. Surely even God would forgive her using the word because she was trying to make Sandra feel better.

She told herself, The Rev Dad would understand, and that's good enough for me. Actually my idea of God is an exalted version of the Rev Dad. A Rev Dad who doubles as a country policeman. That says pretty much everything I need to know about religion.

'It's nothing physical. He's taking control of my head.' Sandra's heart sank. She'd had a wild idea it might help to talk about what was happening to her with Hilary. At least Hilary had a churchy background – her father was a clergyman. A good Protestant. But if Hilary was just going to make silly jokes…

Hilary saw Sandra's face and felt guilty that she wasn't helping. 'What's going on, Sandra? What's wrong?'

She sounded serious enough now.

Sandra started to try to explain. 'William is going to be a minister in the Free Presbyterian Church. That's the

45

church my family belongs to... I belong to. They sent him here to watch over me and now they're making him take me back.'

She looked at Hilary expectantly, but Hilary's expression was blank. Hilary knew vaguely that the Protestant Church in Ulster had many different mansions and she thought that Presbyterian was probably one of them, but so far she couldn't see Sandra's problem.

'So he's a Presbyterian? What's wrong with that?'

'The Free Presbyterian Church is different. It's the Rev Ian Paisley's Church, the church he founded. Dr Paisley believes that he is chosen by God and there will be divine retribution against anyone who goes against him.'

It was ludicrous. Hilary wanted to laugh. She said. 'Does William Carson believe that?'

But Sandra looked deeply troubled. Then, in a flat voice she said, 'He believes absolutely every single syllable. He believes the Bible is God's literal word. He goes back North of the Border most weekends to support Dr Paisley in inciting violent protests against contraception and abortion, or homosexuality and the Pope. '

Hilary still didn't understand what the fuss was about. Why didn't Sandra simply tell William to get lost? And the Rev Ian Paisley, too, if it came to that.

Trying tactfully to probe, she asked, 'But what's it got to do with you what William believes? You've got a mind of your own, tell him to leave you alone.'

'He's dedicated himself to bringing me back onto the path of righteousness. He and my parents.'

Hilary thought, why does she keep saying that Biblical language? That's something new. Is that a sign she's bowing under the brainwashing?

She said, 'Sandra, he's loony. Don't have anything to do with him. He can't do anything to you unless you let him.'

Sandra shook her head. 'My family are Free Presbyterians; it's like a tribal thing, it comes before anything. You can't escape from it. They have ways…'

Hilary first reaction was to say that if so Sandra would be well shot of them.

But before she could say anything, Sandra said, 'They abducted a teenage Catholic girl who'd had doubts about her faith. They took her to Scotland to brainwash her. When she disappeared, her family reported her missing; there was a huge search and the police thought she'd been murdered. It was only when the girl finally escaped that it all came out. They don't stop at anything.'

'But you broke away yourself by coming to Trinity? They can't touch you here. Surely you can't ever want to go back there to live?'

'It's not that simple. That's where I belong. I persuaded my parents to let me come to Trinity because they know Catholics can be excommunicated if they come here, so they thought I'd be protected. OK, I did want to experience another kind of life. But I thought I'd stay the same inside.'

'And you haven't?'

Even as she asked the question, Hilary understood. What else were the swearing, the dyed hair and the garish makeup, if not an act of defiance? 'Oh, Sandra,' she said with real pity.

'If William can't bring me back into the fold, he'll report back and my parents will cut me out of their lives. And all my family and friends, the community I belong to. They'll have to, I've betrayed our faith. I'll be an outcast from everything that's gone to make me who I am.'

Hilary wished she'd paid more attention to some of the Rev Dad's sermons; she might have more idea of what she could say to Sandra now. All she could recall was how he'd often said about Catholics or Buddhists or Muslims, or possibly even Free Presbyterians, if he'd ever heard of them,

47

that there was more road than one to Heaven and Christians should remember that. But, Hilary thought, that isn't very helpful in the present case.

She looked at Sandra's tear-streaked face. We've none of us done much to help her, she thought. We share a room, and we didn't notice what's been going on.

Hilary tried to remember what William looked like. A faceless man, like one sheep in a flock. He certainly wasn't the cliché religious maniac with mad eyes and long dirty hair; more like a nerdy scientist who spent all his time in a research lab under electric light, without access to fresh air.

'Surely your family will understand you want to live your own life. Otherwise why did they let you come to University?'

'So I can qualify as a teacher and be useful.'

'There you are, then.'

'Useful to the Free Presbyterian Church. And God.'

Hilary said under her breath, 'Aka Ian Paisley?'

Sandra managed a small, wan smile.

Hilary went on, 'My Dad says God gave us free will to choose how we live.'

'Mine says we can't be happy unless we make God happy, and that means doing his will.'

'According to the interpretation of a bigoted control freak like Ian Paisley?'

There was a long pause. Hilary was thinking what harm religion could do when it became part of a power game. Once politics came into it…

Hilary stood up. She said, 'We won't let this happen to you. Between us – Ffion, Ellie, me and you – we'll put up a fight. One of us will always be with you from now on. Nobody's going to make you do anything you don't want to.'

She's got another think coming if she thinks she can get Ffion and Ellie to go along with that, Sandra told herself, but she was touched nonetheless.

She shook her head. 'I'm not really sure what I want. Trinity isn't what I hoped, there doesn't seem to be much for me here. Perhaps I'd be better going back.'

There was a sudden rush of cold air as Ellie came in then, heaving behind her a large bag of dirty clothes.

'Matt can't get to a washing machine, I said I'd use the one here.' She dropped the bag and the washing fell out onto the floor.

'Oh, gross,' Sandra said. She swooped on a garment amongst the dirty clothes. She held a pair of very brief women's panties up in front of her. 'Fecking hell, Ellie,' she said, 'don't tell me these are yours?'

Hilary stared at her, asking herself, How come she can be in pieces one minute and positively callous the next?

Ellie started to push the clothes back into the bag. 'Ughh!' she said. 'They must belong to one of the girls who hang around Players. Matt camps out in rooms in College with three of the actors, there's a constant succession of women. I don't think I've ever seen the same one twice.'

The lie came easily; Ellie was learning to pretend she took the young women for granted. Women had to be out of the College rooms by 6pm on pain of being sent down, and she told herself that if Matt was no different from the others and took advantage during daylight hours, it didn't mean anything. Casual sex in the daytime wasn't the same as making love at night. She thought, He'll be picking me up on Friday evening and we'll go down to the cottage on the beach. Home, our place. He's coming to Dartry Road to meet me so I can bring the clean washing. That's love, it's not just sex.

Ellie took off her wet coat and put her dripping umbrella to drain in the dinky hand-basin which was a relic of long ago days when Trinity Hall was the grand Dublin private residence of some member of the Protestant Ascendency, washing facilities in guest bedrooms.

'Have you two been in all evening? Any gossip?'

Hilary and Sandra looked at each other. Hilary shook her head. But Sandra suddenly laughed and blurted out, 'I've lost my fecking faith. Henceforth, I'm officially a fecking atheist.'

Ellie looked blank. 'Oh!' she said. 'What brought that on?'

'I've gone off the idea of spending eternity with most of the people I know on earth who'll most likely get to Heaven.'

'Oh, but isn't that a bit drastic. After all, we'll be there too,' Ellie said. 'Except Fiona, of course,' she added; and smiled.

6

Ffion announced, when they returned to Dublin a week or so before the start of their second year, that she would not return to Trinity Hall. She had moved into a flat at the top of a Regency house in Raglan Road, Ballsbridge. A beautiful flat, with high-ceilinged rooms with original mouldings and floor-length sash windows with antique shutters that folded away into the casement.

At last, she told herself, a place where I can take charge of my own life.

'But...' Hilary had taken it for granted that the four of them were a permanent unit. She was shocked that Ffion hadn't even thought to warn them that she was about to do something so drastic.

'It won't be the same,' Ellie said, uncertain how she felt, but definitely unsettled.

And Sandra, too, was disturbed how insecure she suddenly felt.

Ffion shrugged. 'It's time to move on, we're not children any more, and this place feels like we're still at school.'

Ffion had done a deal with her mother over the summer. Beverly would take a lease on the Raglan Road flat (and pay for it). She would tell the college authorities that she was moving to Dublin, and intended that Fiona should live there with her. That got over college regulations insisting that students live only in approved lodgings or at home.

'But of course you won't set foot in Ireland, ever,' said Ffion with menace in her voice.

'That's a promise.' Beverly was relieved to have her daughter out of sight and mind.

'Otherwise I've decided to leave university for good and come back to London to live with you.'

That clinched it. Ffion knew it would. Beverly had just started a new love affair. She would jump at the chance to pretend that she was childless.

In return, Fiona promised that she would stay away from Beverly's home in London.

Beverly did suspect that she was being short-changed. She said, grumbling, 'I don't see why I should support you anyway, you're over eighteen. I don't believe that *Mi casa es su casa* crap applies to adult children. Home is where the heart is, and that's not anywhere where we're together.'

'*D'accord*,' Fiona said mimicking Jeanne Moreau in an implicit threat – Beverly's new man was French.

It was settled.

Her first evening in the flat, Fiona opened a bottle of red wine and lay on cushions in front of the open window watching a blushing moon sail free above the sepia rooftops. After a year sharing a room in Trinity Hall, she had forgotten silence. It was Sunday, supper would be over; Trinity Hall would be loud with high-pitched girls' voices; rival radio programmes turned up too loud hammered the ears, the ambient sounds too noisy to listen to, you could only try to close your ears to it. But here was no more than a faint moan of traffic on the main road in the distance; the footsteps of passing pedestrians in the street were muffled by a thick damp carpet of red and gold fallen leaves on the pavement. Ffion could smell the sharp, decaying smell they gave off when trodden on. At a certain hour in the evening, the Virginia creeper growing like thick-piled velvet on the walls of the house was full of small brown birds making for bed. They pecked and swore at one another, ignoring Ffion through the open window. She liked to watch them. There was one, fatter and a lighter brown than the others, that reminded her of Ellie.

This, she told herself, is the life.

All this was very nice but two days later she suggested to Ellie, Hilary and Sandra that they move out of Trinity Hall and in with her. I need them, they'll be useful, she told herself, I don't do housework. What decided her, really, were the things her former room-mates couldn't tolerate in daily life. Hilary couldn't stand dust and cobwebs; she'd been brought up to keep her living space as polished and as fragrant as though she was always expecting visitors.

And Sandra, scared of any kind of illness, waged a constant and compulsive war against germs and bugs wherever they lurked in kitchen or bathroom. Probably some sort of weird sublimation of her religious obsessions, Ffion thought. Cleanliness was next to godliness, that kind of thing; except that since she'd officially embraced atheism God and His appointed interpreter, the Rev Ian Paisley, had been replaced by keeping herself fit, and her immune system in tip-top shape.

And Ellie? Why include Ellie? But she didn't hesitate. Well, for one thing, the others might not have wanted to come to Raglan Road without her, not to live alone with Ffion. Ellie had an infuriating motherly superiority that Hilary and Sandra both seemed to find comforting.

And Ellie is a natural housekeeper, Ffion told herself. She likes shopping, and doing the washing; and she'll do all the cooking.

Oh God, Ffion groaned, how boring these young women will be as fully-fledged adults. A year sharing their lives with them, and that's about all the relationship between us amounts to, a list of household chores.

Dammit, she thought, it's not fair! Why should they be so reduced by their own limited expectations? But then she told herself, it's self-inflicted, they don't have to be like that.

She remembered, years ago – she must have been about ten years old at the time – she'd had a crush on an older girl. Funny, I can't even remember her name now. The whole school was in the assembly hall, lined up form by form for some announcement. How I admired her, envied her self-possessed air, her confidence that she had all the equipment within herself to become whatever she wanted to be. Even the teachers respected her.

And then that morning Ffion had suddenly caught sight of this paragon unawares, her attention elsewhere, and saw her the way Ffion knew surely that she saw herself in the mirror with nobody looking at her, with no transforming aura of a chosen one. Ffion's hero-worship evaporated.

My God, Ffion thought, I still remember that moment, it changed my life. That girl had been extraordinary for me because she gave the impression that she was; but when for an unguarded moment she forgot to project that charismatic image, she was nothing, just like everyone else.

It was the most disappointing moment of Ffion's life, realizing that the illusion wasn't real. But it was a gift to see that, Ffion had known that at the time. A gift other girls seemed not to be given. From that moment on, she knew the price she must pay not to be like the others was perpetual vigilance. She looked at Ellie and Hilary and Sandra now and she wondered, how do these others see themselves, what do they think defines them? But then, they wouldn't know what she was talking about.

It was too late to change her mind. She had a moment of panic then at what she had done, bringing the others back into her life. They bore me, she thought, everything about them bores me.

Not everyone, perhaps. Matt Brewer still intrigued her. She had forgotten him over the summer, never given him a thought. But now seeing Ellie reminded Ffion she had

54

unfinished business with the man. And Ellie could perhaps bring her into contact with him. Ffion, who never forgot a grudge, intended to seduce Matt. Preferably under Ellie's rather long nose.

Ffion did not like Ellie. Ffion did not really like anyone very much; at best she was indifferent. But Ellie personified everything about womanhood which made Ffion wish she were a man. A real man, like Genghis Kahn, or King Herod, who got on with the important things in life without wasting time on whimsicalities like putting women and children first.

Bleeding heart females like Ellie, in Ffion's opinion, stood in the way of women achieving important things. To Ffion, the one achievement the girlies were so smug about, motherhood, was actually the greatest threat ever to the future of the world. Over-population.

But when Ellie moved in to Raglan Road there was no sign of Matt. Oh, Ellie expected him to come. She waited in night after night so she'd be there if he called. When the others came in at the end of the evening, she interrogated them – had they seen him? Who was he with? Where did he spend his time? Was he ill?

'Why don't you ring him?' Hilary said.

'Where? He doesn't have a phone.'

'You're making a right fool of yourself,' Ffion said. 'How can he remind himself that you exist when you're making yourself invisible?'

Ellie didn't say anything then, but the next Saturday, she borrowed a car from a student called Betty, and suggested to Hilary and Sandra that they go down to Bray or Greystones and have a picnic on the beach. She went on and on about it. It would be such fun to get out of Dublin and blow away the cobwebs.

In the end they agreed. Perhaps Ellie was at last getting over being lovelorn.

From the start, there was something unreal about that afternoon. The autumn colours of the trees seemed unnatural, brash and garish as though the countryside were playing a part in a Disney movie. It's nearly November, Hilary thought, it's like a summer day. They left the car on a track and walked through the dunes towards the beach. There were families trying to swim among the breakers. It could have been a warm afternoon in August. They were glad of a cooling gusty breeze from the South.

They spent a blustery afternoon on the beach. They ran in and out of the sea and raced each other across the sand, then sprawled among the dunes in intermittent bright spells feeling the warming sun.

When they were hungry, they went back to the car where they'd left the food and bottles of wine.

Ellie said, 'Let's move away from the beach to eat. I hate getting sand in the food.'

She started off up the track with the wine, leaving the others to bring the food. Far too much of it.

'You'd think you're planning to feed the five fecking thousand,' Sandra said grumbling.

'Look,' Ellie said, turning back to them, 'there's a deserted shed or something up ahead. We could eat there out of the wind.'

They came up to her and looked where she was pointing. A green-painted corrugated iron shed on a piece of scrub land beside the track.

'There's someone there,' Hilary said. 'There's a car parked.'

'Let's ask if they mind us having a picnic here,' Ellie said. 'I don't want to lug all this stuff back down to the beach.'

She suddenly shouted, 'Hallo! Is anyone there?'

When there was no answer she walked on and hammered on the door.

There was a long pause. Then the door opened and a rather dishevelled Matt Brewer came out. He was wearing what looked like a skimpy hospital dressing gown.

Sandra said under her breath to Hilary, 'The cow, she's set us up.'

'You mean she knew he'd be here? I can't believe she'd do this,' Hilary said.

Matt looked as if he'd just got out of bed and his eyes hadn't adjusted to the bright light of day.

'Ellie?' he said, as if he weren't sure.

Ellie said over her shoulder to Sandra and Hilary, 'What a bit of luck, it's Matt. He'll have a corkscrew. I'd forgotten to bring one.'

Hilary had the corkscrew in her pocket. She looked at Sandra and said nothing.

'Aren't you going to ask us in, Matt? We come bearing food and wine.' Ellie said, holding the wine in front of her to force him back through the door. 'Come on, you lot, I'm starving.'

Matt stood aside as Hilary and Sandra hung back.

'Hi,' he said. 'You've probably gathered…I'm Matt. Come in, won't you?'

Hilary was used to people barging in on the Rev Dad at inconvenient times, and she knew from the look on Matt's face that he was wishing fervently they were someplace else.

'Glad to meet you, Matt,' she said, 'but if this isn't a good time…'

An exasperated female voice said from inside the shack, 'No, it bloody well isn't. I was just about to come.'

A girl Hilary knew from Anglo Saxon lectures rose naked from a bed in the corner of the room and reached for her underclothes.

'Are these people friends of yours, Matt?' she said.

'We know each other from Anglo Saxon, don't we?' Hilary said to her. 'Aren't you Judy Heald?'

Hilary found herself blushing because the only reason she remembered this girl's name was because she'd overheard two men talking before class one day about interesting things she did with a cucumber.

Ellie, horror of horrors, was setting out the food they'd brought on the table. 'Where've you hidden the glasses, Matt?' she said, taking the wine into the small kitchen. She seemed quite at ease.

Judy's voice was almost a wail. 'Matt?'

'You've got to eat,' Ellie said. She went to the bed and pushed Judy aside, then smoothed the covers.

Hilary and Sandra watched her in disbelief.

Suddenly, Matt began to laugh. 'How lucky you happened to be passing, Ellie,' he said. 'A truly impromptu feast.'

'I want to go back,' Judy told Matt. She managed to give the impression that the others didn't exist.

Ellie said quickly, 'Oh, don't worry, Hilary and Sandra will take you. They've got to go back as soon as they've eaten. Hilary will drive my car. Give it back to Betty Thing, I can't remember her name.'

'And what about you?' Judy said.

'Oh, I'll wash up and give this place a bit of a going over. You must admit it could do with it, Matt.' Ellie added to Judy, 'Matt will bring me back later when he's ready.'

The light began to fade from the sea. The sun sank low behind the outline of the hills; the earth seemed to be on fire.

Hilary, Sandra and Judy drove back to Dublin in silence. Only Hilary spoke once, saying, 'I hope we don't run into anything. I haven't got an Irish driving licence.'

That was it; they drove the rest of the way without saying another word.

Hilary and Sandra told Ffion about it when she came home early from the Soup Bowl. It had been a quiet night.

'Yuck!' she said with a grimace. 'Ellie's like a boa constrictor, she winds herself round people and squeezes every vestige of individuality out of them and then she ingests them. Oh, really, Yuck!'

She smiled. It was going to be interesting. Women's role in society hung in the balance. Ffion thought, Ellie represents an enhanced feminine status quo; she's the educationally-improved housewife and mother, the family-first team player against a new generation of exciting independent lone women intent on their own achievements, women who see marriage and children as secondary, even irrelevant.

And she thought, Poor Matt Brewer, representing the final flourish of the rampant male; he has no idea he's been reduced to a pawn in a game between me and Ellie, her kind of woman and mine. Some prize Matt's going to be; he's a man, he's bound to be the loser whoever wins.

7

'There's something you should know,' Sandra said to Hilary.

They were standing at the open kitchen window of the flat in Raglan Road. The glorious Indian summer continued, and their elderly landlady, Miss O'Connell, who lived in the lower half of the house, was sitting out in the back garden reading a book.

The whistle of the kettle from the top flat sounded to Miss O'Connell like her telephone ringing in the house. Sandra was amusing herself making the kettle boil so that Miss O'Connell jumped up from her deck chair and hurried indoors to answer it. As soon as the old lady disappeared into the house, Sandra took the kettle off the boil; the ringing stopped, and Miss O'Connell returned to her deckchair believing she had missed a real call.

Sandra found it amusing to watch the old woman, getting more and more agitated, return to take up her book. Sandra let her get settled, then put the kettle back on the gas ring and sent her scurrying back into the house.

'Any minute now she'll start crossing herself and calling on the saints to defend her,' Sandra said. 'Catholics are always fecking hysterical. Silly old fool.'

'Oh, stop it. Little things amuse little minds. What's the matter with you?'

Hilary was annoyed; what Sandra was doing was the sort of nonsense even small boys grew out of, surely. But she was also disconcerted by Sandra's almost automatic contempt for Catholics. Almost as though Miss O'Connell was a less developed species of humanity than Ulster Protestants.

Hilary herself was fascinated by the old lady.

Miss O'Connell, according to rumour, had in her youth been the mistress of the former Taoiseach Eamon de Valera, and so part of Ireland's romantic struggle for identity. Actually Hilary disapproved of de Valera, a prejudice based entirely on an irrational preference for Michael Collins, whom she saw as a much more handsome and charismatic figure. But since she'd heard about Miss O'Connell's past – her *alleged* past – Hilary had begun to question her own judgement in Michael Collins' favour. Had not De Valera, after all, proved the better choice for Ireland? Brain above brawn, the rational thinker over the hothead?

Stupid, she thought, I don't know anything about either of them.

The whistling kettle was irritating her. She asked Sandra, 'Well, what is it? What should I know?'

Sandra turned off the gas ring and shut the kitchen window. Her pale skin looked unnatural, as though her face was made of plastic; the doll-like effect enhanced because she wore her bright yellow hair in a beehive rigid with spray, which gave the impression it was built of metal.

'William Carson committed suicide over the summer vac.'

She didn't look at Hilary as she said this in a queer, flat voice which gave no clue as to how she felt about it.

Hilary, probing, said, 'What happened? Are you sure it was suicide? Could it have been an accident?'

She asked herself, What difference does it make, he's dead, isn't he? And then she thought, It must matter to Sandra. She has to blame herself if he committed suicide. She's bound to think he did it because she rejected him and what he believes in. He failed to give her the help he thought she needed, even if she didn't know she did.

'No, he killed himself all right,' Sandra said. 'The scales must've fallen from his eyes. Once he realized how wicked he was, he didn't see any other way out, I suppose.'

61

Was William wicked? Hilary asked herself. Misguided, yes, but wicked? And yet Sandra judged him so easily.

Hilary thought of the lonely old lady in the garden hurrying painfully indoors to answer a telephone in the hope someone wanted to talk to her. Sandra's cruel, she thought. She scrutinised the hard little face for some sign of pity for William. Nothing. God, who is she, what makes her tick? I don't know how she feels, or anything about her, Hilary told herself.

And then she thought it's not just Sandra. We think we're the same people we were when we first got here, but how much we all of us have changed in just two years. It comes as a surprise when we see it in other people, but we each of us think we're the same as we always were. I never understood Ffion. Ellie has become a stranger, too. And we've none of us become nicer people. Is that what happens when you grow up, or is there something wrong with us?

She became aware of Sandra saying, 'He fell out of a window on the top floor of the Royal Avenue Hotel. He must've wanted to make a show of himself; Royal Avenue's the busiest street in Belfast, and he jumped from a front window at lunchtime right down into a crowded street. Who'd kill himself that way unless he saw himself as some sort of martyr?'

'Perhaps he was too unhappy even to plan how he did it, he acted on the spur of the moment,' Hilary said, trying to create some grain of sympathy for William. 'Did he leave a note, or anything explaining why he did it?'

'Oh, just show-boating stuff. He'd scrawled a lot of Biblical texts about not being able to endure the wickedness of the world and the evil about to be visited upon us.'

'How do you feel about it?'

Sandra had rather curious blue-grey eyes; Hilary was astonished that she'd never noticed before. How unusual they were. A lifeless matt colour which did not reflect light.

'William was mad,' Sandra said. And clearly, for her, that was the end of the matter. William was better off dead.

Hilary thought, what does it mean to be religious when it comes down to it? The Rev Dad and William, presumably, would both say they were close to God; but really William's faith seemed more about politics and exercising power. It would never make him happy the way it did the Rev Dad; there was no joy in William. Did his faith make him that way, or did he seek out a faith to suit his nature?

She asked Sandra, 'Do you ever think about the real Irish people outside Trinity? Coming here is a wonderful experience for us, but what about them, struggling to make ends meet in their own country on less than we get in grants, while we live in our ivory tower exploiting their culture and making no effort at all to know or understand who they are or what they hope for? Or, in fact, what they think of us.'

'They make money out of it. Even students must be preferable to tourists, surely?'

Sandra wasn't interested. She wanted to talk about herself. William was dead, she must feel something. So far, she couldn't make herself care, it seemed too remote. He wanted to die so he killed himself. That didn't strike her as tragic.

She said, in answer to Hilary's question, 'They live off our backs, when it comes down to it. They may have made martyrs of themselves fighting for the Republic against the Black and Tans and the Protestant Ascendency, but those self-same freedom-fighters are now earning a living providing digs for us or letting out their slum houses to us as flats. I don't know the figures, but would there even be an Irish economy without Trinity?'

Hilary told herself, Miss O'Connell is the only real Irish person I've had any contact with. She's been part of all that passionate history, all the violence and the hatred — and the only conversation we've ever had together is about the rent. I wouldn't even know which political party Eamon de Valera belonged to. I only know Sinn Fein means Ourselves Alone, but I've no idea what the other political parties call themselves or stand for.

She asked Sandra, 'What are the main Irish political parties?'

'What?' Sandra was still thinking about William. She couldn't tell Hilary, but she was glad he was dead. She had broken away from him, and in doing so from her own past, but she'd hated it that he knew more about her in her misguided youth than she wanted known. Now I'm free, she thought, I can be who and what I like.

'Oh, nothing,' Hilary said. She'd heard a key in the lock of their front door. One of the others must be home. Tomorrow I'll go into the Library and find out, she said to herself, it's the least I could do.'

Ffion came in. She was wearing a minuscule black and white patterned mini-dress and white tights and she didn't look at all like a genuine student coming in from work; more like a socialite who'd been to a garden party.

Hilary thought, perhaps she has been to a garden party, she's seeing an older man who works for the US Embassy. A meal ticket, she calls him. As if Ffion doesn't have more than enough to eat, what with the Soup Bowl and posing as the socially-suitable girlfriend of a medical student who hopes to land a job in one of the fashionable practices in Fitzwilliam Square. That must involve a lot of eating. Howard, his name was. Ffion said she thought he was homosexual, but that could be because he wasn't interested in her.

Hilary smiled to herself. No, that couldn't be right. A heterosexual man who wasn't interested in Ffion would have to have been dead some time.

'God,' Ffion said, coming into the kitchen, 'who died?'

Hilary caught a look of panic on Sandra's face.

64

She said quickly, 'We've been improving the shining hour playing the kettle trick on old Miss O'Connell.'

'I can't believe she still falls for that. She must be thick as Liffey water.' Ffion put the kettle on to make herself a coffee. 'God,' she said, 'there's not a single clean mug in this place. You might at least have washed up.' She glanced out of the window. 'Deirdre of the Sorrows has gone in,' she added.

'Ffion, do you know what are the main political parties in Ireland?' Hilary asked.

'The government party is Fianna Fail and the Opposition is Fine Gael. There are others, but I don't know about them.'

'What's the difference between them?'

'No idea. What's brought this on?

'I just think sometimes it's going to be an awful shock when we leave here and have to go out into the real world.'

'What the hell are you fecking on about, Hilary? We'll have our degrees and that'll open doors to careers and we go from there.'

'I can't help it. I feel being at Trinity is like living in some sort of Brigadoon place beyond reality in a mystical Ireland where we can wallow in a magical literary and historical dream world, but real life for the Irish is an insult to the intelligent.'

'The intelligent what? I don't know what you're fecking talking about.' Sandra wanted to talk about William Carson.

'I do,' Ffion said. 'About insulting the intelligence of the Irish. I went to see a film the other night – *Two Women*, based on Moravia's novel. It was incomprehensible; so much had been cut out. I tried to buy the book to find out what it was about, but I couldn't. It's banned. That's an insult to the intelligence of Protestants too.'

Hilary said, 'The worst thing is the ban on contraceptives. The people are so poor and the women have to go on having babies.'

Ffion nodded. 'You know, the Irish Constitution guarantees freedom to other faiths to practice their religion, which, for Protestants, for instance, allows them to plan their families. So technically the Irish State should provide the means for them to do so. Someone should take the State to court.'

'The State would never go against the Catholic Church,' Hilary said.

Ffion laughed. 'Look,' she said, 'this is how I get round that problem.'

She went to her room and came back with a heavy leather-bound book. 'It's the most turgid-looking tome on Constitutional Law I could buy,' she said. 'I've cut a hole in the pages and I smuggle contraceptives back from England in it. Sometimes I even get the Customs people to help me carry it. No one's bothered to look inside so far.'

'Contraception isn't the only fecking thing; do you know the Catholic Church in Ireland tells girls not to use tampons. It says they're 'a grave source of temptation', if you can believe that?'

There was a sound of something heavy bumping on the stairs.

'That must be Ellie,' Sandra said. 'But didn't she say she was staying over with Matt?'

Ffion said, sounding irritated, 'Oh, Christ, that sounds like another load of Matt's washing she'd bringing here. Can't she tell him we don't have a washing machine now we're not in Trinity Hall?'

'I must say it's a bit much having his fecking Y-fronts dripping on you when you're having a bath,' Sandra said.

'Greater love hath no woman than that she washes her man's Y-fronts by hand,' Hilary said, trying to seem one with them.

'Unless, like Ellie, she hand-washes his girlfriends' knickers too if they're in the laundry bag.'

Ellie came in then, dragging two bursting bags of dirty clothes.

'Matt not around tonight after all?' Sandra said.

Ellie noticed the way they were looking at her. She said, 'Someone would make a fortune starting a chain of launderettes in Dublin, you know. I can't think why no one has.'

Ffion suddenly asked her, 'What do you do about contraception, Ellie?'

'What?' Ellie flushed very red.

Hilary said, 'We were talking about things that are banned in Ireland.'

'Which are almost invariably aimed to suppress women.' They all looked at Ffion as though this had never occurred to them.

'The Catholic Church and the Irish government aren't the only fecking ones,' Sandra said. 'Look at Trinity, the way we're treated. Women must be out of College rooms by 6pm, and we can't belong to the Philosophical Society and debate whether we should be allowed to be full members of the University the same as men.'

'God, I wouldn't join the Phil even if I could,' Ffion said. 'All those immature men sneaking down to the basement in the GMB to swig Dr Collis Browne's cough mixture for the morphine in it. They're not worth competing with. Pathetic.'

'Is that what they do?'

Ffion shrugged. She was watching Ellie. 'Aren't you going to answer my question?' she said. 'You're the only one of us in a regular relationship. What do you do about contraception?'

Ellie sat down suddenly on the bag of dirty laundry.

'Oh, do shut up,' she said. She burst into tears. 'I've only gone and got myself pregnant.'

8

On a gloomy afternoon the Buttery snack bar was almost deserted. At a table by the window Hilary and Sandra were waiting for Ellie.

Outside the day was preparing for the last rites. Black clouds banked in the sky over a grim Museum Building were about to sound the last trump with a Day of Judgement thunderstorm to end the unseasonable autumn heat wave.

Sandra and Hilary stared out of the window, seeing only themselves reflected back at them in the glass. They looked as though they were on stage, had forgotten their lines, and the prompter had lost his place.

Ellie had asked them to wait for her. She was going to break the news that she was pregnant to Matt and she wanted to have her friends there to talk to afterwards about what he'd said and the way he'd said it and what he'd meant to say and what she'd wanted him to say.

'She's been gone an hour already,' Sandra said, looking at her watch. 'How long does it take to say "I'm pregnant", for God's sake?'

Hilary said, 'I'm surprised he hasn't noticed anything before now. They're supposed to be so close, how come he hasn't seen how weird she's been lately?'

'We didn't.'

'I suppose we thought it's normal for someone in love to be a bit mad.'

Sandra shrugged. 'How far gone is she? Three months overdue? She's lucky she's so overweight. Anyone can see if a thin person gets fat, but no one notices a fat person getting fatter.'

'Yes, and the clothes help. Ellie always wears those shapeless, droopy sort of things.'

'Can you imagine Ellie in a mini skirt?'

'I can't wear them either,' Hilary said. 'But no, they don't suit women with our shape, hers and mine.'

'At least you wear brighter colours. It's not just a question of shape; you've got to have the right style,' Sandra said, knowing she'd put her foot in it and thinking it would make Hilary feel better. With her long coltish legs the mini, any mini, suited her; Sandra felt part of the spirit of the Sixties. She thought of Ellie and Hilary as being from an older generation even though they were the same age as herself.

I can't believe we're having this conversation with Ellie's future hanging in the balance, Hilary thought. She said, 'Want another coffee?'

Sandra shook her head. 'No, thanks, I'm awash with the fecking stuff. Do you think Matt's giving Ellie a hard time? I bet he'll walk all over her. She'll get that poor little me look on her face and say sorry all the time. Honestly if I were him I'd give her a good slap.'

Hilary was trying to imagine how Matt would react to Ellie's news. She feared for Ellie. Matt was the ubiquitous man about college; all over the place like vermin, Ffion said. He was involved with Players, and with the production of TCD Magazine; he wrote poetry for *Icarus* and was a leading light in debates in the Phil and Hist. He knew everyone, and went everywhere.

Hilary thought, He's got that shack down the coast near Brittas Bay, but he seems to spend most week nights dossing down in someone's rooms in the Graduates' Memorial Building.

At least, that's what Ellie said. But she would, wouldn't she? It was easier for her to think of him spending his nights in female-free rooms in College than imagining him sleeping with various girls in flats around the city. Hilary and Sandra had never mentioned it to Ellie, but they'd often discussed Matt's reputation as a seducer of women.

Father to that thought, Hilary asked herself, Is he begetting sons by the dozen? She said, 'He may even be married. He's quite a bit older than we are. Do you think Ellie expects him to marry her?'

'You mean settle down in that hovel on the beach and come back to help her change the fecking baby every night? She's in for the hell of a fecking shock if she thinks that'll happen.'

'She thinks he loves her.'

'He'll run a mile. What's she going to do? She'll have to leave College.'

Hilary didn't dare say, 'Oh that poor baby,' but that's what she was thinking. An unwanted child. Even Ellie couldn't want it now, however much she dreamed of having Matt's children one day.

She said, 'Matt'll have to do something, won't he? He can't just wash his hands of her. It's not as if he's an innocent party, is it?' And then she found herself saying, 'If he loves her, surely he'll be pleased. They'd probably have got married one day anyway, don't you think?'

Sandra gave her a scornful look. 'She made all the fecking running. Don't you remember that night she got us to go with her down to Brittas Bay? She positively forced herself on him. I bet that right now he's trying to make her have an abortion. For her own fecking sake, of course, not his. At least he must know someone in England where she could go to get rid of it.'

Since Ellie had announced she was pregnant, Hilary had found it hard to think of anything else. It had even crossed her mind that Ellie was making it up to trap Matt into giving up other women to concentrate on her.

No, Ellie couldn't be that naive. Or could she? Hilary had quite often heard the Rev Dad say to Mother that one or other village girl had deliberately got in trouble to put pressure on a lover who wouldn't commit to her. 'Oh, the silly girl,' Mother always said, 'it'll end in tears.'

Hilary thought, if I ever find someone to impregnate me, I won't tell anyone I'm pregnant. Least of all the father. Hilary fully expected that any man who got her pregnant would be pretty well bound to be drunk when he did it. Almost certainly, he wouldn't want anything more to do with her. I don't want to know that, she thought. No, I'd leave Ireland and get a job and bring it up on my own. Mum would help me. Oh, I wish it was me; I wish I was Ellie. It occurred to her that Matt, too, probably wished she was Ellie at this moment. She'd be far less trouble to him than poor Ellie.

'Do you think she would? Get rid of it?' There was a horrified awe in her voice that any woman could possibly do such a thing. Hilary couldn't imagine it.

Indeed, she was already nurturing a wild hope that she would persuade Ellie to give her the child to bring up. Then Ellie could go ahead and get her degree and have a career and afterwards they'd share the child.

Hilary hadn't dared mention her idea to Ellie, but, lying awake that night, she saw it as a serious option

In the light of morning, of course, it was a bit different, but she still hoped Ellie might consider it.

Sandra said, 'Ffion wouldn't think twice.'

'Oh, Ffion!' Hilary was about to say it wasn't a subject to joke about when Ellie arrived at their table. She was laden with shopping bags which she dropped on the floor as she sat down at the table. She said, 'Oh, God! I'm exhausted.'

Sandra and Hilary looked expectant. Hilary was already wearing her 'oh, poor Ellie, how awful!' expression.

'Well?' she said.

'I'm dying for a coffee – black and strong.'

'That's bad for the baby.'

'For feck's sake, stop stalling, Ellie. We've been sitting here for over an hour dying to know what's happened.'

Ellie bit her lip. She said, 'I didn't tell him.'

Then, when they appeared struck speechless, she said, 'I couldn't. There were people there and he was having terrible trouble finishing an essay he was supposed to've handed in yesterday. He hadn't time to talk. It wasn't the right moment.'

'Ellie!' They protested almost in unison.

'You've got to tell him. He's got a right to know.'

'Or are you going to fecking wait until it's born and then hand it to him and say "Surprise!"'

Tears began to roll slowly down Ellie's plump, pale cheeks.

'It's all very well for you, but it just goes round and round in my head and I don't even know what I want to do.'

Then she added in a whisper, 'I think I'll have to kill myself.'

'Surely there must be ways you could live with it?' Hilary said. Was this the moment to suggest her own solution? She didn't quite dare. Instead she asked Ellie, 'What about your mother, would she look after the baby while you finish your degree?'

'I couldn't ask her.'

Ellie could feel herself going red because it was a lie, she could ask her parents and they would welcome the addition to the family. But Ellie didn't want that. She didn't want her mother involved with this new child. She told herself, Mum's past it; she's not modern, she couldn't do a proper job of preparing a baby for the world it's got to live in. But Ellie couldn't try to explain this. She almost shouted, 'No.'

They sat in stunned silence, except for the sound of Ellie's muffled sobs. Hilary stared at the three of them reflected in the window and the scene seemed unreal and one-dimensional like an old photograph, impersonal and without any trace of emotion.

Sandra said, 'We'd better go.'

She started to pick up Ellie's shopping bags from the floor.

They went back to Raglan Road. Ffion wasn't there. Hilary and Sandra sat in the sitting-room in silence. Ellie went to the bedroom. She sat on the edge of her bed trying to take in the horror of her situation. She wondered, how can I have been so stupid? It was only when I chickened out of telling Matt that I realized what I've done. I can't tell the others, they'd hate me if they knew. They'd never understand I let something momentous like this happen like tossing a coin to decide my future.

She tried to remember what it had been like: wanting Matt with all her heart and body, wanting to bind him to her and herself to him forever. It was the one way she could be sure that he felt about her the same way she did about him.

College, her career, her future hopes and his, weighed against their future together, bonded by the new life they'd created. She'd thrown the dice, telling him it was her safe time of the month so he didn't pull out. Now it was too late to withdraw the stake.

Ellie groaned to herself, My God, what have I done?

Outside the uncurtained windows of the flat, a shaft of lightning split the sky. Hilary counted to four before the crack of thunder followed, and rain started to pound the panes.

Nobody wanted to eat. Sandra opened a bottle of wine but they weren't drinking either. They felt numbed by Ellie's misery, overwhelmed by their first personal awareness of someone they knew grappling with a personal catastrophe.

Hilary, trying to be positive, suddenly said, 'It's not a tragedy, is it? No one's died, or failed, or got cancer; all that's happened is that Ellie will have to change her plans.'

73

Sandra surprised herself by saying, 'She's lost hope, Hilary, her dreams won't come true. That's tragic for her.'

'Then she must get new dreams.'

There were running footsteps in the hall. The door burst open and Ellie, her hair damp and her nightdress clamped to her wet body, burst into the room.

'It's come,' she gasped, 'it's all right. There's no baby. I've got my period.'

Sandra jumped to her feet. She said with fury, 'Fecking Hell, after you sicked up all that self-serving anguish crap on us? I tell you, right now I'd really like to give you a good smack in that fecking gob of yours.'

Ellie, laughing, tried to throw her arms around Sandra but Sandra stepped aside. She was angry.

Ellie said, 'What's the matter? You look as if you're sorry I'm off the hook?'

Sandra glanced at silent Hilary and tried not to notice that there were tears in her naked-looking eyes. 'OK,' Sandra said, grabbing the bottle of wine, 'we should celebrate. Let's drink to anti-climax.'

9

Compared to her flatmates, Hilary spent much more time than they did on her academic studies.

'Parkinson's Law,' said Ffion when the others commented on this one night, accusing Hilary of being a closet blue-stocking. 'Work expands to meet the time available,' she said.

'What's that supposed to mean?' said Ellie, using any opportunity to challenge Ffion.

'Do I really need to spell it out? Hilary has nothing else to do. She doesn't go to parties or go out at all. She hasn't got a boyfriend to feed and keep clean, and she doesn't have any particular interest or talent there's a club for. So she has a lot of time for work. QED.'

They all looked at Hilary to see what she would say in her own defence.

She laughed. 'To coin a phrase, I refuse to join any club that would have a person like me as a member. Anyway I'd always end up with the boring jobs, like club secretary. Just because I'm not good-looking, why should I be the dogsbody? Frankly I'd rather study, if that's what you call reading a good book.'

Sandra giggled. When would she grow out of giggling, it was really irritating? 'At least you didn't say the Good Book.'

Hilary herself had often thought it was ironic that the others had come to University intending to jump start their potential careers with a good degree. Well, perhaps not Ffion, but she also intended to use it as a stepping stone to Top People.

Whatever, Hilary thought, the others give priority to almost everything else TCD offers over serious study, while I, who has no real use for a degree, came here to find someone to marry me and give me children, and I do nothing much except academic work.

She said, 'At least I want to come away with something to show for my time here…'

'Education isn't all about studying. It broadens the mind. Most of us don't have to spend our time in the library; we're out experiencing new things.'

Ffion sneered. 'So Ellie's practising married life with Matt and you're trying to embrace the Swinging Sixties? No wonder the country's going down the tubes, investing all that money on universities to teach us what we could just as easily learn on a dirty weekend in Brighton or even Blackpool.'

Sandra knew that Ffion was mocking her. She could never defend herself against the fecking woman; she never understood why she was being laughed at. She fell silent.

Hilary, too, had nothing to say. She knew none of those aspirations were for her. I'm out of place in my own generation, she told herself. I don't look right, I don't dress right, or speak the lingo. Everyone sees me as an overgrown schoolgirl, preparing for a lifetime as the prototype of a woman Jane Austen might describe as "a maiden aunt".

'Yuck!' Ffion said in disgust.

I don't mind, Hilary told herself, I'll do what I can with what I've got; if I can't have my own kids, I'll be the loving aunt to other people's children. And I'll teach. I'll be the best teacher I can be. If I get a good degree, it'll help me do that.

But the best-laid plans…It was in the vacation before the start of the Trinity term in April of their senior sophomore year that Hilary's cocooned existence fell apart.

She badly needed a friend she could trust to keep her awful secret. But I don't have any friends like that. Mother had friends for life, everyone Mother's age did. But I don't have friends, full stop; I just know people.

That's feminism's fault, she thought. Women don't share their feelings like that anymore, they're afraid of opening up to each other.

To test the water, she said to Ellie, 'I don't know what to do, I need help.'

Ellie started to list what sounded like a shopping list. 'Anna Raeburn's good on relationships. Write to her if you wouldn't die of embarrassment. And the Citizens Advice Bureau is very helpful on legal rights, or money if you get thrown out of home. Of course, if it's something really bad, there's always the Samaritans.'

'Don't you even want to know how unhappy I am? And why?'

'Of course not; I'm not that insensitive. That would be a real invasion of privacy.'

Hilary expected Ellie to say, in that look-on-the-bright-side way she had, 'You of all people must know that God only helps those who help themselves.'

I don't think God ever said anything about "only", Hilary thought. She wanted to say, 'Don't you care?'

But of course Ellie didn't care. Her strongest emotion would be relief that it was happening to someone else, not her.

Well, Hilary thought, when Ellie thought she was pregnant, I suppose I didn't care for her, I just tried to imagine how I'd have felt in her place. I only thought of myself, that I wanted a baby, and that if she gave hers to me, it would solve her problem and mine.

It's no good, Hilary thought. I judge everything by my practically pre-War standards, and that's pre-World War Two, not the Sex War. Compared with other women my age, I'm morally retarded.

She wanted to confide in Sandra because possibly Sandra knew a little about the bonds of guilt which rendered Hilary in her troubled state unable to decide anything for herself. The Rev Dad left such decisions to the Will of God; her mother referred them to an unwritten code of convention. But Sandra had fought long and hard to escape from similar, even more bizarre, terms of moral reference.

And all I know to do about what's happened is to deny it and blank it out of my mind because my mind isn't where I can solve the problem.

Hilary tried to imagine how Sandra would react. But really they didn't know each other at all, not well enough to feel responsible for each other. Hilary was afraid to trust Sandra with the power that the knowledge she wanted to share would give her.

So, there's no help for it. She stands hunched against the wind on the dark deck of the ferry to Ireland with the waves breaking against the side of the long-suffering vessel. The spray starches her face with salt, or maybe it's tears that leave a crust on her skin.

Her hands clamped on the metal rail she thinks how easy it would be to let go, to lean forward and let the sea take her. The water is kind, fondling her gently as she slips down into a wave's trough.

It's too tempting. She stepped back away from the rail and clung to the wooden rim of a lifeboat.

Fool, she told herself, it is a sin. A sin against people who need me.

She seems to hear a mocking laugh somewhere nearby. Ffion's laugh. And Ffion's voice, unsentimental as the wind. 'You're on your own. Deal with it,' Ffion said.

I'm trying to turn what's happened into history, she tells herself, but it's now, it's the urgent present. So, decide.

Spring had started like all the other spring times Hilary remembered since she was a little girl. The Rev Dad mowing the lawn or preparing his Sunday sermon in the conservatory after tea; Mother weeding or dead-heading the daffodils, bending broad-beamed in her old slacks tied at the waist with a dog lead; always a succession of visitors wanting to talk to one or other of them and Hilary always on the side-lines, a passing presence on her way out of all their lives, nodding and smiling as she carried trays of tea and scones, or fetched pen and paper for note-taking.

And on the surface she still was that little girl; that's how everyone still saw her.

'How are you liking university, dear?' her mother asked, and was echoed by everyone from the organist to the postman, the cleaning lady to the bell ringers.

Hilary knew from the way they asked that they didn't want to be told.

And then suddenly this spring was different.

There were children there, two girls and a boy, Hilary's nephew and nieces. Their mother, Hilary's elder sister, Susan, hadn't been home to Surrey for years. Once or twice Mum and Dad had taken the train up to Edinburgh to see the kids, but Sue was always too busy to bring them to stay. Now she was here for at least a month. Her husband, Duncan, was tied up with work; he'd agreed to cope on his own while Sue brought the family down for a break with the grandparents. Duncan was so thoughtful, they all said. Not many husbands would want to be apart from their families for so long.

Hilary and her parents knew something was wrong. At least Hilary did and she was sure the Rev Dad and Mother must, the way they all nodded and smiled and were careful not to ask questions. When one of the children barked her knee and cried for her Daddy to make it better, they all made noises about Daddy having to be away working because he loved them so much. No one asked why Duncan hadn't rung to find out how they were. Instead Grandma took the children out to buy sweets; Granddad got back to his sermon.

79

Hilary, ignorant then of what it felt like to need a friend, played hoydenish games with the children and talked to Susan as it were through the mouths of the kids. 'Grandma and Grandpa are planning to take Susan and Hilary and Lizzie and Jenny and Teddy-boy to Chessington Zoo this weekend if we're good' – that sort of thing until one night when the children were in bed Susan burst out, 'For God's sake, Hilary, will you shut up and be quiet before I kill you or myself.'

'Sorry, I'm sure,' Hilary said, so awfully hurt.

Susan looked at her and made a helpless sort of wringing-of-her-hands gesture, then burst into tears and ran out of the room.

Hilary didn't follow her; she thought Sue would want to be alone with her tears. Or her bad temper.

Then one Friday afternoon Duncan suddenly turned up unannounced on the doorstep.

'Oh, how lovely, the children will be over the moon,' Mother said. 'Susan took them shopping in Guildford, but they'll be back soon.'

'I've come to see Susan,' he said, 'Something's come up and we need to talk.'

'Promotion,' I hope,' the Rev Dad said. 'She's told us how hard you're having to work; I guessed you might be in line for a step up. It would be nice if it meant you could move a bit nearer.'

Duncan smiled but said nothing. 'Here, give us a hug,' he said to Hilary, 'how's my little sister-in-law? How's university? You've grown up; you were just a kid when I last saw you.'

'And you're almost an old man,' she said. She hugged him, laughing.

Feeling his arms round her, smelling the man smell of him, Hilary was suddenly overwhelmed by envy of Susan. The pain took her breath away and her knees went weak. If Duncan hadn't been holding her she felt she would have fallen. She knew that Duncan had been aware of her reaction and was embarrassed.

Oh God, she thought, but he can't possibly have known what I was thinking.

And then the kids were there, all over him. And Susan too, suddenly years younger and all smiles. Hilary brought tea to the terrace as though Duncan were another visitor on parish business. Everyone made polite conversation about the weather and the garden and the lack of local public transport.

Mother said, 'Do you have to go back on Sunday, dear?'

Duncan took Susan's hand. 'I can't stay that long, I'm afraid, darling, I've got to fly back tonight.'

'Oh, no, surely not.' Susan looked stricken. She said, 'They can't make you work all weekend.'

He said, 'It'll soon be over. But we've got to talk.'

Hilary, noticing the sulky, stubborn expression on her sister's face, wanted to kick her under the table to warn her that she wasn't behaving well when Duncan had made the effort to come all this way to see her. She wanted to say, 'Be nice to him, show him how pleased you are that he's here,' but she couldn't make Susan hear without the others asking what she'd said, so she said nothing.

Then Mum and the Reverend Dad, being tactful, took the children out for a walk to the village to buy more sweets. Hilary cleared away the tea things and washed them up, while Susan took Duncan upstairs.

Hilary was embarrassed again when she heard them shouting. She tried not to listen, but she couldn't help it. They were having a terrible row and she didn't want to know what they were saying, but even when she put her hands over her ears she couldn't shut out Susan's high-pitched whine. Like a chain saw; on and on it went, repeating itself. Duncan said nothing much, he seemed to be trying to calm her, but her painful tones continued, on and on.

Until, just as Hilary thought she could stand it no longer, there was a thump and the sound stopped. Then there was a long silence.

Hilary ran upstairs to Susan's room. She threw open the door. Sue was on the floor, holding herself up on her arms, her face white and shocked, staring at Duncan who was sitting on the side of the bed, his head in his hands.

When she saw Hilary, Susan manoeuvred herself on to her knees and pointed at Duncan.

'He hit me, the bastard, he knocked me down.'

She said to Hilary, 'You're my witness, he hit me; he struck a woman.' And then she returned to Duncan, 'I'll get you for this,' she said, 'you'll never see your children again as long as I live.'

Hilary went to her and put her arms round her, trying to help her to her feet. Susan struck her hands away.

'Don't touch me, get away from me.' She was screaming. God, this is just awful, Hilary thought

'Don't, Sue,' Hilary said, 'let me help. You can't let the children see you like this.'

'Why not, why the hell not, why hide it from them that their father beats up their mother? And what do you know with your mealy-mouthed ways and your baby-talk and your happily-ever-after platitudes. No man's ever wanted you, what do you know? Get away from me, Hilary, I don't want you here.' She sniffed and pointed at Duncan. 'Do me a favour and take that brute with you.'

Hilary knelt down beside her, careful not to touch her.

'Don't, Sue. You don't mean it. Mum and Dad will be home soon, and the kids-'

Susan lashed out at her. Hilary ducked and the punch grazed her shoulder.

'Don't you understand, get out, both of you? I'll think of something to tell Mum and Dad, just get rid of him.' She fumbled in her pockets and found the keys to her car. She sounded calmer now, with a new steely look on her face. 'Take my car and put him on a train. Take him to Heathrow to catch a plane. I don't care what you do, but get rid of him.'

Hilary didn't know what else to do. She took the car keys and went to Duncan. He didn't seem to have moved but when she put her hand on his arm she could feel him trembling.

'Come on,' she said. 'You can't do anything here at the moment; we'll sort it out later.'

He followed her out of the house and into the car. It was a long time since she'd driven, and she made a few false starts to find the controls in a strange car. Duncan made no effort to help her. He looked punch drunk.

As she drove shakily out of the drive he said, 'I've never hit her before in my life.'

Hilary heard again that high-pitched screech, saw the sulky accusing expression on her sister's face and all the memories of years of sibling jealousy and resentment flooded back to her. Susan, always the first, always deferred to, always the winner. Hilary felt guiltily glad. The blow Duncan dealt Susan was her revenge too.

At the crossroads in the village, she saw her parents and the children coming out of the shop. The children were calling out to each other. Hilary's heart missed a beat and tears came to her eyes; they were so small, so confident that all was well. The girls were holding hands, and Mum and the Rev Dad were swinging Teddy between them. Hilary was almost sure they were singing one of the bracing hymns; Onward Christian Soldiers, perhaps. That was their favourite.

'Oh, please God, not now,' she said under her breath, turning away from them down the lane past the church to avoid them seeing her.

'What?' Duncan said.

She said, 'Where do you want to go?'

83

'I can't leave it like that,' he said. 'Do you think she'll come round?'

'Why did she get so mad? Apart from you hitting her, I mean. Are you having an affair, is that what you came to tell her?'

He looked affronted. 'Of course not. The firm wants me to go to Saudi Arabia. I can't turn it down, really, but that's what Susan wants me to do. The company will get rid of me if I don't go.'

'God, is that all? I thought at least you wanted a divorce to marry someone else.'

'I've never seen her like that. Do you think she'll cool off and let me talk to her?'

'Not by tonight. Find a hotel and try again in the morning.'

'Yes. That's what I'll do.'

She took him to a roadhouse somewhere outside Woking. He checked in and came back to the car.

'Come in and have a coffee or something, at least,' he said. 'You've been great. On second thoughts, I need whisky. I'll get a bottle from room service.'

Vaguely, she thought they'd had a drink and then another, and then there was the issue of driving home so she said she'd have a quick nap and then she'd be all right to drive.

She awoke in bed beside Duncan. Her clothes were scattered across the room and the wet sheet felt cold under her thighs. It was 4.30 in the morning. She felt sick.

She tried to wake Duncan but all that happened was that he shifted position and the tone of his snoring changed. At least he wasn't dead. She put the car keys on the bedside table.

She put on her clothes and found her way to reception where a night porter was dozing with the radio on. She made him call her a taxi and as she waited for it to come she found herself burning with shame. She knew exactly what the porter was thinking, even before he grinned at her.

The taxi driver took her into Woking, where she drew £100 out of a cash machine so she could pay him. When they got to the vicarage the man met her eyes in the driving mirror. 'Shall I drive in, or would you rather I dropped you here?'

She got out. He winked at her as he took her money.

She let herself into the house and went upstairs to Susan's room. Her sister sat up in bed as she came in.

'Hilary?'

'It's me. Are you all right?'

Susan put on the light. She looked much better for a good night's sleep. Quite normal, in fact.

'I took Duncan to a hotel and left him there. I left your car so he can get back here in the morning.'

'My God, how did you get back here alone? You should've taken a room too, and come back in the morning.'

'I thought you'd imagine God knows what and accuse him of seducing me.'

Susan laughed. 'You wish. He'd never make love to you, however far gone he was.'

Shut up, Hilary told herself, don't say a word. But how she wanted to...

'I hitched. There are quite a lot of lorries about in the wee small hours.'

'What did he say? Is he sorry?'

'He's devastated. How do you feel?'

'Better. I suppose I owe you an apology?'

'What did you tell Mum and the Rev Dad?'

'Oh, I said Duncan had taken my car to make a business call, which is why he really came here in the first place. Then we'll all drive back to Edinburgh tomorrow. I said you'd gone off to study, you didn't want any supper.'

'Did they believe you?'

'Of course they did.'

'You've done this sort of thing before.'

'I like a good fight; it helps to keep a man like Duncan on his toes.'

Hilary went to the bathroom and turned the shower on full, letting the water buffet her body. She was surprised that Susan hadn't smelled Duncan on her, it seemed to her she reeked of him.

In her own bed she tried to sleep but all she could do was cry. Hilary was horribly afraid. Her body already felt different: of course it was much too early to know she was pregnant but she was sure. She clenched her fists and ground them into her temples. It was so damned unfair, this was the moment which should have crowned her life but now it had happened, if it had, it was all wrong. It was impossible, the family had too strong a hold on her, she couldn't do it. Their standards, their morals, their values, they were still hers, she couldn't betray them; she could not throw back in their faces everything they'd done to make her what she was. Vicar's daughters were married when their children were born, even if it was a shotgun wedding. Duncan was married already, to her own sister, and his children - well, she could never do anything to risk their happiness.

But what of the child she might be carrying? Her own child. Hilary pulled the pillow overhead and howled, unable to stop herself.

Downstairs at breakfast, one of the children asked, 'What's Auntie Hilary doing making that noise?'

Mrs Taylor smiled, 'She's pretending to be a wolf, darling. I expect it's a new game.'

'Can we go and play it with her?'

'Of course dear, off you go. You can be the wolf's puppies.'

Later that same day Duncan returned with Susan's car and after lunch he and Susan and the kids set off for Edinburgh as though nothing had happened.

Now, not many weeks later, she was back in Dublin fooling herself and everyone else that everything was normal. She was in no doubt now that she was pregnant. She tried to ignore it, pretend it wasn't real, but it definitely was. When she was sick, she said she'd got a stomach bug and took Milk of Magnesia. She told herself, it's just as well everyone takes it for granted that I'll always be the same old Hilary that they don't notice any difference. Even if I have to kill myself because there's no other way out, they'll scarcely realize I've gone.

But she knew it could not go on like this.

I wonder if, if there is a God, He minds always being people's last resort? She thought this as she walked into St Patrick's Cathedral early one morning.

The predominantly lime-greenish tiled floor of the vast nave startled her; it wasn't what she'd have picked as a holy colour. This is where Jonathan Swift once walked, his mind in torment, she told herself, and wished that he was here now for her to talk to.

She imagined that the interior represented contempt for weakness; the arched pillars and stern grey stone daunted her; she was a little afraid of losing confidence in herself under the eye of a judgmental God.

Perhaps Ffion should think of being a bishop, she thought.

She sat alone beside a pillar near the nave. Silently, helpless to stop herself, she found herself crying. It wasn't like real weeping, no screwed-up expression or painful gasping; it felt like the inside of her head were leaking out of her eyes and overflowing down her face to drip on to a dark patch on her blue blouse.

Someone sat down in the seat beside her. Hilary turned; she wanted very much to be alone and there was a sea of empty seats around her. She wondered if it would be rude to move.

Then she recognized the man as Ffion's friend, Howard.

'Hi,' he said, 'do you mind if I sit with you?'

She shook her head and tried to smile. He must be horrified he butted in when he saw my face, she thought. She wondered why he was here. He wasn't looking well, he'd lost a lot of weight. He'd been working out of College in the city's public hospitals most of the year, and she hadn't seen him for some time.

She got up to go out of the cathedral and he came with her. Outside he said, 'I'm sorry I barged in. I was glad to see someone I knew and I didn't think. I took it for granted you were a regular.'

'It's the first time I've come,' she said. 'I didn't expect to see you here.'

He looked around and up at the massive grey building. 'This place is so enduring. I like that. It puts things in proportion.'

'I was thinking of my father, hoping he'll be imbued with Christian mercy and forgiveness when he finds out what I've done.'

She smiled, hoping that Howard would think she was joking but at the same time unable to stop herself telling him more. She'd been bottling things up too long; she'd come here to try to tell God, if there was a God. Howard might not look like much of a stand-in for Him, but at least Howard was here, a friendly presence.

'I don't know what to do,' she whispered. Her lips were trembling so much she could scarcely speak. 'I've got to tell someone.'

He took her arm and guided her round the outside of the building to a wooden seat against the massive wall. He said, 'You can tell me. I'm almost a doctor; I'm bound by the confidentiality agreement, even if you're not my patient.'

So she told him; about Susan and what happened with Duncan that dreadful night; and that now she was pregnant. A baby was what she wanted most in the world but, if she went ahead, it would destroy the lives people she loved. Susan's marriage, Sue's children's relationship with their father; her parents' trust, their hopes for her. She couldn't help it, and maybe her values were as old-fashioned as theirs, but she loved her family. That, and their love for her, sustained her.

Now I know why Sandra couldn't tell William Carson to go to hell, she thought.

She said, 'And my own life, I destroy that too, I need them,' she added. 'I'll be an outcast in my own family and they're everything to me.'

They sat for a while without speaking. It was a beautiful morning, the sun catching the ruffled surface of the grass. At this time of day the churchyard was almost deserted; all around in the bushes birds sang; outside the Cathedral boundary a jogger passed them, absorbed in the rhythm of running, not noticing them; some people were exercising dogs, and a couple of homeless tramps sat against the railings using a bottle of water to try to wash their feet.

At last Howard said, 'I was on duty all night, I think I'd better get something to eat.'

He didn't look up as they walked past the tramps, who were laughing as they splashed each other. Hilary thought, I've never heard a tramp laugh, I'd expect it to sound different to regular people laughing but it isn't, it's the same sound we all make when we're happy.

Howard took her to his flat in Merrion Square. It was nice, she thought, not at all like she'd expected a man's flat to be.

He made toast and marmalade for them, and coffee. After he'd eaten he began to look better, more relaxed. Hilary found herself thinking how this was the first time she'd been alone with a man in his room. Except of course with Duncan that awful night, but that was different. That was a hotel; it wasn't his own private room, the place he'd made to be his shelter when he was alone, with his precious things in it. It was practically public property. Howard's room was full of books and bright cushions and photographs of Howard with other people. She wondered if the girls were his sisters, most of the pictures were of boys. They looked like friends from schooldays. Hilary began to feel that she'd found a real friend.

She looked up to find Howard looking at her with an odd expression on his face.

'What is it?' she said. 'Why are you looking at me like that?'

'Hilary, I've got to say this, even if you hate me for it. What do you think you're doing? You can't just carry on as though nothing has happened and hope it goes away. You've got to make some sort of decision. What do you want to do?'

'I think I have decided, but I don't know how to do it. I can't have this child, Howard. It's breaking my heart, but somehow I'll find a way of getting over it. I don't think the other people involved would be able to, and I feel I'd rather bear the pain myself than hurt them. I can't put my happiness before theirs. I could never be happy if I did, anyway.'

'What about the child?'

Hilary went white.

She said, mumbling, 'Do you think I haven't thought of that? But it hasn't life except as part of me. It hasn't got a view, it doesn't know. Haven't you heard Ffion on the subject? She says seeing it any other way is like saying it would be wicked to cut out a cancerous growth to save someone's life. Only the mother can decide because it's part of her body.'

'But you're not Ffion. Are you sure about what you're doing?'

'Yes, I'm sure.'

He said, gently, 'Right or wrong, I think you're very brave.'

'If you only knew how much I'm not brave. I'm scared out of my mind. What do I do now? I've heard there are girls in College who've had abortions in London. Girls in that fast crowd round Players. Perhaps they can give me the name of someone. I've saved a bit of money. I've been putting money aside for years in case I ever had a baby of my own.'

She broke off because she was afraid she would lose control of her voice. Then she went on, 'And how can I keep it secret? It's got to be a secret, for everyone's sake. No one must know about this or it'll all have been for nothing.'

Howard put his arms round her. It felt odd to her, sweet, like being hugged by a child.

'Don't be afraid. I'll look after you.'

'Oh, Howard, will you tell me what to do? Do you know anyone? Should I go to London? At least no one would know me there.'

'I'll do what's necessary.'

She pulled away from him, staring into his face. 'You can't do that. Do you realize what you're saying?'

'Yes, I can. I'm a doctor. I'll do it for you.'

'But Howard, suppose you were found out? You'd be ruined; you might even go to prison. You'd be barred before you'd even been registered.'

'I know what to do. I want to do it for you, so you can start again without anyone ever knowing anything about it. I must do it, now you've told me. I can't let you destroy your life.'

'Howard, you can't do it.'

'Your father's a vicar, you must've been brought up believing in God. Don't you think it's possible that's why I was in the Cathedral this morning, so I could help you? I've never been there before but today I felt I should. Do you think it's too far-fetched to say it was meant to be?'

Hilary laughed and said, 'That's what my mother always used to say. And the Rev Dad would say it was the Hand of God – except he wouldn't if he knew the truth because he'd think I was too wicked!'

'That doesn't sound very Christian of him.'

'The Rev Dad may be a bit set in his ways. Personally I think Christianity has to adapt to the times.'

'Christianity's one thing,' Howard said. 'But if I were you, I wouldn't say a word to your father any time soon.'

10

Some nights at the Soup Bowl were more rewarding than others; this was not one of Ffion's best. The party atmosphere that often took over late on didn't happen. The film crowd, mostly Americans tonight, had left early, and quietly. They seemed overawed by the presence of the pride of the Abbey Theatre and Broadway actress, Siobhan McKenna.

Ffion had never heard of her. As the actress and her party came into the restaurant, she overheard diners at the other tables whispering the famous name and talking about her run on Broadway as St Joan a few years ago, but Ffion assumed they were talking about a film.

She didn't pay the home-grown international star particular attention. There was no point; Ffion knew from experience that she could not expect anything special in the way of a tip from a woman.

She did remark to her boss on the actress's exceptionally carrying and beautiful voice, but it was not in admiration. 'She treats me like dirt, and she lets everyone know it,' Ffion complained.

'She doesn't like the English,' her boss said. 'But she's a great actress. The Divine McKenna.'

Fat lot you'd know, Ffion thought. Her boss's main interest outside the restaurant was karate and watching children's programmes on the television in the afternoons.

The Divine McKenna gave a command performance that night. The faint-hearted slunk away as the evening wore on, daunted as the actress trumpeted orchestral invective against the wickedness of the Saxons.

On nights like these, which carried on sometimes till dawn, Ffion was usually invited to join the party. She heard her boss, now well away himself, suggest it.

'No,' the actress boomed, 'let her stay in the kitchen.'

Ffion could think of quite a few cutting things she could have said to the drunken bitch. She thought she might manage to pour wine over her when she brought a fresh bottle to the table. Or hot strong black coffee; that might add insult to injury, she thought, except nobody was sober enough to notice.

And Ffion had to admit that the voice was beautiful, whatever it was saying. Quite a lot of the vituperation was in Irish. She makes it sound like poetry, Ffion thought.

There was a funny little fat man, a junior lecturer in the English Department, who liked to mount the marble Chapel steps in Trinity to proclaim poetry. God knows what he said, but he, too, had a beautiful voice; mesmerising also, like listening to obscure classical music. Perhaps it was something the Irish did, Ffion thought. There was also an old woman used to play the harp on a street corner near Grafton Street.

Ffion had had a few drinks herself by now. She thought, wasn't it Walter Pater who said that all art aspires to the condition of music? So were the obscene outpourings of an old actress and a vertically-retarded drunk on the way to being art? Yuck! Double yuck!

There was no seat in the narrow kitchen; the staff didn't usually get much chance to sit down. Ffion, tired of leaning against the stove, finally sat on the floor with her back against the cupboard under the sink.

Ffion wasn't used to not being noticed. She was a budding dress designer's awkward coltish child, and Beverly made sure she always looked stylish. Beverly claimed that against tax on her advertising budget. Ffion was always the one the others wanted to look like. And then, of course, she grew up to be beautiful, with all the right Sixties attributes – huge eyes, strong cheekbones, luxuriant thick hair, and enviable long, long legs.

Ffion took this beauty for granted, but she knew its value and how to exploit it. She never had the awkwardness with men which she found so off-putting in most girls her age. Women like Hilary and Sandra treated perfectly ordinary boys as though they were some kind of minor gods. Or, as Ellie did, acted like their mothers or a bossy older sister. As though what men thought of them was what defined women as people.

Sitting there on the chill tiled floor of the Soup Bowl kitchen, Ffion suddenly asked herself if she had got it all wrong.

Perhaps that bloody woman shouting the odds like an operatic race-course bookie has a point. Even the film crowd were overawed by her; they knew they couldn't compete. She's nothing to look at, not really, and she's old – no, not old, but in her forties – not young anyway, but she dominates everyone.

She thought, it wasn't just Siobhan McKenna who didn't notice me; tonight no one else even registered me. I couldn't hold a candle to her. But why?

On these long nights in the Soup Bowl, her boss always provided her with a bottle of wine to drink while she was waiting to finish work. She got to her feet and poured herself another glass.

I've been on the wrong tack, she thought, it isn't men I have to work on to get ahead. Women will be the problem, they're the ones who'll hold me back. Women like Ellie who think I'm betraying my sex. It's women I should be looking to influence and impress. Men won't get in my way, but women will.

Women are jealous of me, they gang up against me, and they don't trust me. That's going to matter one day; they're going to stop me getting anywhere in a career.

Ffion made a face and drank more wine. How humiliating, she thought, I'm going to have to take women like Ellie and Hilary and Sandra seriously and try to see that they might be able to teach me something I don't know about people. What do I have to do to get them on my side? Make them sorry for me? Make them feel in some way better than me? Or at least happier? Oh, Yuck!

The night was almost over when Ffion finally walked away from the Soup Bowl. She'd been right; the Divine McKenna hadn't left a tip. She thinks her presence is recompense enough for serving her, Ffion thought, and found herself being satisfied with that. She told herself, Thanks to her, I had a mind-changing revelation tonight.

But it meant she didn't have money for a taxi. No matter, she could do with the exercise. Dawn was breaking as she walked up Kildare Street and past the Shelbourne Hotel along the north side of Stephen's Green. A rather half-hearted kind of a dawn, she thought, as though the day was thinking better of getting up at all. There was something intimate about the city at that time of the morning, as though everyone up and about was a family member getting a theatrical show ready to open to the public.

When Ffion got to the corner of Fitzwilliam Street she turned left towards Merrion Square. That's where Howard lived. Her feet hurt and her back ached from standing up so long. She thought Howard might be prevailed upon to give her breakfast before she faced her room-mates with her new, respectful, *ingratiating* attitude.

A car slowed down beside her.

'Bloody kerb crawler,' she said as the driver leaned across and opened the passenger door.

Then she recognized him. 'Matt! What are you doing trawling for talent at this time of night? Why aren't you tucked up in bed with Ellie in nice clean pyjamas wondering how long you've got before the Teasmade goes off?'

'No Teasmade,' he said. 'No electricity in the mornings till Ellie gets the generator going. It's easier for her to boil a kettle on the Calor gas. Want a lift?'

She got into the car. She said, 'You know what I'd really like? I'd like to go up into the hills beyond Sandyford, out of the city.'

'OK. Funny I never figured you as a country girl.'

'I'm not, I just need to get some fresh air.'

He turned the car and headed for Leopardstown. As the road started to climb beyond Dundrum the sun dragged itself above the clear-edged shapes of the two Sugar Loaf mountains. She turned to look at Matt's face as he drove. He felt her eyes on him and smiled. He looked tired, but then, so must she.

He stopped the car at a point where the City of Dublin was spread out below them. They were in the shadow of the hill, but the city was bathed in the watery spotlight of the early sun.

She thought he might be going to seduce her, but then realized he was not another student; he was a grown man, way past the age when he wanted a fumble in the back of a small car.

He made no move to touch her. He said, 'Isn't it about time we slept together? We both know it's going to happen sometime.'

'Yes, I know. But what about Ellie? I share a flat with her, and the rest of the time she's at your place. Where can we go to do the deed?'

'She's like a faithful dog, wherever I go, whatever I do, there's Ellie. She ignores the fact that I shag other women. Sometimes I do it to wind her up.'

He didn't look guilty. Ffion laughed.

He said, 'There seems to be nothing I can do to put her off. Our best bet might be to ask her to make an appointment for us to be together.'

He laughed. She thought, He has beautiful teeth. What a funny thing to notice.

She said, 'How can you stand it? Can't you tell her she should wait to be invited?'

'Have you ever tried to put Ellie off when she wants something? Even if I'm in bed with another girl, she barges in and starts cooking dinner for the three of us. I'd swear she listens at the door for the crucial moment before she comes in; she's the most effective contraceptive I know. It's doing my love-life in altogether; girls can't cope with it.'

Ffion was thinking, though she didn't say it, that there was something obsessive about Ellie's devotion. She thought, She's like a woman in that 18th century French novel by Choderlos de Laclos, *Les Liaisons Dangereuses*. Surely most women aren't like that? But then she thought, Or are they, even though they pretend they're not? I've been after Matt for months now, but at least I've kept it to myself.

She thought, I wouldn't have given Matt a second glance if Ellie hadn't been so crazy about him.

Matt said, 'Ellie's a terrific cook, though. I've never known another student who cooks like her. Or cooks at all, come to think of it.'

I know where Matt and I can go, Ffion said to herself. Howard's always said I can use his flat whenever I want and he'll be at work all day.

She turned away from the city sprawled below. The sun had given up and hidden behind dull cloud, and the sprawling town was no longer shining. There was a ferry coming slowly into Dun Laoghaire harbour. Full of tourists, she thought, all wanting to visit the *Book of Kells* and getting misty-eyed about leprechauns and *Danny Boy*. The government should put that Siobhan woman in charge of Tourism, she'd soon put them off.

'I know somewhere we can go,' she said. 'This friend of mine said I could use his flat. He leaves a key under a stone in his window box.'

Matt raised one questioning eyebrow, but he said nothing.

What's he thinking? she thought. Does he think Howard is some kind of pimp? It amuses him.

They drove back into town in companionable silence, as though they were old friends and knew what the other was thinking. They were both looking forward to making love, as something special they'd prepared for over a long time. Like drinking a really special bottle of wine they'd kept for a momentous occasion.

In Howard's spare bedroom, they undressed without haste. Ffion got into the bed and slid across the cool sheet to leave room for Matt.

He collected their clothes, folded them carefully and laid them on a chair. Ffion wanted to laugh. Did he do that before he started going with Ellie? He looks like a leprechaun when he's naked, she thought.

There was no foreplay. 'You've got an interesting belly,' he said, 'it's like a wooden puppet's, not functional in itself, just somewhere to attach the legs to. Open up, will you?'

'Oh, yuck! she thought.

And their lovemaking was disappointing. Matt came before Ffion was ready. She had a vague sense of anti-climax but she was curiously relieved. She wasn't missing out on anything special that Ellie had.

'Perhaps I'm too big for you,' Matt said.

Too small more like, she thought, it's like a stick insect. But she just smiled, moving into the crook of his arm.

It was hours later when she woke. She heard a loud clatter from the kitchen and started up. She shook Matt's shoulder. 'Howard's back,' she said.

He opened his eyes, recognized her, and smiled. Then he turned over and went back to sleep.

He's used to this, she thought. His half-conscious mind probably thinks it's Ellie.

She got up and put on her clothes. Then she went to meet Howard. She was going to have some explaining to do.

He was in the kitchen. She asked herself, What the hell's he doing in there? What are those noises?

She opened the kitchen door.

For a moment she thought there was a spaceman in the room, not Howard. Somehow this didn't surprise her. Then she realized that Howard was wearing his surgeon's gear, down to the mask and the cap and the blood-streaked rubber gloves. There was a lump of something on the kitchen table which looked like a body covered in a sheet. Howard was leaning over it, a blood-tipped instrument in his raised hand.

He looked up and stared at Ffion in horror, his eyes glaring over the mask covering his nose and mouth.

'Get out,' he shouted at her. 'This is a sterile area.'

Ffion backed out of the door and closed it behind her.

She thought, He's rehearsing one of those stage things medical students do as a joke at a party, setting up an operation table and then pulling all sorts of things like strings of sausages or carving knives out of the patient's stomach.

But she knew he wasn't. The smell of carbolic and the saucepan of boiling water with instruments standing in it – it was too real. And it was real blood on the sheet.

Ffion did not return to the spare room. Matt presumably slept on, and she hoped he wouldn't wake. She sat for some time on the sofa in the sitting-room watching the kitchen door.

At last Howard came out. The operating gown, the mask and rubber gloves were gone. He came and sat beside her.

'Don't say anything,' he said.

He looked ghastly; white under the sweat and all out at the eyes. 'Oh, my God,' he said.

She took his trembling hands in hers. 'Is the girl all right?' she asked. 'She's not dead?'

He shook his head, not meeting her eyes. 'She's fine,' he said. 'She'll be fine.'

'Oh, Howard,' she said, 'are you all right?'

She wasn't sure if he was weeping or just terrified. Perhaps both.

She said, 'I've got a friend here. He's asleep in the spare room. Can you get out of here so he won't see you?'

'There's the girl,' he said. 'She needs someone with her.'

'I'll look after her. It's all over, isn't it? She doesn't have to wait...for anything to happen?'

He shook his head. 'No, it's all over. It's only like a heavy period, she should rest.'

'Get out of here for a while, and I'll get rid of him...' She jerked her thumb towards the spare room.

She got up and pulled Howard to his feet, bundling him out of the front door of the flat.

'Go on,' she said, pushing him towards the stairs. She thought, Let's hope anyone who sees him in the street will think he's drunk.

Then, taking a deep breath, she opened the door of the kitchen.

Ffion glanced round, but everything looked normal. Only there was a lingering smell of carbolic; as though Ellie has been here cleaning, she thought.

And then she forced herself to look at the girl sitting hunched in a chair by the table with a cup of tea beside her.

'My God,' she said. 'Hilary, is that you?'

101

11

The party ended, almost. This was the last term of their undergraduate last year; even the most laidback students were beginning to think that time was running out for them.

One Sunday night in Raglan Road Ffion came in and found her room-mates together and the gaps between their beds piled with books.

'What's happened?' she said.

'We're panicking,' Hilary said.

'Do you realize it's less than three months to our Finals?' Ellie said.

Sandra picked a book at random from the pile and opened it, frowning. 'Has anyone ever heard of *Penguin Island*? It says here that no student of 20th century satire can afford to ignore fecking Anatole France's influence on Huxley or Orwell. Do you know about it?'

Hilary shook her head. 'I've never even read *Brave New World*. I couldn't get on with *1984* but I loved *Animal Farm*.'

'We've got the summer to study,' Ellie said. 'Thank God that Finals aren't till September.'

Ffion laughed and said, 'The University won't have been thinking of the students' benefit when they decided that. They know that if the exams were held in June no one would pass. That wouldn't be much of an advertisement for Trinity, would it?'

'Ellie would pass,' Sandra said. 'And Hilary.'

'I wouldn't,' Hilary said. 'It's ages since I did any real work.'

Ffion was about to say that Ellie and Hilary were the students least likely to make any impact on the world outside, and that wouldn't do much good for TCD either. Then she thought of why Hilary hadn't done any work lately, and held her tongue.

But they were all thinking suddenly that four years was a long time to waste if they weren't going to get a degree at the end of it.

'I refuse to think about it,' Ffion said. 'As far as I'm concerned the future starts the week after Trinity Ball. Time enough then to think what I'm going to do next. I may not take my Finals.'

'Eat, drink and be merry, for tomorrow we die,' Ellie said, but she still looked doubtful.

Sandra, in particular, felt that time was running out for her. This had nothing to do with getting her degree. She had to face facts.

After the William episode, Sandra had avoided fellow students from Northern Ireland. She felt that as a group, they were different from the other undergraduates, who were mostly English or West Britons from the Protestant Ascendancy in Ireland. "Protestant on horseback" Brendan Behan called them. There was also a sprinkling from middle-class local families who'd been educated at middle-class Church of Ireland private day schools round Dublin.

Sandra did not identify herself as one of the Northerners. She did not want to return over the Border to Ulster, not ever.

And Trinity, she told herself, is the best chance I'll ever have to find a wealthy, well-connected young man with few brains and a large circle of similar friends who'll be part of the English social élite, spend a large part of the year in his holiday homes abroad, and automatically send his offspring away to boarding school as early as possible to get them out of our way. That'll suit me fine.

After all, she thought, this was a long established historical tradition in the English upper classes. The Raj was a case in point.

But there's the rub, she told herself. Sure, the rich young Englishmen who were out in India had chi-chi mistresses and girlfriends, but they didn't marry them and take them home to be their wives in England. They knew they'd be cut off without a penny by their family if they did that.

To Sandra, Trinity was a bit like the Raj. Rich and well-connected families send their sons to Ireland to sow their wild oats in a country they don't think of as altogether foreign, just vaguely inferior. There the girls were fine for future English gentlemen to learn sex on, but not to wed.

Ok, she asked herself, but how do they know I'm not one of them? I've got a British passport, I'm the same colour as them, I speak the same language…

'What's to stop some rich English aristocrat marrying me and taking me to his stately home to live a life of luxury?' Sandra asked her flatmates.

'They're not interested in intelligent women…' Hilary said.

'You don't vote Tory,' Ellie said.

'I could, I don't know how I'd vote. If I bothered to.'

Ellie was scandalized. 'Don't be silly,' she said.

Ffion said, 'No one with any social pretentions is going to marry someone who speaks in that awful accent.'

It was a shock; Sandra had never given a thought to how she sounded.

'That's rubbish,' Ellie said. 'Local accents are attractive. Look at Matt, he's got a strong South London accent and women find it really sexy.'

'They're looking for a bit of rough, that's all. These days guys put on a Cockney accent because that's where the money is.'

'What money?'

'Oh Ellie you know what I mean. Anyone who is anyone these days needs working class credentials like a local accent.

Look at the people who make money – hairdressers, designers, stock brokers, the media, footballers. But Sandra's after old money and a pedigree longer than a Derby winner.'

Hilary said, 'Well, I've got a face like a horse and it doesn't do the trick for me.'

Hilary had got in the habit of making fun of her own looks to pre-empt comments about her lover-less state.

'It wouldn't matter how much like a thoroughbred Sandra looked, she'll never get anywhere when she sounds like a braying donkey.'

'My God, Ffion, how can you be so horrible?' Ellie said.

'You're not doing Sandra any favours being so mealy-mouthed. Friends should help each other face the truth.'

'Surely they should be there for each other, whatever?'

'And what's that supposed to mean?'

Hilary interrupted, 'Children, children, can't you play nicely?'

That night Sandra lay awake, thinking about what the others had said.

What's wrong with the way I speak? My accent is part of my identity, she thought. But why is the only thing I remember from Bernard Shaw is a line about it being impossible for an Englishman to open his mouth without making another Englishman hate or despise him?

Sandra suddenly remembered, too, that ages ago at some sort of Freshers' hop, Hilary had asked her to stop swearing because it put people off.

Worst of all, though, was what had happened a few nights ago. She'd been trying to cheer Hilary up – she'd been so down recently – but it hadn't helped, probably because Hilary wasn't drinking. Anyway, coming home they'd made a bit of a noise on the stairs. Hilary had tried to shut her up because of Miss O'Connell but Sandra hadn't taken any notice.

Rather worse than that, actually. She remembered bawling at the top of her voice: 'Up the 'Tans! Go paddy whackers!' She didn't think Miss O'Connell would hear anyway because she was quite deaf, which was why the whistling kettle trick worked.

But Miss O'Connell had a parrot. It was a furious-looking red and green bird with a malevolent eye and a gift for mimicry. From time to time Sandra had thought all sorts of famous people were in Miss O'Connell's sitting-room with her, only to find it was the bird imitating them.

The next day Sandra came in with Ellie and Hilary. They heard, through the closed door of Miss O'Connell's sitting-room, someone ranting at the old lady. They couldn't believe it. A screeching woman with a fierce Ulster accent was swearing and screaming at De Valera's former mistress in her own front room.

'What on earth's going on?' Ellie said.

They wondered what they should do.

'It's all right,' Hilary said. 'Miss O'Connell's laughing.'

And it was true; Miss O'Connell sounded as if she were splitting her sides to hear the raucous war-cry of the Black and Tans.

Sandra ran ahead of the others up the stairs, too shocked and embarrassed to speak. That fecking bird is imitating me, she thought. It was grotesque, but Sandra wasn't laughing.

She hadn't said anything to the others, but they couldn't not know who the parrot was imitating. Sandra was sure she'd heard Ellie say, 'He sounds better than she does.'

Sandra might be imagining that, but she didn't have to imagine how any upper crust English family with social pretensions would react to being associated with the human version of Miss O'Connell's parrot.

The next day she asked Ffion, 'Is my voice that bad?'.

'Depends what you're after. There must be some people who find an Ulster accent charming.'

'But not…?'

'No, not the sort of people you're aiming at.'

'What would you do if you were me?'

Ffion considered for a moment. 'I'd start drinking in the Bailey. That's where the sort of men you're after hang out. Try not to talk; just smile and look mysterious.'

'Me, mysterious?'

'That Bailey lot aren't hard to please. They get all the intellectual stimulation they need talking to each other about ball games. All they want is for you to be sweet and smile and think they're wonderful.'

'That doesn't sound too difficult.'

'On the contrary, it's very difficult indeed if you have a single firing brain cell in your head.'

Then Ffion looked Sandra up and down; she shook her head. 'You look far too sexy,' she said. 'No, not sexy, bloody cheap. You're looking to enter a world where the typical man isn't looking for someone to screw long term; he wants you to give him children. After that he most likely only has sex when he's very drunk, and then only with someone who looks like she's employed by his mother as some sort of uniformed skivvy; a nurse, or the housemaids, even a nanny.

Two evenings later, Sandra sat on the low wall in front of the next house up to Miss O'Connell's on Raglan Road. She wanted to intercept Matt when he came to pick up Ellie.

At last his battered Morris Minor stopped outside the house. Before he could turn off the engine she rushed across the pavement and opened the passenger door.

He grinned at her. 'What's up?'

'Can I talk to you for a minute?' He's got such twinkling eyes, he doesn't take anything seriously, Sandra thought. Her courage was already failing her.

She panicked then. How could she say to him that he was the only person she knew who'd got an accent as off-putting

107

as hers? 'The moment I open my mouth everyone knows I'm an Ulster Protestant and not worth knowing,' she said.

That's not what I meant to say, she thought. 'I'm talking about fecking men,' she added. 'I want a rich husband.'

I'm making it worse, she thought.

Matt looked at his watch and started to get out of the car. 'You are joking, aren't you? It's the Sixties, Betty Freidan Lives, Women Rule, OK. If you want money, make your own And keep your accent, it's wonderful, like the blades of Boudicca's chariot cutting swathes though men.'

He got out of the car and put his hand on the horn until Ellie opened the bedroom window in the flat and waved.

'She'll be down in a minute,' he said. 'Don't forget, you don't need a man to provide, you're your own woman. No surrender, right?'

He got back into the driving seat, grinning at her.

Sandra went scarlet. Ellie must have told him about... she looked back to the house. The dark curtains in Miss O'Connell's front room dropped back across the window.

She's been watching me, Sandra thought, she's spying on me.

Sandra passed Ellie on the front steps. Ellie was carrying a suitcase full of clean and ironed washing.

'You're the first home,' she said to Sandra, 'don't wait up.' She ran to Matt.

Sandra waited to go into the house. She was mortified. She wasn't sure if Matt had said anything useful or not, but she had a suspicion he'd been laughing at her.

Then as she went into the hall, there came a rough, throaty voice singing:

...And then I prayed I might yet see
our fetters rent in twain
and Ireland, long a province, be
A nation once again...

Sandra asked herself, Can that be Miss O'Connell singing? It sounds more like the parrot? And then she thought, She's ancient, she might be dying.

She knocked on Miss O'Connell's door.

There was a crescendo of *A Nation Once Again* before the door opened and Miss O'Connell peered out.

Sandra said, 'I thought someone must be strangling your parrot. Is everything all right?'

Miss O'Connell, somewhat red in the face from singing, smiled.

The parrot, from its cage in the window, screeched.

'The bird likes you,' Miss O'Connell said. 'It must like your voice.'

'It's probably glad you stopped singing.'

The old woman smiled. 'Come in and have a cup of tea with me and I'll tell you about how I once met W B Yeats. The poet, not a scion of the Yates's Wine Lodges. Of course he was an old man then. But he hadn't lost his marbles. He knew that religion would drive a wedge in the midst of this nation. That's how he put it. Come inside, can't you, you're letting the fresh air in.'

Sandra stepped inside the room and closed the door behind her. 'Coming from the North, I feel excluded from Ireland. But I don't feel I belong in England either.'

Miss O'Connell nodded. 'You should go to London. London has nothing to do with the rest of England. Everyone feels they belong in London, as much as anyone else does, anyway.'

Sandra heard the others come in. She didn't say a word to them about Miss O'Connell, who had met Yeats and then told her that London was the place for her. It seemed to her that her entire time at Trinity she'd been preparing her mind for that one silly incident.

England doesn't have to be my only place in the world, she told herself; it's just another cage. There's all Europe, and

America. There's a big world out there that's a long, long way from the dot on the globe that's Belfast; and so many rich foreign men who speak English with an accent and like the way I talk.

We'll all be gone from here after our Finals in October, she thought. I've left Belfast behind, and soon Dublin. And after that the nearest I'll ever get to Ireland will be maybe late at night in some foreign bar listening to a pub drunk with tears running down his face as he sings *Danny Boy.*

And she said to herself, I might send Miss O'Connell a Christmas card.

12

Ffion stood on the steps of the Exam Hall. It was over. She looked around at milling students who'd just finished the last of their Finals exams and were now loitering in Front Square wondering what to do next.

It's funny how wearing our gowns makes us all look so alike, she thought. I don't seem to recognize any of these people, but I must know them all.

How different it was our first day, she said to herself, almost exactly four years ago. All of us feeling our way, not knowing where to go, scared and excited at the same time; all of us watching each other suspiciously and wondering about these strangers and what part they would play in our lives. We were most of us wearing our gowns then; we'd been told we had to wear them to lectures. That didn't last long. I used to carry mine around in case, but no one ever bothered.

Today was the same sort of misty, indeterminate Dublin day as it had been then; a pall of soft rain and the invisible sun when the cloud thinned, turning the sky to florescent strip lighting. Then as now, the trees on the grass in front of the Rubrics were beginning to turn golden, and surely the same abandoned bicycles were still piled against the chain railings in New Square.

Four years, and nothing external had changed; not even us, Ffion thought, we look much the same. But inside we're changed utterly.

She turned and started to walk slowly towards the Buttery. Is there a terrible beauty born? She asked herself. In a small way they had all gone through fire, been forged from base metal into finer stuff. We'll never know, she thought. All together here we're ready to explode on the world in fallout to flash briefly across the globe. But that's it, we won't know what happens then, we'll probably none of us ever see each other again.

To her own surprise, Ffion felt deserted. It was the last thing she'd expected to feel; didn't she want to start out straight away on the adventure of life. And yet… She thought, I won't forget this moment, I know for certain that I shall never in my life be as happy again as I've been here.

The bell in the Campanile began to toll.

Hilary, dragging her gown and her damp hair standing on end, frizzy like a bush of thorns, appeared beside Ffion. She was smiling, but her voice was uncertain. She burst out in cliché, 'Today is the first day of the rest of our lives,' she said. 'How do you feel?'

Ffion looked at Hilary's anxious, homely face and saw in her mind's eye the Hilary of that morning in Howard's kitchen, when she'd found her, bereft and appalled, sitting like a photograph of a Blitz victim among the ruins of her home.

'That's good, isn't it?' she said. 'We can draw a line under the past.'

Hilary smiled as she said, 'I'm rather dreading it. My parents should've called me Daphne. I'm the sort of person who puts down roots and doesn't like to be transplanted.'

Ffion was about to ask her what she planned to do now when Ellie and Sandra came up.

Sandra grimaced towards the Campanile. 'You know they say that students walking under that thing when the bell starts to toll will fail their exams. Well, it's too late now, let tradition do its worst. We're free.'

She darted across the grass and stood waving her arms in defiance under the bell.

The tolling stopped and Sandra returned to Ellie and the others.

Ellie said, 'There's a party tonight, one final fling. Matt's got a crowd coming down to Brittas Bay. Come on, you can come with me. I've got a lift with a friend of Matt's. We're going early with the food and Matt's coming on later with the booze.'

'Putting off the evil hour,' Hilary said. 'It's probably the last time we'll all be together. I'll miss you all.'

Ffion hung back. Damp sand and a biting wind – there was always a biting wind by the sea – wasn't her idea of fun.

Ellie took her arm. 'Come on,' she said, 'you've never been there, have you. After all, it's our last night, we might as well spend it together.'

Matt had obviously planned this party for some time. He and his friends had built a huge fire in the dunes. The weather had cleared, too, and there was no wind. Even Ffion acknowledged that there was something magical about this night, with the sighing of the sea and the scream of seagulls overhead.

Ellie collected storm lanterns from the shack and as people moved along the beach and through the dunes, the bobbing lights were like glow-worms in the dark.

The heat of the fire drove groups of people gathered there to move outside the immediate circle of the flames. A transistor radio played Radio Luxembourg; Acker Bilk's yearning clarinet in *Stranger on the Shore* expressed a sort of general shared emotion.

Matt hadn't yet turned up with the booze, but that wasn't why people weren't getting drunk. Most of them had brought drink with them, and some of Matt's regular visitors had brought canteens full of beer up the track from the local pub. They had also brought a roasted pig, par-cooked the night before in a commercial oven at a hotel in Bray, to be finished over the flames of the fire on the beach.

'What's the matter with us?' a disembodied voice said from the darkness. 'Why are we sober? If ever there was a night for getting blitzed, this should be it.'

'We've grown up,' Ellie said. 'Suddenly we're facing being responsible for what we do.'

Hilary said, 'I'm scared. I don't feel ready to grow up yet.'

From the transistor, Cliff Richard had now started to sing: Howard sang along softly: *The Young Ones, Darling we're the Young Ones, and young ones shouldn't be afraid...* He smiled at Hilary. She got up and went to sit beside him in the shadows.

Sandra asked, 'What are you going to do now, Hilary? Have you got a job lined up?'

Hilary shook her head, but of course the others couldn't see her. Sandra, thinking she wasn't going to answer, suddenly burst out, 'I'm going to America. I've got a cousin in Madison, Wisconsin, I'll go visit her and maybe she'll get me temporary work at the university.'

'What do your parents say?'

'I haven't asked them. I don't intend to tell them. If I did they'd probably write to my cousin telling her to have nothing to do with me, I'm a traitor to the Protestant religion. I don't want to know what they think, anyway.'

Ffion said, 'But surely you've got some idea in your head about the sort of career you want?'

'I don't want a career at all. I want to find a rich old man to support me in the way to which I hope to become accustomed.'

Ellie laughed. 'You don't really mean that, do you?'

'Why not? I intend to write lurid novels about the perversions of the rich and famous and be much envied.'

It sounded positively prudish, the way Sandra said it. Ellie thought so, anyway. She said, 'Don't you have any ambitions to be an actor or a politician or an architect or something fulfilling?'

'I haven't,' Hilary said. 'I'll go to London and do a secretarial course and then I'll work for a company, preferably one which does interesting work. All I want is to earn my own living and have a little bedsit somewhere in the Home Counties.'

'If that's all you want, why bother getting a degree at all?' Ffion said.

Howard said, 'Haven't you ever heard of education for its own sake, Ffion. There are more important things than getting on in the world.'

Hilary said quickly, to pre-empt an argument, 'What I want is the same as it always was – to get married and have a family. You may not think much of that as an ambition, Ffion, but surely you'd agree that whatever we do, we should make the best job of it we can. I wanted to get a degree because I think as an educated women I'll be a more interesting wife to my husband and a more stimulating mother to my children.'

'And if you don't have husband or children, you won't actually use your education at all?'

'I'll be more interesting to myself.'

There was an awkward silence. Then Howard asked Ellie, 'What about you? You haven't said a word about yourself.'

Ellie put some more wood on the fire. 'Oh,' she said, 'Matt's going to be a teaching assistant at UCLA for a year and I'll go to California with him and do a PhD there. And then we'll come back to England and he'll be a lecturer at Oxford for a few years and we'll have a couple of children and I'll write books about feminist politics.'

Someone – a man's voice – said from the shadows, 'Feminism? They'll be short books. Most women don't want equality; they just want something to complain about.'

'Have you told Matt all this?'

Ffion's question fell into a sudden silence.

Sandra said quickly, 'Oh, yes, I want children, too.'

'Really?' Howard feared he'd opened some old wound. He added quickly, 'Are you sure rich older men want kids?'

'Of course they do; kids prove that they haven't lost their virility. I want lots of kids; the more there are, the more alimony my husbands will have to pay when we divorce.'

'So you expect to get divorced.'

'Several times, if the old boys don't die soon enough.'

Sandra laughed merrily, but none of them was sure if she was joking.

Hilary said to Ffion, 'What about you? Are you looking forward to having kids?'

'I won't have children. I don't want them. None of you seem to realize how lucky we are to be living at a time when there's so much more a woman can do with her life than just breed.'

'But a woman can't feel really fulfilled until she has a child.' Hilary sounded as though she were pleading with Ffion not to contradict her.

'Pure selfishness, if you ask me,' Ffion said. 'There are already far too many people in the world. Eejits like you seem to think that's wonderful. It isn't wonderful; it's a bloody disaster. In some places in South America the police have to go round shooting feral children as vermin, and still women go on breeding regardless.'

'What would happen if more women felt like you do? Society would break down.' Ellie sounded distressed now. This evidently didn't fit in with her idea of feminism.

Ffion now felt she had the wind beneath her wings. She went on, 'People have children because they realize they're never going to achieve what they hoped for themselves. They think the kids will do it for them. Don't kid yourself, there's not a single unselfish reason to have children in this day and age.'

There was a pause. Then Ellie said, 'But surely you want children one day?'

Ffion didn't hesitate. 'No,' she said. 'I really don't. I'm not interested in them.'

They all looked at her, not sure whether to take her seriously or not. Then Howard said, 'Of course you'll have children, just like everybody else. What makes you different?'

'I know what I want,' Ffion said. 'I'm not going to let children get in my way.'

Howard said, 'I bet you anything that in five years' time you'll be married and have at least two kids.' His tone made it clear that to him Ffion was just a silly girl to be dismissed.

Ffion jumped to her feet. She looked furious. She's going to hit him, Hilary thought.

And then there came the blare of a car horn down the track, and a car engine being driven at full stretch.

Ellie jumped up and stirred the fire embers to heat the remains of the roast pig.

'Matt's here,' she called. Slowly couples and groups moved in from the shadows beyond the fire.

The car came to a halt and two men jumped out. They all recognized them – Gordon and Damian, the friends who occupied the college rooms in the Graduates Memorial Building where Matt crashed most week nights in term time.

Everyone around the fire fell silent. Someone turned off the transistor radio. They were all suddenly aware of the smell of roast pork.

Then Ellie said, 'Where's Matt?'

Damian said, 'There's been a pile-up on the Stillorgan Road.'

Then his voice broke and Gordon cried out against the crashing of waves on the beach as the tide peaked, 'Matt's dead.'

117

Part Two

13

There was a letter from Ellie's mother tucked into a book in the drawer of Ellie's bedside table in Raglan Road.

Ffion found it when she was sorting Ellie's things. Ellie wouldn't return to the flat now. On that dreadful night, Damian and Gordon had driven Ellie away as soon as they'd made their shocking announcement. Ffion, Hilary and Sandra, with Howard and some of his friends, had put out the fire and done what they could to clear up before they left.

Their way back to town took them along the Stillorgan Road, where police were still directing the traffic in single file past the smouldering site of the fatal car crash. Men were working under arc lights to clear the wrecked vehicles.

Hilary started to weep then. 'Oh, my God,' she moaned, 'I saw Matt's car. That old Morris Minor of his, it looked like a toy compared to the smashed truck.'

It was mid-morning by the time they got back to Raglan Road. Ellie had evidently been there already. Ffion knew she would not return. She'd put most of her personal stuff into a suitcase with some of her clothes and abandoned everything else. In the kitchen there was a bag of Matt's dirty laundry. The room had been closed up and they all caught the male odour of him as they came in. Sandra rushed to the bathroom and threw up.

'Is he really dead?' Hilary said, 'It's hard to believe all that zest for life can be snuffed out like that.'

Ffion said nothing. All she could think of was what Matt's body would look like in his coffin. No one except me will ever know what a small prick he had, she thought.

Hilary and Sandra both already had flights booked out of Dublin that afternoon. They packed their things and left together. Nobody said much.

Ffion, left alone at the flat, looked at the letter. Ellie's mother had big loopy handwriting. Ellie was exactly the daughter I would have expected a woman who wrote like that would have, Ffion thought.

The envelope was addressed to Ellie – Miss Eleanor Bassett – at Trinity Hall. The postmark on the envelope was less than a week ago.

It was headed Acacia Drive, Wembley Park, Middlesex. Thursday.

Ffion had never heard of Wembley Park. She read on:

'Dear Ellie,
'We're all looking forward so much to having you home next week. All of us wish you the very best of luck in your exams. We know you'll come out top of the class, especially because we know how hard you've worked over the summer giving up your holiday time to do all that revising.

'I hope you are making sure that you and the other girls are eating properly in the run up to your ordeal, and not overdoing the study. At least in the Hall of Residence they'll be taking good care of you. We're so proud of you, dear. Dad's been telling his mates in the pub about his brilliant daughter who'll soon have BA after her name. I don't know if they know what it means exactly but he's basking in your glory all right.

'Enclosed is a small cheque for you to buy something pretty to wear. You'll want to look good for something as important as your Finals. I'm only sorry it couldn't be a bit more, but you know how it is with all the kids wanting new shoes and Linda's suddenly put on so much weight she was bursting out of her school uniform at the start of the new scholastic year. I had to buy her a new skirt. But I'm sure things will be easier when you come home. I'm sure several of the people with *businesses round here will jump at the chance of employing a real graduate.*

'We can't wait to see you.
'With best love, Mum and Dad.'

When Ffion put the letter back in its envelope, her hands were unsteady. There was no cheque; Ellie had obviously cashed it. Was she wearing the special dress for Matt's party that last night? Ffion tried to remember but she hadn't noticed.

She felt guilty at reading the letter. She wished she'd never seen it. She thought, I never made any effort to really get to know Ellie, we were just natural enemies. Poor Ellie. To have all that burden of love and expectation on her back, knowing she wasn't at all the person her family took her for, and didn't want to be.

Obviously Ellie had never told her Mum about Matt; nor, apparently that she'd moved out of Trinity Hall. Someone there must have been bringing the letters into College and leaving them for her in her pigeon hole in No.6.

Ffion thought, How Ellie must've hated the thought of going home and dropping her bombshell about what she intended to do with her life, and who with. She won't have to do that now. But what will she do?

And Ffion told herself, She won't say a word now. She's too broken to do anything else. Poor, poor Ellie.

She wondered what to do with Ellie's things. The clothes were simple enough; she knew without any doubt that Ellie would never want to wear them again, so she left them in the wardrobe. But there were other things which she guessed had been part of Ellie's life since childhood – her elephant alarm-clock with the broken trunk; a silly stuffed monkey with one eye; her maddening charm bracelet which rattled so irritatingly. Ellie used to shake it deliberately, Ffion suspected, like a school teacher ringing a bell to bring the class to order. Yuck!

In the end Ffion put everything into a black plastic bag and put it aside. She couldn't send the stuff to Ellie, she didn't know where she was. The parents' address would find her, but Ffion couldn't physically bring herself to write Acacia Drive, Wembley Park, Middlesex on anything.

It's weird to think I shared a room with Ellie - and with Hilary and Sandra, too – for four years, and I don't know anything, really, about where they come from. Except Hilary came from a Surrey village, and presumably The Vicarage would find her. If I could remember the name of the wretched place, which I can't.

And Sandra's family lived in Belfast; a Protestant area of Belfast, presumably. But Sandra herself had been careful not to reveal more than that. Ffion thought, I suppose she knew it might tell too much she wanted to keep hidden. Ffion admitted to herself that Sandra and she had that in common. That's what people who weren't sure of their identities did. Ffion said to herself, People looking for me might know where to find Beverly's business address, but that's the last place they'd ever find me.

Ffion went down to see Miss O'Connell. She told her what had happened.

The old woman crossed herself. She remembered noticing Matt's antique Morris Minor, she said. Her father had driven something like it in the old days.

'He was always saying he was going to teach me to drive,' she said. 'But my mother wouldn't let him. She didn't approve of women driving cars.'

Miss O'Connell agreed to Ffion's request that they should leave their furniture and fittings in the flat. Why wouldn't she?

'You could let it furnished next time,' Ffion said. 'It's easier to get the tenants out then if you don't like them. And my mother bought everything new, so it's not rubbish.'

124

Miss O'Connell was understanding. 'I'll send anything personal, the clothes and things, to the Home for Fallen Girls in Harrington Street,' she said.

Oh, my God, Ffion thought, a Home For Fallen Girls! Ireland is like something out of P G Wodehouse. Not at all real. Except, of course, for those poor fallen girls who have to live in it.

Miss O'Connell came with Ffion to the door. 'I'm sorry for your loss,' she said. 'But God's will be done.'

'We've all been happy here,' Ffion said. 'We'll miss this flat.'

Miss O'Connell put a thin hand on Ffion's arm. 'The little girl, the little Prod from the North, will you wish her well from me?'

Ffion was startled. 'I don't expect to see her any time soon, or ever, but if I do, of course I shall. Her name was Sandra Redmond, I expect Trinity could give you her address.'

She thought, I said 'was'. Sandra's not dead. Why do I think of them all in the past tense now?

Two days later, in London, Ffion took the Bakerloo Line to Wembley Park. She'd found only one Bassett on the telephone living in Acacia Road.

One good thing about Beverly, Ffion thought, she always lived in the centre of whatever city she was in. She wanted no truck with the suburbs or anyone who inhabited them. Her London flat, which she'd recently abandoned in favour of Los Angeles, was in Sloane Street.

On the Tube train, Ffion stood up rather than sit on one of the filthy-looking seats in her dull-pink Biba mini skirt. She tried to ignore a couple of scruffy boys of eleven or twelve who watched her trying to stay upright against the movement of the train, sniggering behind their hands. Their fingernails were black. My God, she thought, are we in the Industrial North already?

It was raining as she walked from the Underground station. She hadn't thought to bring an umbrella, expecting there would be a taxi at the station to take her to Ellie's house. She told herself, There must be something wrong with Ellie to come back here, however devastated she is. The 1944 Education Act and the County Grant System which had supported her through TCD had given her the chance to escape. Of course Matt's death was bad, but coming back here must be making everything much worse. Ffion asked herself, Hasn't four years in Ireland taught her anything?

Ffion reached Acacia Drive and stopped in confusion. She thought, which one is it? *Little boxes made of ticky-tacky, Little boxes all the same...*

She asked an old woman carrying a shopping bag which house was the Bassetts.

'I'm not sure, but I think it's the one with the green front door,' the old woman said, pointing. 'But if it's not, you can ask them there which is the Bassetts. I know they're here somewhere. All those great big children!'

Ffion walked up the paved path to the green front door and rang the bell. Oh, no, chimes! This isn't a good idea, she thought, and turned to go. She told herself, Ellie won't want to see me, and I sure as hell don't want to see her.

But it was too late. A scruffy younger version of Ellie had opened the door. 'Yes? What do you want?

'Is Ellie here?'

The child turned and yelled up the stairs. 'Ellie, someone wants you.' Then she pounded away down the hall and left Ffion on the doorstep.

A window opened above Ffion's head. A voice that didn't sound like Ellie's but like a much older woman said, 'Yes?' and then, when Ffion looked up, cried, 'Ffion!' sounding so pleased that Ffion stopped regretting coming.

'Can we get out of here?' Ffion said.

'Wait, I'm coming down.'

On the front path, they looked at each other: Ffion in her pink Biba skirt and T-shirt, a rather bedraggled feather boa dripping on her shoulders; Ellie in jeans and a grey Sloppy Joe sweater that like all Sloppy Joes had seen better days.

'Oh, Ffion,' Ellie said, almost weeping, 'I'm so glad to see you.'

Ffion looked around at the weedy sycamore saplings on the pavement, and the little patches of flowers in the front gardens. No wonder, she thought.

They walked together down the street, back towards the Underground.

'You look awful,' Ffion said.

'So would you. Why've you come?'

'What do your parents think has happened to you? They must've noticed something's wrong.'

'Studying for Finals. And I told them I was dieting.'

'You really look like death. Not warmed up.'

'I wish I were dead. Or I did. It's different now you've come. What do you want?'

'I wanted to see you were OK.'

Ffion felt foolish. It seemed so inadequate, but, after all, it was true in a way. Ellie didn't know it, but now Matt was dead Ffion felt she'd done Ellie a wrong by seducing and then belittling him. It had been unsporting, like a man hitting a drunk. It was on her conscience.

Ellie didn't say anything. It would be too disloyal to Mum and Dad to say she was not OK, that nothing would make things all right if she stayed here. But she found she couldn't lie, her tongue positively swelled up and stopped the words before she could say she was. So she just looked miserable.

Ffion took a deep breath. She thought, I hope I'm not going to regret this.

And then she said, 'Beverly's gone to America and I've taken over her flat near Sloane Square. I wondered if you'd come and be my flatmate? At least it's got to be better than living in this dump.'

Ellie started to laugh. There was something hysterical about the way she laughed.

'What's so funny?'

'Oh Ffion, you are. Of all people, I never expected you to be anyone's saviour, but I can't tell you … yes, yes, I'd love to be your flatmate.'

Christ Almighty, Ffion asked herself, what have I done?

14

Under the clock on Waterloo Station, Hilary was waiting for Sandra.

She'd been hovering around there for nearly an hour. From time to time she walked off to browse through the magazines in W H Smith's, and once she bought aspirin at Boots the Chemists, hoping that when she came back to the clock Sandra would be there complaining that Hilary was late.

Hilary was annoyed with herself. Why do I always come early to everything? Sandra's never on time. And, she thought, what's even more annoying is that I'm almost certain she won't come at all; and yet I've come anyway.

That awful day when they'd stood together feeling lost on the concourse at the West London Air Terminal among crowds of people who all seemed to know where they were going and were in a mighty hurry to get there, they'd found it very hard to sever their connection.

'Let's not lose touch,' Hilary said. 'We could meet up again, just to catch up.'

And Sandra said, 'I'd like that. If I'm still in London, that is. Where and when?'

Sandra was as pleased as I was to keep a hold on each other, Hilary thought. But it was a natural reaction to Matt suddenly being killed like that. We both felt insecure. She even changed her flight so she could be on the same plane as me. If death could be so random and sudden as it was for Matt, we didn't want to be with strangers if it was going to happen to us. That's all it was, she'll have forgotten all about it.

She looked at her watch. I should have known better than to come, she told herself. It's been months, of course she's probably working, or gone somewhere else, to America or somewhere. Sandra's not like me, she'll have moved on.

There was twenty minutes before the next train back to Guildford. I'll have a coffee, she thought, at least I can watch the people.

'Hilary, you came!' Sandra rushed towards her from the station entrance. 'I thought you'd have given up on me.'

'I nearly did.'

I wouldn't have recognized her, Hilary thought. She looks so different, like Twiggy with that surely chemically-induced platinum hair that looks as if it was cut by an engineer using precision tools. And the way she's made up her eyes. Except Twiggy doesn't have that imposing bust.

'I'm so sorry I'm late. I took a train going the wrong way on the Circle Line and I didn't notice and there was nowhere else to change to the Northern.' She hesitated, then admitted, 'I wasn't sure you'd come. I thought you might have forgotten.'

'It's good to see you.' Hilary was surprised at how pleased she was. Perhaps they could recapture some of the hope and enthusiasm they'd had at Trinity before Matt was killed.

They sat in the coffee bar on the station drinking disgusting frothy coffee made with milk and served half-cold in thick-rimmed shallow green cups. They stared at each other, smiling but not able to think of anything to say.

'How did you do in the exams? What did you get?' Hilary said.

'I scraped a Second. Better than I expected. I thought I'd failed. What about you?'

'A 2(1). Ellie got a First.'

'You've been in touch with her?'

'I wrote. I didn't know what to say but I couldn't let her think I didn't care.'

'I would have written too, but I didn't know where to send it.'

'I got her address through Ffion.' Hilary paused, then thought more explanation was necessary. 'I went to the mother's shop and asked where I could find Ffion. The girl could see I wasn't going to buy anything and took pity on me. She told me.'

'You mean she thought you'd put her smart customers off and wanted to get rid of you.'

'Thanks for that.' They laughed and then it was like old times.

Sandra asked, 'What about Ffion, did she get her degree?'

'I forgot to ask. I don't suppose so, do you? But an amazing thing, she and Ellie are sharing a flat.'

'No! Good God, how did that happen? Ffion and Ellie living together? I can't believe it.'

'Me neither, but it's true. Apparently the mother – Beverly, wasn't it? – she's moved to America so Ffion's taken over her flat and she asked Ellie to move in with her.'

'What on earth made her do that?'

Hilary shook her head and sounded puzzled as she said, 'Did you ever think there might've been something between Ffion and Matt?'

Sandra frowned, considering, 'You mean Ffion screwed him? Well, she fucked everyone who had something a bit special about them. And Matt just fecking fucked anyone. So what?'

Hilary shrugged, dismissing her own speculation. 'There was just something... I've sometimes wondered if Ffion didn't feel guilty about Ellie. I mean, it would just've been a bit of fun for her, but if Ellie found out...'

'Ellie must've known Matt slept around.'

'Yes, but Ffion would be different.'

Sandra wasn't convinced. 'Perhaps Ffion was jealous because she wanted something more from Matt but she couldn't take him away from Ellie.'

'That, too… We'll never know. What about you, are you working?'

Sandra suddenly looked embarrassed. She said, 'You remember how you left me that day at the BEA Coach terminal in Gloucester Road? Well, I hadn't meant to come to London at all. I was actually booked to go back to Belfast and I changed my booking on the spur of the moment to go with you.'

Hilary didn't smile, though she wanted to. Poor girl, she thought, she's finding it really hard to admit that in spite of all her protestations she was going to have to go home.

'I'm glad you did,' she said, 'I was glad of the company.'

'When you went I'd nowhere to go, so I walked along the Cromwell Road and booked myself into a hotel. One of those small places up a side street, you know, No Coloureds, No Dogs, No Irish. Well the woman who ran it was from Antrim and she was nice to me.'

'Don't tell me you're working in a hotel?'

'No. Why I'm telling you this is that I spent most of that night really thinking things out. I sorted out a lot of things in my head. And in the morning I asked this woman from Antrim if she knew of any jobs going to tide me over, because I wanted to stay in London. We had a really good talk. She said I reminded her of herself when she was young, though she'd never had a university education. Anyway, she made a few calls.'

Hilary said, 'Heavens, she might've been contacting white slave traders…'

Sandra laughed. 'Not quite. I'm working for a filthy rich widower in property development who pays me as a crammer to get his son through Oxford Entrance.'

'How old is he? The property developer, not the son?'

'Old enough.' Sandra grinned.

And Hilary laughed. She's fun to be with, she thought; I think the spiritual politics of Trinity made it hard for me to see that in Dublin. Sandra's geared to the future, she has no base in the past. But if I said that to her, she wouldn't know what I'm talking about.

Sandra lit a cigarette and leaned back, tipping her chair. 'So what are you doing? Do you know what you want to do yet?'

Hilary was suddenly embarrassed. It would be too feeble to admit she hadn't done anything since she last saw Sandra; at least, nothing anyone could describe as doing anything with her life. She thought, I must've made a ton of scones and enough gingerbread to surface a car park, as well as poured thousands of cups of tea, but I haven't moved my life forward an inch.

Sandra surprised her then. She said, 'Hilary, you've got to stop this. If you don't decide soon what you want to do and make an effort to go for it, you'll be bogged down doing nothing forever. I know they don't mean to, but honestly your parents are exploiting you.'

She gave Hilary a sideways look, trying to decide if she dared say what she was really thinking. 'You know, being an old maid isn't just not getting any sex; it's a state of mind, an attitude.'

There, she'd said it. She didn't know how Hilary would react. But Hilary just said, 'I know.'

Sandra moved to safer ground. 'What's Ellie doing, apart from living with Ffion?'

'She's working in the Social Services Department of Hackney Council. Basically I think she checks up on problem families and tells them how they should be bringing up their children.'

'She must be a glutton for punishment. Or is it something she's doing as part of the grieving process?'

Hilary smiled, then felt guilty. It was nothing to laugh at. She said, 'Could well be. According to Ffion she's going out with Patrick Somebody who was a friend of Matt's. Ffion thinks they'll get married so she can get as close as possible to being with Matt, with the bonus that Patrick isn't the type to put himself in a situation where he might get killed. Ffion says Ellie tells him what to do and he does it.'

Sandra laughed and looked at her watch. 'My God, look at the time. It's nearly 6.00. I promised my old boy I'd go with him to dinner with a prospective client tonight. He likes me to do that sometimes, he says it gives a family-friendly feeling to business proceedings, whatever that means.'

'Oh, I think I can guess. But we must do this again. I thought you wouldn't turn up today and I'm so glad you did. You run along, I'll pay the bill.'

'Next time's on me, then. Take care.'

Hilary watched her go, startling bouncing blonde hair like a streak of lightning dividing the crowded dark grey suits of commuters hurrying to catch trains home.

She's right, Hilary told herself, it's the 60s; the daughter of the vicar role has been obsolete for the last century.

She pushed her way against the flow of home-goers out on to Waterloo Bridge. It had been a dull day and was now almost dark. Office blocks loomed like cliffs along the river were they now rose in bands of light, except for dark floors where the workers had left for the night. Then the bright tiers above the strip of black seemed to float like the superstructure of liners on an unseen ocean.

And across the bridge queues of buses, insect-like, butted their way slowly forward in a haze of diesel fumes. Hilary had never suffered from agoraphobia but she was scared now by the crush of grey zombies bearing down on her, their intent pale faces set and unseeing. They'd mow me down and trample me without even noticing, Hilary thought.

But she struggled on against the crowd; she wasn't going to stop now. If Sandra could do it, so could she. She walked down the Strand. To make herself feel better she thought of Handel in the Strand. She thought she might hum it. At Aldwych the sight of trees made her feel happy. They were a touch of Nature; a hint of it anyway. Where everything else proclaimed the works of Man, Hilary rejoiced at the defiant survival of those trees.

Outside the main door of the Waldorf Hotel she went into a telephone box and rang the operator to reverse the charges for a call to the Vicarage.

Mum sounded hassled. 'Oh, it's you darling. Have you missed the train? Well, supper's going to be late. The Rev Dad's been called away to talk about the funeral arrangements for Walter Carey — he died earlier this afternoon. So inconsiderate, really; people seem to treat the Vicar like their own property...'

'Don't worry about me, Mum. I've decided I'm going to stay the night up here. Expect me sometime tomorrow.'

'Oh, darling, are you sure? It's no trouble keeping the food warm. I'd hoped you'd help me with the coffee morning in the Church Hall...'

'Sorry, Mum, I've things to do. See you tomorrow.'

'When?'

Hilary didn't answer that.

'See you soon, then?' her mother said.

'Sometime. Bye.' She put the phone down.

Then she walked into the Waldorf and up to the reception desk.

'I want a room for the night,' she said.

15

Beverly's flat near Sloane Square was the sort of apartment dreamed up in the fantasies of plutocrat villains on the set of James Bond movies.

It comprised the entire second floor of a small block overlooking a garden square behind Sloane Street. It had been bequeathed to Beverly by the Arab Sheikh who originally launched her on her career as a fashion designer. He was the one who gave her the only piece of advice she ever took: 'However bad things are, behave as though you're on top of the world. Success is down to the impression people have of you.' Ffion asked about him once and Beverly said, 'You know, I've forgotten how to spell his name.'

The day Ellie was to move in, Ffion delayed returning to the flat.

Was I off my head asking her to come here? she asked herself. Why did I do it? I don't want to share, I don't want a home and all that companionship crap that goes with it.

So why?

A stupid gesture on a whim. Of course I'd never really thought Ellie would agree to come. I was just trying to be nice to make her feel better, Ffion said to herself. And now look what I've done. She'll hate it here but she'll never admit she'd much rather be somewhere else. She'd think she was being rude or ungrateful and she'd hurt my feelings. As if!

Ffion still hoped that when it came down to it, Ellie would stick to the familiar and stay in Wembley Park, where there were lots of common people living in proper homes with all the trimmings.

When Ffion couldn't put off the dreaded moment any longer, she let herself into the flat.

She found Ellie sitting on an upright wooden chair in the hallway in her duffle coat and College scarf. Suitcases at her feet. Like fucking Little Orphan Annie.

Ffion wanted to slap her.

She said, 'If you're cold, why haven't you turned up the heating?'

Ellie said, 'I don't know where you keep the coal.'

And Ffion knew that this wasn't going to work. She thought, I haven't done her any favours asking her to live here. Or myself, either.

'You're not a guest here, Ellie. This is where you live.'

'Shall I put the kettle on?'

'No, I will. You go and unpack and take your bloody coat off. Your room's the one with Ellie on the nameplate on the door.'

'Is your name on the door of your room?'

'Of course. If you don't like it, pick another one. Your room used to be Beverly's. We don't want boyfriends walking into the wrong rooms.'

Boyfriends? Ellie was shocked. She had not thought ahead to a future with boyfriends in it. Not hers, not now Matt had gone, but of course Ffion must have loads of lovers. I wish I hadn't come, she thought, all I want to do is to remember Matt. I've no interest in men, especially not Ffion's.

Ffion saw the look on Ellie's face. 'Don't worry,' she said, 'There's no time in my little life at the moment for lovers. I put your name on the door as a gesture; it helps me make myself believe that Beverly doesn't live here anymore.'

At first, it wasn't so bad sharing the flat. Not on weekdays, anyway. Ellie went off to work early. She took to cycling to work.

'You're off your rocker. You're taking your life in your hands,' Ffion told her. She hesitated, then said, 'This isn't some sort of death wish, is it?'

'If you really want to know, it's because I'm less likely to be recognized by someone from work wearing a cycling helmet.'

'What the hell are you talking about?'

'My life won't be worth living if anyone at work finds out where I live. I'd be ostracized as a class enemy.'

Ffion thought, And do you still give your address as Acacia Avenue, Wembley Park, the same as when we were living in Raglan Road you got your letters sent to Trinity Hall?

'You could always say I employ you as a live-in skivvy.'

Ellie didn't notice the sour note in Ffion's voice. Ffion thought, God, there's nothing worse than someone thinking you're being nice when you're trying to be bitchy.

Why would Ellie want to cling to her underprivileged background rather than embrace her opportunities? Ffion asked herself, Is she looking for an excuse for failure before she even tries to succeed?

'Why do you care what those dogsbodies think?'

'Because I'm doing an important job and if my colleagues thought I was a bloated plutocrat I'd lose my job.'

Ffion raised her perfectly arched eyebrows, 'Do you mean that you've got to have bona fide underprivileged credentials to help deprived and inadequate people? Admit it, Ellie, you're scared of no longer belonging to the working classes.'

Ellie looked irritated. 'Why do you talk as though my background is something to be ashamed of? It was wonderful, even if it was tough sometimes. I was loved, we all were. I know I was loved and I know that whatever happens my family's there to support me.'

At last, Ffion told herself, I'm making her angry.

'But Ellie, that's a lie. Well, it's an illusion. If you feel loved you would see no reason to change.'

'As long as I'm happy, and make others as happy as I can, what more should I want?'

Sanctimonious bitch, Ffion thought, no one could be that simple-minded.

She said, 'All that love won't help you in the real world. Out there, if you want to get on, you won't be loved. Respected, maybe, but not loved.'

She's trailing her coat, Ellie told herself, I won't rise to it. Ffion never has been loved, that's why she's the way she is.

She said, 'If that's the case, with Beverly for a mother, you should be setting the world on fire by now. But you're not, are you?'

Ffion smirked and said, 'I've got things under control.'

Smug cow, Ellie thought.

Us living together is going to be a disaster, Fiona told herself.

Why did I agree to move in with her? Ellie thought.

It was worse at weekends, though. At first Ffion thought a grateful Ellie was trying to be helpful when she tapped at Ffion's door at 7am on Saturdays and Sundays to tell her that it was time to get up, that breakfast was almost ready, and housework beckoned.

Ffion protested, 'But it's Saturday. At weekends I lie in.'

But Ellie wouldn't be told. 'You don't want to miss the best of the day. Chop chop.'

God how I hate people who say chop chop, Ffion thought.

Then, worse: Ellie said, 'Matt wouldn't want us to turn into slobs. He was never lazy. He used to say there was always so much to do at weekends. He hated lazy people.'

Ffion in her head cried out, Oh no he didn't. He was the most laidback person I ever met, he wanted people to do their own thing. You're turning him into a monster.

God, she thought, we're turning him into a pantomime joke. Oh yes he is, Oh no he isn't.

Ffion said, 'You scarcely knew him, after all.'

And then there'd be the painful hours when Ellie would talk about Matt and how she missed him. Wallowing, Ffion called it. If Ffion said anything, anything at all, Ellie said, 'You've never lost anybody close to you, have you, Ffion? Someone in the family?'

'Several stepfathers.' Ffion said.

'They're not family.'

'Matt and you weren't family. You weren't married.'

In desperation, Ffion once said, 'I miss Matt too, you know.'

I do, she thought. Even though he had the smallest penis.

'He wasn't yours to miss.'

Then Ellie was aghast at what she'd said. She started to explain, she hadn't meant it; but Ffion stopped her.

'You've accomplished what you set out to do. I'm up and dressed at half seven in the morning. Now what do we do?'

And she asked herself, Oh, God, how long is this nightmare going to go on?

Then one Sunday morning in the local off-licence Ffion ran into Howard.

'Where did you get that suntan?' she wanted to know. 'Have you just come back from Hollywood?'

He gave her one of those one-two-three air kisses. 'You look fabulous,' he said.

'Well I don't feel it. Oh, you mean the Vidal Sassoon haircut? It's good, isn't it? It cost the earth. Probably five times the weekly wage of one of Ellie's inadequate.'

Funny, she thought, we haven't seen each other for ages, and it's as though it was only last week. I wonder what he's doing; in spite of the tan he doesn't look too good. A bit gaunt, and older, definitely older.

But he was the one who asked, 'What's wrong?'

Why do medical people ask you what's wrong in that tone of voice as if they don't want you to tell them? Ffion supposed Howard suffered from people telling him about their boring ailments.

'Oh, life in general. And Ellie in particular.'

'Ellie Bassett? What's she got to do with your life?'

Ffion's eyes narrowed.

Howard knew the signs. He said, 'You've had an idea and you're going to ask me to do you a favour which you know I won't want to do.'

Ffion laughed. 'There's a place we can get real coffee and croissants on Ken High Street. Surely you can spare the time to catch up? Don't tell me you're working?'

'Yes and no. I've been out in Central Africa on secondment in the Democratic Republic of Congo for the last six months. Hence the tan. Funny how people kid themselves a tan is a sign of health. I picked up some so far unidentified virus and I'm on sick leave.'

'Howard, I'm so sorry. That jibe about Hollywood...'

'Very flattering actually. It's just till they find out what it is. As a precaution. So what is it you want me to do?'

She could tell he didn't want to talk about himself.

It was a bright autumn day; not warm, with a brisk breeze chasing paper and discarded cartons down the street. It had blown away the fumes and dust of the previous humid week and the air was fresh and clear. There were a few tables set out on the pavement and they brought their coffee out to sit there.

He said, 'Tell me about yourself first, Ffion. Any "Significant Other" about to make an honest woman of you?'

She felt the old irritation when Howard talked like this. He always assumed her life centred on a husband and children, or a lack of them, in spite of her protestations that they didn't feature on her 'To Do' list.

She said with asperity, 'Certainly not. Unless you count Ellie. She's as bad as a wife. She's a social worker in darkest North London and she comes home and talks incessantly about her problem children.'

'What sort of work do you do?'

'I'm personal assistant to a junior Minister in the Treasury. It's part research and part propaganda, a bit like Squealer in *Animal Farm*.'

Seeing his face, Ffion thought, He's never read Animal Farm. She said, 'My Minister's son was at Trinity. That's how I got the job. I'm biding my time. I don't think Harold Wilson will be round for long and I'm waiting to see what happens next.'

Howard's mind was still on Ffion's problem with Ellie

'Can't you just ask her to move out?'

Ffion hesitated. Why couldn't she do that? It was the simple solution. Ellie wasn't happy in the flat. The chrome and stainless steel kitchen could never be the heart of any 'home' Ellie aspired to. Ffion thought, She'd be much happier somewhere with fitted carpets and a three piece suite with flower-patterned chintz covers. So why not turf her out?

I don't want to have to admit failure, that's really it. Asking Ellie to share wasn't just trying to be nice because I was sorry for her; it was some sort of bid on my part to show I'm a normal woman. It's a test I have to pass.

And she thought, It's no good, I don't like women. I can't communicate with them. I don't share the values they think define them, and, Jesus, they bore me rigid. Asking Ellie to share the flat was supposed to prove I can change. And I can't.

Howard waved his fingers in her face. 'Hey,' he said, 'come back. You were miles away.'

Ffion said, 'Look, now we've found each other again why don't you come to dinner with us one night soon. Ellie would love to see you again, and I'll try to get in touch with Hilary. She's probably still buried in Little-Nowhere-on-the-Wold with the Rev Dad. You remember Hilary, don't you? The last virgin on earth?'

Ffion paused, struck by a momentary expression on Howard's face. She wondered why did he look like that. Perhaps he's forgotten her.

Then he said, 'No, actually. I've heard about her. Apparently she spends a lot of time in Northern Ireland.'

Ffion was startled. This was disconcerting. Ffion didn't like to admit it, but it made her feel good to think of Hilary still re-living her old life before Trinity.

'Why?' she said.

'Why the North? Don't ask me. But it would be good to see her again if you're planning a reunion.'

'All hell's breaking loose in Northern Ireland. Has she gone out of her mind?'

Howard shrugged and said, 'Search me. More coffee?'

Ffion nodded absentmindedly and said, 'Well OK, not Hilary. But you were a friend of Matt's, weren't you? Don't you still know any of his men friends?'

Howard frowned, trying to think. Then he said, 'He didn't really have men friends, did he? Being a few years older than the rest of us he probably found the men in his year very immature.'

'There was that guy who came from up North. Patrick something or other. A bit of a hanger-on. He'd be perfect.'

'Patrick Grant, you mean? Yes, he and Matt used to go off on trips *sur le Continent*. But what do you mean, perfect? What do you have in mind?'

'Bring this Patrick Grant person along. I want Ellie to get married. Then she'd want to have a home of her own and start a family and she'd move out of my place.'

'But why someone who was Matt's friend?'

'Trust me. Ellie loved Matt. Personally I think her way of showing it was grotesque, but she did. She's not going to love anyone else like that, but she needs to be married.'

'Who appointed you God?'

Ffion ignored the cliché. 'Don't you see? She's much more likely to marry this Patrick guy than someone new. She'll and marry him exactly because he was Matt's friend.'

'And how are you planning to get him to fall in love with her.'

Ffion was losing interest.

'Will you bring Patrick to dinner?' she said.

'I wouldn't miss it for the world,' Howard said.

16

Old friends from Trinity, that was what was wanted. What friends? No matter, it was enough to have been at TCD at the same time. Ffion telephoned to ask Hilary to her dinner party.

'It's to celebrate Ellie's birthday,' Ffion explained. 'Very small and select, all old friends from Trinity.'

Hilary knew that Fiona was in manipulative mode. As when wasn't she?

'Ffion, what are you up to? We've never celebrated Ellie's birthday in our lives.' she said.

'Stop being paranoid, there's always a first time. After Matt and everything, I thought it would be nice. Howard's coming.'

'Howard? Is he in London? The last I heard, he was working in the depths of Africa.'

'He's back. He particularly said how pleased he'd be to see you again.'

Hilary, bemused, said yes before she realized what she'd agreed to. She stood staring at the phone for several minutes, wishing she'd had the presence of mind to say no. She thought, What is Ffion up to? Is she trying to get Howard off with Ellie? I suppose she thinks Ellie would make a good doctor's wife, and that's just what Howard needs.

It was ages since she'd spoken to Ffion; before Ellie first moved into the flat in Chelsea.

Hilary was amazed that Ffion and Ellie were still living together. I didn't think that would last a week, let alone till now, she thought. I wonder what Ellie's doing for a job? I

145

can't see her still being a social worker in the shabby part of Islington and living in up-market Chelsea. But I can't see her fitting in on the King's Road either, unless Evans Outsize has opened a branch down the Fulham end.

She surprised herself at the thought, it was unlike her to be so unkind. Or was it? Had she without realizing it grown mean-spirited?

Hilary wasn't only interested in finding out what was happening to the others; she was curious to see how they would react to the changed Hilary. So much is different in my life, she thought, I've changed beyond all recognition.

Or perhaps not, she told herself. People identify others by the way they perceive them, and I don't look very different. OK, I do my hair in a French pleat now, and I get my eyebrows plucked sometimes; but the outline's much the same and no one's going to give me a second glance to notice that I'm no longer a pushover.

She looked around her pretty basement bedroom, which was also her office. It was a long way away from the fusty Victorian paterfamilias of a house which was the Vicarage, with its brown aura of middle age and huge light-absorbing heavy furniture. Here the sliding glass door on to the patio had a view of the apple tree on her patch of lawn, the grass now looking covered in theatrical snow from fallen blossom.

I'm a new person in a new life, she thought.

And then she asked herself, How did Ffion get my telephone number? Has she really been in contact with Howard? Why would she?

She surprised herself by a flash of jealousy, resentful that Ffion could claim any part of Howard. She thought, Ffion can have anyone she wants, why can't she leave a sweet man like Howard alone? She never even liked him, he used to wind her up asking her when she was going to get married and have children. His teasing drove her mad. She's got no sense of humour.

Hilary's first reaction was to ring Ffion back and say she couldn't come after all. And then she thought, If she thinks she can put Howard down all evening, he won't defend himself. I must go, just to stand up for him.

She thought of the last time she'd seen Howard, that night she'd had some sort of crisis after meeting Sandra under the clock at Waterloo Station and ended up in the Waldorf Hotel.

She had marched into the hotel full of good intentions about sorting herself out. It was actually Sandra who'd made her feel that if she could only be alone in some place to which she had no emotional connection, she might be able to find some answers to questions about what she wanted to do with her life.

Alone in that silent hotel room, aware of the teeming life of London all around her and herself insulated from contact with it, she admitted, Seeing Sandra has make me realize that I do want something more than hang around at home making myself useful.

But why? And what? Why can't I just be the dutiful daughter helping the Rev Dad out in the parish and mucking in with Mother in the house?

Hilary now laughed at that not-so-former self. But then she remembered how at the time she hadn't dared ring Room Service to order something to eat. She wouldn't know what to tip the waiter, she wouldn't know what to do with the used dishes and she wouldn't be able to go to bed because she hadn't got a nightdress, and the chambermaid might see her naked.

Yet the thought of eating alone in the hotel dining-room was too terrifying to contemplate. But how she longed to be there: mysterious, cosmopolitan, aloof from the glamorous people watching her and wondering who she was. But overriding that was crippling reality; an overweight, unfashionable woman, no longer a girl, placed out of the way behind a pillar and noticed only if someone pitied her in passing.

In the end she'd gone back down to the street and bought the last two sandwiches in a kiosk which was closing for the night. Then she returned to the room and rang Reception to put her through to the Westminster Hospital. At least that held no fears for her; that's the sort of thing the dutiful daughters of vicars knew how to do.

Howard was going off duty. He sounded pleased to hear her. If she'd called next week, he said, he'd be on his way to Africa to do research on SIV.

'What's SIV?'

He laughed. 'Simian immunodeficieny virus. We're basically looking into whether this retrovirus could cross the species barrier to infect humans. Pretty esoteric stuff, don't worry about it.'

'Yuck, as Ffion used to say. Can we have a drink?'

He came right over to the Waldorf. He was so thoughtful; he brought a bottle of wine with him to drink in her room.

She drank too much too quickly; he scarcely touched a drop. She only just stopped herself from telling him about the only other time she had been drunk with a man in a hotel room, but then she remembered why that wouldn't do. To him of all people it couldn't be an amusing anecdote.

While she was still sober enough to know what she was saying she said, 'I was afraid to ring. I thought that what you did for me might get in the way of us being friends. But it's all right, isn't it?'

'Of course it is,' he said.

She looked at him and thought what a doctor he looked. Funny how some professions seemed to attract people who looked a certain way, like bankers looked as though they'd been born wearing dark grey suits, and tax men all appeared to have been weaned on pickles. Doctors, to her mind, were earnest and concerned-looking; and very clean, with nice teeth and pink plump fingers.

What rubbish, she told herself, I'm drunk and he's sober, he must decide for me.

She said, 'Will you marry me, Howard?'

He smiled. 'Too much work on at the moment, I'm afraid.'

'You could make love to me. I love you, Howard, I want your baby. Oh, please, give me a baby.'

He tried to make light of it and said, 'Where I'm going they may eat white babies.'

Even Hilary's befuddled mind noticed how embarrassed Howard was. 'Don't look so scared, I didn't mean it. Surely you don't think I'm serious?'

She started to cry.

'What's up?' he said.

Weeping sobered her. So she told him. Perhaps because of the enormous thing he'd done for her, and the intimate things he knew about her, she couldn't help treating him as though he'd accepted some sort of special responsibility for her happiness.

He asked her, 'Do you have to do anything? Aren't you happy as you are?'

'I'm content, I suppose. I don't think I'm happy. I want more out of life.'

'Have you any interests you could use as a basis for a job?'

Hilary shook her head. 'No,' she said, looking miserable.

'Nothing at all? Hilary, you're still a young woman, you must be interested in something.'

'I miss Ireland. I loved it there. I think about Trinity a lot, the way we were. And with all the trouble that's going on in the North, it's on my mind.'

'That's it, then,' he said. 'Go and see for yourself.'

That's how she'd got her first journalistic commission. Howard knew someone on the New Statesman. This friend agreed to look at anything she wrote. No promises.

149

She wrote about what it meant to be Irish, about Ireland as a tribal nation. She'd thought hard about that, from the time when she'd first recognized Dublin as the capital of a foreign country and felt ashamed to be an Englishwoman there, an English girl.

Howard's friend agreed to publish the piece.

Now, with Ireland in the spotlight because of the Troubles, both British and American magazines and newspapers asked her to write for them.

She telephoned Sandra when her New Statesman article appeared in print. 'I want to thank you. If you hadn't put a bomb under me that day on Waterloo Station, I'd never have got out of my rut.'

'I didn't mean you to take it literally,' Sandra said. 'Where are you living?'

'Still with Mum and the Rev Dad, of course. It'll be a while before I can afford a place of my own.'

'Hey, you know I married my old boy?'

Hilary thought, She doesn't have to make it quite so obvious that I'm boring her.

She tried to sound interested; she asked herself, Is that good of bad?

She said, 'The property developer with the thick son?'

'Well, he wasn't really all that thick; he got into Oxford. But yes, that old boy.'

'Congratulations. Are you happy?'

'Of course I'm happy – I'm rich. I hope you will be, too.'

'I am. At least now I feel I've got a purpose in life.'

'No, not that sentimental stuff. I can help you. You can live in one of our flats.'

'Sandra…?'

'It's obvious. We did a flat conversion in Barnsbury. We took over three adjoining houses and turned them into apartments. We keep it empty, waiting for the prices to go up. But it'll be much safer with someone living there to keep an eye on it and put off the dreaded squatters. There's a staff flat in the basement, you can have that. You'd be doing me a favour, because the place will all be mine when my old boy kicks the bucket.'

Now, months later, walking out in the spring sunshine on to her private patio to water pots full of daffodils, Hilary smiled to herself.

She was quite looking forward to Ffion's dinner party.

Hilary had not seen Ellie since that disastrous night at Matt Brewer's so-called beach cottage at Brittas Bay. There had been so much confusion Hilary didn't remember what happened to Ellie. Someone must have taken her back into town, she was certainly not there when she and Sandra and Ffion of all people started to clear up and put out the fire.

Ellie looks older, Hilary thought; but more attractive. More a person somehow. The puppy fat's gone, with that vapid little-girl look which always seemed to come to the surface, however much she tried to look grown up and soignée. I used to think she was like a half-modelled lump of plasticine waiting to be finished off. But that's only because that's how I saw myself.

Ffion looked stunning, of course. She greeted Hilary at the front door of a flat so like a science laboratory that Hilary thought she should be wearing a protective mask. Ffion wore sizzling tangerine bell-bottomed trousers and a filmy peasant blouse with wide sleeves in citrus green. The high-gloss surface of her thick dark hair might as well have been signed like glass with a diamond: Vidal Sassoon.

Hilary was rather late. The others were already on their second drink when Ffion ushered her into the sitting-room.

Howard, looked brown and strained, stood up as she came in. His hair was bleached blonder than usual, presumably from working in the open under the African sun.

But it was the other man she noticed. Of course, I remember, she thought, he's the one who took Ellie away that awful night. He got into the back of a car with her and had an arm around her while someone drove them away. He was a friend of Matt's.

Ffion said, 'This is Patrick Grant, Hilary. Do you remember him at TCD?'

Why is she looking so smug? Hilary asked herself. She was practically winking at me.

Halfway through the meal – all supplied ready-prepared from Harrods Food Hall, Hilary guessed – Ffion asked her to come into the kitchen for a moment.

Ffion could scarcely contain herself.

'Didn't I tell you?' she said.

'Tell me what?'

'They're falling in love.'

'Who?'

'Oh, Hilary, don't be dense. Ellie and Patrick, or course. I knew it would work. It's the solution to everything.'

'What? What are you talking about?'

'Getting Ellie out of the flat, of course. I hope you won't wear that midi skirt to the wedding, it doesn't suit you at all. It would look better with platform boots, they'd hide your less than slender ankles.'

'For God's sake, Ffion, what are you playing at?'

Ffion tossed her black mane and laughed. 'You know me,' she said, 'I only want everybody to be happy.'

'Yuck!' Hilary said. Ffion failed to take that in.

17

Ellie, in reflective mood as she pushed Saffron in her pram along the towpath beside the canal, asked herself, What is it about water that's conducive to melancholy? Particularly dirty water.

But that's nonsense. The sea is never melancholic, nor white water rapids, nor even rippling trout streams. It's water without movement that's depressing. Dirty stagnant water.

Actually the surface of the canal didn't look like water at all. More like oil spilled on a sheet of black plastic under a thin December sun, definitely toxic.

But on the opposite bank to Ellie, in the shadow of a rundown block of council flats, three small boys (who should surely be in school?) squatted on the bank with home-made rods, trying to fish. Fly-fishing, no less, or a form of it, flinging their lines out across the canal and then winding them in quickly.

She wondered, Should I shout out to them and tell them they're wasting their time? No fish could live there. But why spoil their fun? If one had been on his own perhaps she would have called. But three of them would just let fly a stream of obscenities. Why invite trouble?

I must try to stop thinking that if three or more kids are gathered together in this part of London they're bound to be members of a criminal gang, she thought. But the moment had passed anyway.

One boy shouted. He started to reel in his line. The others gathered round, excited. One boy flung himself flat on the bank and tried to reach over to grasp the line. He pulled out a bent bicycle wheel dripping mud.

The boys took it out of the water as carefully as if it were a salmon. Ellie thought, Will that old bike wheel become something more impressive when that kid describes his catch to his friends later?

She was suddenly cheered. Perhaps the wheel disturbing the surface of the water had something to do with it. How wonderful children are, she told herself, they make everything life-affirming.

Hold on to that as long as you can, she said, bending over the sleeping baby.

And then, as so often happened now, she felt overwhelmed by the responsibility she had taken on so lightly in having a child. I thought a baby would be like the ultimate family pet, she thought, but it's so much more. Having a baby proves you have the power of life and death, you're part of God. I must ask Hilary one day if that's significant.

Ellie found it hard to put into words, even for herself, the guilty ambivalence she felt now about becoming a mother. She thought, Why don't other women tell you how it'll be before it happens? Nobody tries to warn you about this reservation, this feeling that I have to pay for the miracle of Saffron's life by giving up something of myself. *Everything* of myself; my independence, my free will, my own time; even my relationship with Patrick. Everything I hoped and dreamed is now subsumed by Saffron, I have to live for her.

Saffron, awake now, was staring at Ellie from the pram.

Ellie said to her, 'I wish I'd known, that's all. I could've prepared myself better. I promise you I'll warn you when the time comes.'

She felt vindicated now, though she would never tell Patrick about her promise to Ellie. If he'd had his way and made her take the baby out in one of those buggies instead of a pram, this precious mother-and-child bonding moment would never have happened.

Patrick wanted the baby to face outwards to welcome the wider world of the massed human experience; Ellie took the view that a child so young should always face the security and love represented by her mother's adoring face.

Ellie stopped and stared down into the water, watching the leafless urban trees reflected in the oily surface. What was it Hilary had said once, one night in their first year at TCD, when the four of them were still sharing a room in Trinity Hall?

Hilary was upset. They'd been teasing her about her virginal state.

Ffion had expounded one of her outlandish theories that normal men were put off women who wanted children as much as Hilary did. They avoided them like the plague.

'It's as though you walk around like an old-time leper ringing a bell to warn them to keep off,' Ffion said.

And Hilary took her seriously. She said, 'What else can I do? The person I really am can't be born until I have a child.'

A breeze appeared from nowhere and ruffled the water. Ellie smiled at Saffron and walked on. Poor Hilary, she thought, I know what she was trying to say; at least now I do.

Saffron held out her arms and laughed. Ellie took her up and hugged and kissed her.

'Oh God, I love you so much,' she said. 'You've made the world so much bigger and better.'

Other years at this time she'd be thinking of parties, of what she was going to wear and eat and do; when she could find time to get to Kensington High Street to the shops, and where she and Patrick would spend the Christmas break: Wembley Park, or with Patrick's parents on the Grants' farm in Ireland.

But this year would be Saffron's first Christmas. And the first for Ellie and Patrick in their new home. Ellie would rather have waited a year or two and saved up for a nice bijou little terraced house in Prebend Street, but with the baby coming they had to settle for an unrenovated two-bedroom cottage well the other side of the New North Road.

'It's all that nasty Ffion's fault,' Ellie said in a baby-voice to Saffron, leaning forward over the pram. 'I don't know why she didn't want Patrick and me living in that great big flat of hers while we got on our feet.'

Ellie, thinking back, wondered again why Ffion had behaved as she did. She'd forked out for her and Patrick to stay in a hotel for a fortnight after the wedding. Her wedding present, she said. And then she suggested Ellie went to live at home in Wembley Park. She said she didn't want a man living in her flat. As if Patrick could really be counted as a man once we were married. She must've been jealous that I'd married before her.

Ellie could hear the twigs on the leafless trees stirring. She leaned over and tucked the blanket more closely round the baby. It had all turned out for the best. Ellie was very happy living in her own little nest of a house. Patrick liked his job lecturing at the new City University. 'We're a perfect ickle nuclear family,' she told Baby. She didn't feel in the least embarrassed by the baby talk.

This year she'd be doing her Christmas shopping at Mothercare, instead of Harvey Nicks. As for presents for herself, well, all her friends would buy her things for the baby. As for Patrick, he'd probably give her a new baby buggy. Well, if he did, she'd make him take it back to the shop and get a refund.

Ellie did rather wish that Patrick didn't call her Mummy all the time, even when they were with their friends and Saffron wasn't there. She sometimes wondered if he even remembered that she did have a name of her own. But then he had so many names to remember, with all those students of his.

She smiled, remembering how Ffion had once asked Patrick how he introduced Ellie to strangers? 'It must be awfully confusing if you tell everyone she's called Mummy,' Ffion said. 'After all, aren't they all?'

Honestly, Ffion was beyond the pale sometimes. I miss the old days, Ellie thought, all those times we'd sit around in Raglan Road and put the world to rights and Ffion would say the most outrageous things just to wind us up.

No, don't go there, she thought. Don't start thinking about Matt. He's dead and I've moved on. It's not Patrick's fault that he's not Matt, but Matt loved him, too; he'd be happy we're together, two people he loved.

It had all been so light-hearted then, so innocent. Things seemed much more grim and serious now. All the paramilitary killings there've been in Ulster, and the British Ambassador to Ireland murdered. And then the rumours about the SAS going over the border to capture Republicans. All that in Ireland, that Land of Dreams.

Ellie tripped and jerked the pram handle. Saffron began to cry. Ellie thought, I wonder what Sandra's doing now? We never talked about what it was like for her, coming from Belfast. She must've grown up knowing what it feels like to be scared of the people around her in the street. She seemed to have been indoctrinated by where she came from, as though she had no practice before she came to Trinity at having a mind of her own. But that was long before the Troubles started.

None of that has anything to do with me, Ellie said to herself. My future's taken care of.

But there wasn't much else to celebrate here at home either. Ellie wasn't looking forward to returning to Social Services after her statutory maternity leave. People seemed so indifferent to the sufferings of others. The poor were getting poorer and more vulnerable but the rich seemed to be ignoring any social responsibility to help people who couldn't help themselves.

The sun was gone; it was getting dark. Ellie started to hurry. She was afraid of being alone in empty streets in London. I never felt like this in Dublin, she told herself, and then thought, But I suppose what's been happening in the North has changed things even there.

She had reached an up-market part of Islington. Here the elegant Georgian houses which backed on to the canal were screened from public view. Impenetrable Russian vine and thorny climbing roses spilled over the walls to hide locked doors in the garden walls.

They should call it hostile planting, Ellie thought. And when did people start cementing discreet spirals of barbed wire and coloured shards of broken bottles on top of their walls? Perhaps it's not paranoia, perhaps it really is taking sensible precautions. But it never used to be like this in Wembley Park. We didn't even bother to lock the back door. People trusted each other. Who knows, perhaps that's changed, too.

She was going to cry. She cried so often these days. 'Oh, God,' she said aloud, 'What a bloody waste. And I never even found out what I was wasting.'

It had been easy to be optimistic then. But then hope didn't mean much if it came so easy. It was tougher later, when you had to fight to hold on to it. But, she supposed, that was what growing up was all about.

Beside the towpath she passed a drunk lying covered with cardboard and newspapers on the canal bank under a wall overrun with yellow winter jasmine. It struck her as a sign of the resurgent human spirit that a derelict inhabiting a body she could smell from five feet away should seek out a refuge close to the sweet-scented flower.

She tucked a five pound note into the drunk's sleeve.

There's no comparison, she told herself, there's so much more to living now. People don't have to beg for charity, there are institutions who want to do their bit to help society's victims. It comes naturally to most people to want to care; it's just these days they don't realize they're still needed.

She paused, asking herself if this comforting thought was true. Well perhaps not everyone thinks like that, she told herself, but there must be enough like us to change things for the better. Patrick and I are a force to be reckoned with because we care, we can make a difference to other people. And that's why we're happy.

Ellie walked more quickly now, under the bridge where the view on the opposite side of the canal became more industrial, dominated by Sixties office buildings and rows of council houses. The canal itself could be a metaphor for the social divide, Ellie told herself. No, that wasn't true; the canal, choked with old bedsteads and supermarket trolleys and plastic shopping bags hiding God knows what, was a statement of nothing but the dysfunctional lives of city dwellers. It was she herself who represented new hope for the future. She was an ordinary wife and mother, but through her the outcasts of society, like that poor drunk on the bench, could be included in a better way of life for everyone. People like me, she thought, me and Patrick, we're the shape of things to come.

The baby was awake; she stared at Ellie through unfocussed violet eyes. It was all Ellie could do not to stop herself picking her up and hugging her because she was going to be the most precious thing in her life from now on. Saffron was the future, and Ellie would keep her safe. She and Patrick, a happy family.

She left the canal and walked up Charlton Place to Camden Passage. With the street lights lit, she felt less nervous. It was only just after four o'clock.

I hate winter, she thought, making her way towards Islington Green, where she could catch a bus along Essex Road.

Further down the Passage, she saw a couple laughing as they came down the steps of a small restaurant to the street. The woman tripped and clung to the man's arm.

Drunk, Ellie told herself. Disgusting, at this time of the day.

Then she saw that the man was Patrick. The woman he was holding was beautiful, tall and dark and bloody perfect, even under the orange tint of the street light: Ffion.

18

Ffion said, 'Why the hell did Ellie ring you?'

Hilary sighed. She was asking herself the same question, but Ellie was in such a state, she hadn't been able to get much sense out of her. She'd known that tackling Ffion was going to be difficult. That's why she'd rung her at work; Ffion couldn't go berserk at work.

Hilary told Ffion, 'People do when they're upset. They always have, they did at Trinity. God knows why. I suppose there's something about the way I look that makes other women think I'm on their side. They don't see me as competition.

Ffion sounded irritated. 'It's probably because you're a vicar's daughter and they associate you with the Church and being a good person. But I suppose that amounts to much the same thing.'

Is Ffion really having an affair with Ellie's husband? Hilary asked herself. Ellie was so sure. According to her, she saw Patrick and Ffion come staggering out of a restaurant at 4.30 in the afternoon and practically fornicate in the street.

Hilary thought, It doesn't sound right to me. Patrick's far too buttoned up even to snog in public. Or get drunk, come to that.

Ffion was saying, 'What's happening to Ellie? She seems to have lost all reason since she had that baby.'

'Hormones, probably.'

'Well, what does she expect you to do about it? Ask me to give him back?'

'Ffion, you're not, are you?'

'Don't be so bloody stupid. I'm not that desperate. Don't forget I set them up together. He's duller than a wet weekend; and anyway I wouldn't be seen dead with anyone with that beak of a nose and no chin.'

'I hope you'd also lay off him because he's your best friend's husband.'

Hilary was winding Ffion up with her priggish tone, but Ffion never knew when she was being teased.

'Is Ellie my best friend?' Ffion sounded surprised. The idea had never occurred to her, obviously.

'You asked her to share your flat, didn't you? And you fixed her up with Patrick.'

'I wanted to be rid of her.'

Hilary was in a hurry. She was due to take the Shuttle to Belfast later in the day.

She said, 'It's nothing to do with me. Ellie asked me to find out if there's anything going on between you and Patrick, that's all. She's terrified of losing him, what with the baby and all.'

'Oh, yuck! I don't believe a word of it. She's wallowing in victimhood and elephantine and boring and she's jealous as hell of me because I'm free, size 10, single, and I can do what I like. That makes her hate me and she wants to give you a reason for hating me too.'

'Poor Ellie.'

'Poor Ellie my backside. Don't you see what she's doing? She's creating a crisis where there isn't one, so she can dramatize herself. I've problems of my own without having to suffer for hers.'

Hilary laughed. 'You, problems? The future growth rate of the economy for the next ten years put in jeopardy by misguided job creation schemes and your Minister's being made the scapegoat? Or trouble keeping the real rate of inflation out of the newspapers? It's a different thing entirely to what's happening to Ellie.'

'And much more important.'

Later that day, though, Ffion thought about what Hilary had said. The night at the Soup Bowl, when she'd had her Siobhan McKenna moment and decided that career success depended on empathizing with other women, had had a profound effect on her. Indeed, Ffion thought it likely that women got so emotionally involved in feminism because without the unity from fighting a common enemy – men — they were afraid women would start scratching each other's eyes out. Which, she told herself, was exactly what was happening.

Now we don't have to like or support each other; at last we're free to hate each other. What a relief to admit it.

But that means that if the mass of women like Ellie oppose me, I'm pretty well bound to fail, Ffion thought. If Ellie really does feel she has reasons for hating me, I need to know more. Do most stay-at-home mothers feel the way she does about women like me? And if they do, why?

But the real question, she thought, is who or what *are* women like me? Do we count as women at all? And if not, who or what do the Ellies of this world think we are?

Ffion telephoned Ellie.

'What do you want?' Ellie said.

'Can you get rid of that baby for a bit and meet me for a drink. Or tea.'

'Patrick and Saffron have been spending a few days with her Granny and Gramps at the farm. I'm waiting in for a telephone call to tell me what time their train gets in.' Ellie hesitated, then added, 'If you've something you want to say to me, you'd better come here.'

Ffion took a cab. She had little on at work that day. Her Minister was on a break with his family in the country.

It was the first time Ffion had visited Ellie's home, in a street amidst a maze of small terraced former artisans' dwelling in the back of beyond off the New North Road. Or maybe Kingsland Road, Ffion had lost her bearings once the taxi turned down the Essex Road.

Ellie's house was one of the few in the street which had been gentrified; Ffion took that to mean it had an indoors lavatory. There was a pram chained to a bicycle padlocked to the railing in front of the house.

'This is it,' she told the taxi driver.

Ellie heard the cab stop. The door slammed. Ellie told herself, If she's got that 'I've just stepped in dog poo' look of hers on her face, I shan't let her in.

She went to open the door.

'It's quite a pretty street; I should think the house is a good investment.' It was a compliment.

Ellie thought, Who the hell does she think she is. As if I need her approval.

She said, 'Thanks for that. There's still a lot to do.'

Ffion followed Ellie down the twisting staircase to the big basement kitchen. You dare, Ellie thought, you dare say anything at all and I'll tell you what I think of you.

There was a pile of Saffron's toys in a corner, and on the table a heap of case histories Patrick had brought home for Ellie to read. He liked her to take an interest in his work, and usually tried out his lectures on her. What, she wondered, would Ffion think of that as an idea of fun.

'Sorry about the mess,' Ellie said, going to fill the kettle. 'Coffee or tea?'

Ffion was looking about her with the curious pitying expression of a tourist visiting a primitive hovel in Africa or somewhere, as though it was wonderful that people could survive such hardship.

Ellie said, 'We'd better have coffee; the milk's slightly off and it won't taste so bad in coffee.'

'I'll take it black.'

She's thinking, What kind of stay at home mother with nothing else to do has no fresh milk in the house, Ellie told herself. Patronising cow!

She made coffee and Ffion sat herself down at the kitchen table. Ellie sat down opposite and waited for her to start talking.

Ffion said, 'I'm not having an affair with Patrick.'

'I saw you.'

God, Ffion thought, she looks as though someone knitted her out of dishcloth cotton. Grubby dishcloth cotton that's worn out from washing up. She looks about fifty; she's only in her thirties.

'Listen to me, will you. Patrick wanted to get you a Christmas present, something for yourself. He asked me for suggestions.'

'A likely story. He's going to give me a baby buggy.'

Ffion was trying not to lose patience. 'I suggested an antique Victorian ring. You used to have some good Victorian jewellery, and your hands are your best feature.'

Ffion glanced at Ellie's hands and knew Ellie saw her realize her mistake. Cow, Ellie thought, with your unchipped nail varnish and manicured cuticles.

She said, 'Have you and Patrick cooked this story up between you?'

Keep your temper, Ffion told herself. She's tormented by hormones.

'He asked me to come with him to find something in Camden Passage. He said he'd no idea about women's stuff and he was quite right. I picked you a lovely ruby cluster set in gold. That's what he's going to give you for Christmas. For God's sake, don't spoil it.'

'He can't afford it. Or eating out in Italian restaurants.'

'That was my treat.'

'Why would you do that?'

Ffion nearly told her that she owed Patrick because by marrying Ellie he had given her back her flat. Her life, actually.

She said, 'I was hungry.'

Ellie still wasn't sure that Ffion wasn't lying. Or, even more insulting, was she saying the idea of Patrick even aspiring to have an affair with her was beyond preposterous?

But Ellie let it go. She changed the subject.

'Have you seen anything of the others?' she said. 'Hilary seems to be spending a lot of time in Ulster. She shouldn't mess in what she doesn't understand, if you want my opinion.'

'Still a virgin, is she?'

Ellie shrugged. 'What about Sandra? Someone said her husband died and left her his property development business. Apparently Sandra's taken up with the head of the funeral directors who arranged the funeral. She didn't ask any of us to go to it.'

'Was it in Belfast?'

'No, in Israel, I think.' Then Ellie said, 'What about you, Ffion?'

'Me? It's a bit of a bugger, actually. I'm in love.'

'Well, that's good, isn't it? After all, it's not the first time, is it?'

'Yes, actually it is. I didn't want it to happen but when it did it was cataclysmic.'

Ellie stared at her in disbelief. She thought, Whoever he is, he has my sympathy; he must be a glutton for punishment, Ffion hasn't a clue how to be in a real relationship.

But she said, 'Ffion, that's great. Where did you meet him? What does he do?'

Was Ffion actually blushing, Ellie wondered. Her voice sounded soft, too, gentler.

'His name's Vaclav. Vaclav Novak. He's a violinist, he gives concerts at the Wigmore Hall. Perhaps you've heard of him...'

'No, but we don't get out much since Saffron was born. Honestly I'm so tired most of the time I don't think I could stay awake through a whole concert, however good your Vaclav is.'

He's older than her, then, Ellie thought. Of course, Ffion would always go for someone older, someone who would give her space to do her own thing. She'd always want someone with a successful career; she didn't want to have to help anyone else up the ladder. Older men aren't so needy, either, they've already made a life of their own.

Ffion was saying in her surprising new girlie voice, 'I met him on a government trade mission I headed in Prague. He was a guest soloist playing with the Czech Philharmonic. The moment we met we were mad for each other, but then when the job was over I thought that was it, I'd never see him again.'

'But you did?'

'He came to London to give a series of concerts, and now he's based here.'

'Do you live together?'

Ffion raised an eyebrow. What does that raised eyebrow mean? Ellie asked herself.

Ffion said, 'Of course we do. But this is IT. I thought you'd gone haywire over Matt, Ellie, but now I understand. Not that I'd let Vaclav reduce me to a domestic slave.'

Ffion smiled, almost apologetic. Then she said, 'Vaclav needed somewhere quieter than Chelsea. I moved out anyway because Beverly came back to London. Vaclav and I rent a house on Wandsworth Common.'

She frowned, as though not sure if she wanted to go on.

Spit it out, can't you, Ellie thought, what's the problem? Don't tell me you're so worried because you've just discovered what it's like to be happy.

Ellie tried to prompt her. 'It sounds idyllic,' she said. 'What's wrong?'

'Would you say I was the jealous type? I'm not unreasonable, am I, would you say?'

Ellie said to herself, Guilty on both counts. Aloud she said, 'Of course not. Anyway you've never had any reason to be jealous; it's other people who were jealous of you.'

'That's true, of course that's true. Ellie, you've put your finger on it. That's why the bitch is doing this.'

'Who's she, and what's she doing?'

'Beverly. She's having an affair with him. With Vaclav.'

'Who is?'

'Beverly.'

'Your mother?' Ellie didn't know what to say.

Ffion held her head in her hands. Her thick dark hair hid her face. Her voice was muffled. 'Vaclav told me he was giving a concert in Vienna and he'd be away for a week. I hadn't seen Beverly for ages and I'd nothing to do so I went round to Sloane Street. She didn't answer the door but I've got a key so I let myself in. I thought she might possibly be ill, she's not as young as she was.'

Ffion paused and then went on, 'She was in bed all right, but she wasn't ill. She was at it with Vaclav. They were making love.'

'Wow!' Ellie said. She hesitated, imagining the scene. It was like something on television. I mustn't laugh, she thought.

'What are you going to do now?' she asked.

Ffion frowned. 'I had it out with them, then and there. Vaclav actually said he was in love with her, she was everything he'd ever wanted in a woman. He'd thought at first he loved me, he said, but apparently … this is what he said, I think he's gone mad… apparently I'm not a complete woman like her. He said I'm like a spoiled child, that I don't know how to love anyone except myself.'

'What happened then?'

'I mean, I ask you, what's the matter with the man? She's incapable of loving anyone. Not even me. And she's years older than him; it's grotesque-'

'What did your mother say?'

'Well, there wasn't much she could say. She looked ridiculous, trying to pull the sheet up to cover herself. She mumbled something about it being one of those things, that they were both helpless in the grip of passion.'

'What did you say to that?'

'I told her she was gross, that I'd never forgive her, that I hated her, that I never wanted to see her again for the rest of my life.'

Ellie began to feel sorry for Ffion 'You could've told her she's the worst mother in the world.'

'She wouldn't see that as an insult.'

'What did Vaclav do?'

'Christ, what a wimp! He told me not to speak to my mother like that. So I picked up her bedside lamp and brought it down on his hand.'

'My God! What was it made of?'

'Marble. It had a marble base.' Then she added, 'I thought it was plastic.'

'So what happened then?'

'He squealed like a pig and burst into tears.'

'Did you actually break his hand?'

'I don't know, I didn't hang around. If I did he deserved it, he's broken my heart.'

Then Ffion smiled and added, 'One thing I do know, if he does ever play again he'll never be able to pick up a violin for the rest of his life without remembering me and how he made me suffer.'

She's a monster, Ellie thought. But what a great story. She couldn't wait to tell the others. And Patrick!

19

'If you see an accident beside the road, drive on.'

'But…'

'Even when a hysterical motorist seems to be trying to get help for injured people lying in the road, keep going. It could be an ambush.'

'For God's sake…'

'Listen, even if a man with blood streaming down his face drags himself into the path of your car waving desperately for you to give him a lift to hospital, avoid him if you can, but in any case, don't stop.'

Hilary had been told the rules about driving in Northern Ireland. Sandra, sounding like an instructor giving last minute tips to an L-driver taking the driving test, had rung her specially to warn her.

'For God's sake, you can't leave injured people bleeding to death at the side of a road,' Hilary said.

Hilary could almost hear Sandra shrug as she said, 'Suit yourself, but if you do stop, chances are there'll suddenly be masked men pointing guns at you. They'll force you to go to an ATM cashpoint and take out money on every credit card you've got.'

'You mean the blood is probably tomato ketchup?'

Sandra ignored that. 'Or they'll abduct you and hold you for ransom.'

'I've only got one credit card, and nobody would pay a ransom for me.'

'At the very least they'll put a load of explosives in your car boot and make you drive somewhere they want to bomb.

Whatever happens they won't let you survive to tell the tale. And you'll go down in history as a terrorist.'

Hilary couldn't take all this seriously. Since the William incident at TCD, Sandra seemed to have become seriously paranoid about what really went on in Northern Ireland.

Hilary had thought it was just about feasible when Sandra told her family she was the target of rogue paramilitaries who blamed her for William's death, and that's why she wouldn't return to Belfast.

But she made that up as an excuse, Hilary thought, she didn't believe it. Surely she didn't?

'You've been reading too many trash paperbacks,' she said.

Hilary wondered what Sandra was trying to do, unless she just wanted to create some vicarious drama to spice up her life. Hilary thought, It must be very boring to have all that money and nothing she really wants to do with it.

Hilary was thinking about Sandra as she drove her hire car towards Belfast. It was late evening, a night with a fitful moon and sudden bursts of heavy rain. There was a lot of debris on the road. That was another of Sandra's warnings – fallen boughs or trees across the road could indicate an ambush.

'Do you mean they pick stormy nights for an ambush? Like poachers? Don't tell me there's such a thing as an abductors' moon?'

God, she thought, as she peered ahead, trying to see the road, I wish I hadn't laughed at her. This is really spooky.

Hilary was a daytime driver at the best of times. She'd never liked taking the Rev Dad's car out after dark when she lived at home. She got confused in mist or even heavy spray from big vehicles, and she was blinded by oncoming headlights.

At least tonight there was no other traffic; not a car in sight although this was the main road to Belfast.

She'd spent the day in Newry. The town, on the border with the Republic, was traditionally a mixed community where Catholics and Protestants co-existed amicably enough until the late 1960s. There had actually been a Catholic majority in the Town Council when a People's Democracy civil rights protest in 1969 effectively fired the starting gun on the Troubles. Now, with Northern Ireland polarised by civil war, Hilary wanted to learn how things had changed for the now divided community.

She was approaching a sharp bend and changed gear as she slowed down. As she straightened the car coming out of the corner, a movement on the other side of the road caught her eye.

Next moment something – a human or a large animal – staggered into the road and fell into the path of her car.

She stopped.

For a moment which seemed to last forever, she stared into the terrified eyes of a young man on his knees in the road and blinded by her headlights.

Oh, my God, Sandra's right, she thought. What's going to happen to me?

But whatever her head (and Sandra's voice in her head) was telling her, she acted on instinct.

She opened the car door. The man tried to get up. She ran towards him.

'Help me,' he said, 'please, help me.'

She got him into the car. There was blood on his clothes, and in his hair.

He was wearing a bright satin shirt of a light colour, with extravagant ruffles; incongruous, that struck her in passing.

She started the car. She was blocking the road on a dangerous bend, another car could run into them.

'No,' he said. 'Don't drive on, for God's sake.'

'Do you want us to be killed? We can't stay here.'

She saw the look of horror on his face. He put his hand on her arm. 'Turn round,' he said, 'for the love of God turn round and go back.'

His fear was infectious. Her heart was thumping and she could hear her own breathing sound hoarse as though she'd been running.

She found a gateway and turned the car.

'Get away from here,' he said over and over again, his fingers digging into her arm.

She felt she was driving for her life as she sped back down the road.

At last she saw a layby and pulled into it. After she turned off the engine, the two of them sat without moving, staring ahead at nothing.

Hilary tried to pull herself together. It was very quiet; even the wind had dropped.

The boy said, 'They were British soldiers. They were British soldiers and the van blew up and they'd got us lined up on top of the ditch and then they fired. British soldiers did.'

Hilary felt suddenly very cold.

'What's happened? Who are you? Why did you stop me going on?'

She got it out of him at last. He and his friends were musicians; they'd been playing a gig in a pub somewhere outside Newry. They were on their way back to Belfast.

'There was a road block. British soldiers in uniform. Five or six of them, and two men who weren't in uniform. We were all having a laugh. We knew they wouldn't find anything. It was routine, they said, they had to check everyone.

'They told us to get out of the van and get in line with our hands up while two of them searched the vehicle. Routine, they said.'

He stopped. He was shaking so much she could feel the car rocking.

'Hang on a minute,' she said, and got out of the car. She went round to the boot and brought him her heavy winter coat to wrap around him.

He finished telling her then. 'Liam went to help the men in the van so they didn't damage our musical instruments. And then there was a God-Almighty blast and the van exploded.

'And then we tried to run down the ditch into a field and they fired at us. The British soldiers did, they just kept firing and firing and I could see the other guys fall and I did too.'

'How could you see?'

'The van was on fire. And the moon, there was a bloody moon.

'What happened then?'

'I just lay there wondering if I was dying or maimed. Denny was lying half on top of me. I could tell he was dead.'

He retched then and she leaned across him and opened the window. A burst of rain hit him in the face.

My God, is he dying? He could be shot, she thought.

'Did you get hit?'

'No…I think Denny's body protected me.'

'What did they do after they finished firing at you?'

'They came into the field to check we were dead. One of my mates was still alive, I heard him groaning. And then a shot. I didn't hear him after that. They kicked Denny's body as they passed to make sure he was dead; I played dead and they moved on.'

Hilary found it hard to believe him; there must be some mistake.

'They can't have been British soldiers. Surely they can't.'

'They were in UDR uniforms. But the one in charge wasn't in uniform. He was definitely English. He talked like Terry Thomas.'

'For God's sake, why would they do it?'

'They were talking among themselves while they checked to make sure we were dead. They meant to plant explosives in the van set to go off later. They planned to give us the all-clear and we'd drive on. When the van blew up later in Belfast, the police and the politicians would say we were bringing the stuff over the border for the IRA.'

The boy paused and put a hand up to his hair. Then he looked at his fingers, which were sticky with blood. He looked as though he couldn't believe what he was seeing.

Hilary was afraid she might be sick. She heard her voice shaking as she said, 'What do we do now?'

He hesitated, then he sighed and said, 'If you want to help me, you're going to have to take me back there.'

'What? Are you crazy?'

She really thought he was mad. Perhaps he'd made the whole thing up after all. With what was going on in Ulster, there must be a lot of people who'd been driven insane and couldn't tell fantasy from reality.

He took her hand and squeezed it. Hers was cold, but his felt like part of a refrigerated corpse. He said, 'Listen, please. There's no other way. I've got friends around Lisburn. The Army'll know I should've been there in the van. My friends will back me up that I wasn't, I was with them. We'll say I was sick.'

'But how will you get there?'

Hilary knew the answer to her question before she asked it.

He said, 'All they'll do is stop you, and maybe ask you to get out of the car. But you're English, you'll have English papers on you, they won't suspect you.'

'And how do I explain you?'

He squeezed her hand. 'You're a wonderful woman yourself.'

Hilary had no choice. She thought, What else can I do? I can't leave him here.

'OK, get in the back and crouch down in the well behind the front seats. Pull my coat over you, they might get a flash of that neon shirt if they shine a torch into the car. And pray.'

He did as he was told. Hilary got out and took her suitcase and hand luggage out of the boot and piled it on the back seat.

The boy's voice was muffled when she got back in the car and started the engine.

'I won't forget what you've done for me.'

'Let's hope you live long enough to have a chance to.'

She thought the strangled sound he made might be a laugh.'

She turned the car round and drove back towards Belfast. Neither of them spoke. About a mile further along the road from where she'd found the young man, she saw Army and police vehicles blocking the highway.

The car smelled faintly of tobacco, and sweat. She opened the driver's window to clear the air and then drove slowly on towards the road-block spotlighted in a reddish glow where a burned-out vehicle smouldered on the verge.

The police had taken charge. It was a cop who stepped forward to shine a torch in her face and then briefly into the back of the car.

She said, to distract him, 'Oh dear, has there been an accident. It looks bad, I hope no one was badly hurt? Is there anything I can do to help, officer.'

She couldn't take her eyes off the handgun in its black leather holster so close to her face.

'It's a rough night to be out, to be sure,' he said. 'May I ask the nature of your business here?'

She turned to pull her handbag from the glove compartment and fumble through it for the papers for the hire car.

'I'm on my way back to Belfast from Newry. I'm a journalist from London, researching an article. I've been interviewing people all day in Newry.'

'Have you any proof of identity? A passport, perhaps?'

'I didn't think I needed a passport to travel in my own country, officer.' No, no, she told herself, don't antagonize him. She said, 'I'm afraid it's at home in London.'

This isn't going well, she thought.

Another man, a soldier this time, approached to find out what was going on. Oh, God, he's going to ask me to get out of the car, she thought. My legs feel so weak I might fall down.

She smiled at the soldier, 'I know how you can check me out. You're based at Tiepval barracks in Lisburn, aren't you? You can ask them there to check me out with Ffion Finlay. She's the personal political and press advisor to the Secretary of State for the Home Office or the Ministry of Defence, one of the Cabinet Ministers, anyway. It won't be difficult to find out. Or I've got her personal number in my diary. She knows what I'm working on.'

There were headlights approaching the roadblock. A farm lorry, followed by three or four vehicles that had been held up behind it.

'That's all right, Miss, move along,' the RUC man said. He waved his torch to men up ahead and turned away to check the lorry.

The soldier said to Hilary, 'Where can I read your article, which paper?'

Hilary, already driving forward, said, 'The New Statesman, I hope.'

'Never heard of it,' he said.

As she shut the window, Hilary said, 'I hope you soon will.'

She was trembling. Trying to get away, she stalled the car, then over-revved it to start and almost flooded the engine.

The boy's voice behind her told her to slow down. 'For the love of God,' he said, 'calm down. You're acting like a woman with something to hide.'

She said, 'I feel guilty, I lied to them. I'm a vicar's daughter, I'm a hopeless liar at the best of times.'

The young man had come out of hiding now and sat hunched in the back seat, frequently looking behind to see that they weren't being followed.

He said, 'Are you really a journalist?'

'Well, I'm trying to be. What happened to your band tonight should be a big story.'

'You won't be able to write it.'

'Of course I will. And if those soldiers are to be brought to justice, the police will need you to be a witness.'

He looked at her with a resigned pity that shocked her.

'C'mon, you know what's going to happen. There's no chance that scum will get what's coming to them and you know it. This will all be hushed up. Officially, it never happened.'

'But two British soldiers were killed. How can they cover that up?'

'Oh, if it came to it they'd say there were explosives in the van and when the soldiers went to search, they set them off?' Now he managed a shaky smile. 'If I came forward as a witness, sure as hell they'd do me for their murder, don't you see?'

Hilary didn't say anything. There was nothing she could say. She remembered how when she first went to Ireland, she'd wanted to say to all the Irish 'I'm sorry for what we did to you.' But she had nothing to say to this boy that would help either of them.

She drove on in silence. She felt she was driving and driving along this faceless road and getting nowhere. Then the boy said, 'There's a wood beyond that corner ahead, and a turning to the left. Stop there. Then turn on the inside light and check your map; that'll cover the light coming on when I open the door.'

She looked doubtful, not believing him again. There was no one around for miles.

'There are spotter planes,' he said, 'if there's one above us they'll see you checking the map and that'll satisfy them.'

'For God's sake, you must be paranoid.'

'We need to be,' he said.

She did as he'd said. She heard and saw nothing, but she knew he had gone as she drove on. A mile or so on, she passed the turning to Lisburn.

She drove straight to Aldergrove airport to catch the first available flight to London. She was obsessed with the need to get home. She had to wait for the flight. She could not keep still. The terminal was almost deserted at that time of the morning; she walked up and down distractedly staring across the drab grass surrounding the runway.

Even the hares have run away, she thought; usually it cheered her to watch the animals ignoring the aircraft landing and taking off within feet of them.

Stupid of me, she thought, but those hares ignoring the monstrous machines makes me think that the goodness in ordinary people in Ireland can survive the terrible things going on around them.

You fool, she told herself, why do I do it? Why do I keep on looking on the bright side?

But not today. Today Hilary saw the hares' absence as an ominous sign. She was oppressed by fear that something or someone would stop her leaving; that she would be trapped in this alien country by forces outside civilised control; invaders who had taken over by stealth.

As the time of her flight grew nearer, she moved to watch the entrance to the terminal building, keeping a lookout for armoured vehicles she expected to roll up and disgorge armed soldiers who would take over the airport.

An announcement over the tannoy informed would-be passengers that the flight was delayed. Hilary found herself weeping.

She suddenly wanted to telephone the Rev Dad to ask him to make sense of all this for her. He was English, he had been through the Second World War. Maybe it was what he'd seen there had made him become a vicar. But he was a moral man, and intelligent. He knew the worst of men and he still believed in the good of humanity. Surely there could be no question that he would condemn what those soldiers did, ultimately in his name. In our name, I'm English too.

And then she thought, No, not in my name. Dad knows how to forgive, but I don't.

Someone had left a newspaper on a seat. Hilary picked it up, looking for headlines reflecting the enormity of what happened last night. British Soldiers Massacre Musicians, something along those lines at least.

Hilary found the story in the News Extra box at the bottom of the front page.

Four members of folk-singing group The Boyos killed late last night when their van crashed and was destroyed by fire thirty miles north of Newry. No other vehicles were involved. A police spokesman said the most likely cause of the tragedy was that the driver had fallen asleep at the wheel.

That was it. The lad was right, it was being hushed up.

Hilary thought, it's beyond outrage. It undermines everything a civilised country is supposed to stand for.

And then – and it was almost as if the Rev Dad was asking the question – she said to herself, So what are you going to do about it?

20

Howard celebrated his fortieth birthday with a party in the garden of the Chelsea Arts Club. A surprise party. His housemate Andy had organised it as a surprise.

None of Howard's Trinity friends had met Andy. Patrick was the only one of them who saw Howard himself on any kind of regular basis, but when Ellie quizzed him about Howard's new friend, Patrick knew no more than the others.

'He's younger, he's got his own friends,' Patrick said. 'I'm guessing he's a connection from work, that's all.'

The fortieth birthday party was Andy's idea. Andy had found their names in Howard's Filofax and sent out the invitations. Howard knew nothing about it; the party was to be a surprise.

'Why's he doing it? Howard will hate the idea,' Ellie said to Patrick.

'I don't suppose there'll be many people there. Howard was never really one of us, was he? Doing medicine he mixed with a different crowd.'

The day of the party was one of those freak beautiful afternoons which unexpectedly appear sometimes in October like a jewel in a dull piece of pewter. In the sheltered garden behind the club they luxuriated in the sun. B-b-basking like seals, Andy thought, and most of them more like elephant seals than they'd like.

Ellie thought, Is the stutter for real? Or is he imitating Anthony Blanche from the *Brideshead* television adaptation? She'd expected Andy to be like one of them except younger.

But he's like a different species, a new decorative strain of domestic young man bred for exhibition.

They looked good together, though. Howard so blond and Dr Kildarish, if anyone remembered that 1950s TV show; and Andy like the kid brother, a tall, diffident young man with a rather sweet expression, who hung on Howard's every word as though he were trying to sweep them up behind him.

Ellie smiled at them, approving.

The afternoon dozed on. On a bed of fallen leaves on top of the low wall surrounding the patio, an unknown guest lay asleep.

'He must be a doctor,' Andy said, 'they're used to sleeping on narrow b-b-beds.'

Howard walked round the table dispensing wine. He was smiling. 'Whoever he is, it's nice to have friends you didn't know you had.'

He smiled at Andy and said, 'I'd always thought that if anyone ever gave me a surprise party, I'd never speak to him again, but this has been great.'

He leaned over and kissed Andy on the mouth.

The university friends tried to pretend they had seen nothing extraordinary, if they'd seen it at all. Ellie started to burble about a sweet little robin picking up crumbs from the table. 'Look at those delicate little legs,' she cried, 'it's a miracle they can carry the weight of its body.'

Andy giggled and whispered to Howard, 'The robin's probably wondering the same thing about her.' Andy was relieved that Howard wasn't annoyed with him about the surprise party.

Patrick recovered quickly from the shock of seeing two men share such a kiss. And it was a shock. But he stood up and hugged Howard, and then Andy. 'Oh, God, it's good to see you happy, mate,' he said.

'Sit down, Patrick, you're embarrassing everyone,' Ellie said. She smiled at Howard.

The guests sat on into the evening after they finished eating. A few of Howard's colleagues from the hospital had left earlier to go back on duty. 'Where's Hilary?' Ellie asked. 'I was sure she would be here.'

Sandra said, 'She's in Ireland, doing another of her Getting To Know you trips round Ulster.'

'Oh, that's right; she's been there several times, hasn't she? I saw her on television some months ago on one of those Peace Women protests. I wondered then what she was doing there.'

Sandra thought, Ellie's always did have a way of talking about Hilary as though she isn't quite all there. She said, 'I suppose she's trying to make a living from writing about it.'

Ellie dismissed this. 'No, it's not that. Everything would be different if Hilary had had kids. She's sort of taken up Ireland as a surrogate child, to sublimate her thwarted maternal instincts.'

Howard could see that Ellie was getting argumentative. He said, 'Ellie, your glass is empty, have another drink.'

Better she should drink herself under the table than that she starts laying down the law, he thought. Then he said, 'I like this place. Sitting here looking in at the bar with those walls covered in paintings, and a buxom wench serving all those old roués in there, I feel I'm part of an Impressionist painting.'

Ellie allowed herself to be diverted. 'It's hard to believe that the country's falling apart around us, with two and a half million unemployed and riots all over hell, and a place like this can still exist. It's a real anachronism, don't you think?'

She smiled at Patrick. Recently he had taken to wearing his greying hair in a ponytail; he made his students call him Paddy instead of Patrick; Ellie didn't approve, but just now, thinking of the superiority of her life over Hilary's, she wasn't going to make an issue of it.

'In spite of the sound of fecking bloody aircraft overhead going in and out of Heathrow,' Sandra said, rummaging in her new sack-like Enny handbag for a cigarette.

Howard offered her his silver cigarette case. 'Here,' he said, 'have one of these, best black hash from Afghanistan, they're special. Very calming.'

Sandra tipped up her outsize black satin eye patch to peer at his offering. 'No, thanks,' she said. 'I'm going to the fecking loo.'

They watched her go, tottering on precipitous heels and twitching her ass between the tables in her skin-tight vinyl leopard-print skirt.

'What do you think happened to her?' Andy said.

'She's gone to meet Charlie,' Howard said in an undertone. 'She'll be back soon.'

'But what's she done to her eye?'

Ellie said, 'Perhaps she banged into a door in the dark?'

'It may be a fashion statement, it does give her an air of mystery,' Patrick said.

'That could be true,' Ellie said. 'If she'd had an accident, the NHS would only provide pink plastic patches, not a great big black piratical socket-cover like that thing she's wearing. She must've gone to a theatrical costumiers to find that.'

Ellie folded her hands happily across the baby bump that still remained after the birth of Saffron's little brother Dylan more than two years ago.

Andy said, 'Who's Charlie? She didn't say she was b-b-bringing someone.'

Howard looked embarrassed. 'Keep your voice down,' he said, 'I don't know, of course, but I'd guess she's giving herself a quick chemical pick-me-up in the Ladies.'

Ellie was aghast. She said, 'Howard, that's not funny. How can you say something like that?'

Howard shrugged and said to Ellie, 'Suit yourself, but speaking as a doctor I'd say there are clear signs…'

Sandra returned to the table then. She was smiling and seemed to have forgotten her grouch against aircraft noise. She said, 'Champagne, let's have champagne. On me. I'm soon coming into money and I want to celebrate.'

'Are you getting married again?' Patrick asked her.

Ffion, who had held herself apart from the group, sitting in a shady corner smoking a Bolivar cigar, now cut in, 'I like the black patch, Sandra. Who hit you?'

'Oh, that? My latest ex, the fecking playboy with the filthy-rich father.'

'My God,' Ellie said, 'you must report him. Seriously, Sandra, I don't care how rich he is, you've got to tell the authorities.' She half got up as though she intended to march Sandra straight to the nearest police station.

Sandra made a dismissive gesture with her hand. 'Oh, I have. He's on remand at this moment, charged with whatever technical crime they call it when a man knocks a woman around. Personally, I call it marriage.'

Howard raised an eyebrow. He said, 'But you're not married to this one, are you?'

'No, worse luck. If I were I could divorce him and I'd have rights.'

Ffion asked, 'Do you really have a black eye? Take that thing off and show us. I bet you're wearing that patch because you want people to think he's beating you up.'

Ellie was impatient, she wanted to voice her outrage at what a wealthy male thug gets away with. 'You've got to make sure he gets put in jail.'

Ffion gave Sandra a hard look. 'What are you up to, you cunning cow? You think his Dad will buy you off to keep him out of court, don't you?'

Ellie scowled at Ffion, warning her to lay off. She smiled to encourage Sandra. 'Of course it's true, no one doubts you,' she said. She added to Ffion, 'Just because you're prepared to inflict grievous bodily harm at the drop of a hat, don't you dare pretend that women aren't victims of men's violence.'

Ffion glared at her. 'You call what happened "the drop of a hat"?'

Howard said, 'What are you two talking about?'

Ellie laughed. 'Oh, didn't I tell you about Ffion's little drama? She found her boyfriend in bed with her mother and, mad with jealousy, she hit him with the bedside lamp. A real crime of passion, I don't think.'

Patrick tried to shut her up. 'Ellie…' He put his hand on her arm.

Ellie shook him off. 'You know what she's like,' she said, her voice rising, 'lovers are like buses with Ffion, you miss one, another will be along in a minute. It's not comparable to what's happening to Sandra, who's being systematically abused, for God's sake.'

Sandra said, 'Please Ellie, I don't want the whole street to know. I haven't decided yet what I'm going to do about it.'

Patrick said, 'You mean you don't intend that this will actually come to court?'

Ffion, cool and curious, raised her glass in a mocking toast.

Sandra mumbled, 'Feck it, I'm going to the loo.' She turned and walked away.

In the Ladies, Sandra locked herself into a cubicle and sat on the lowered lid of the lavatory trying to gather her thoughts. She asked herself, Why can't fecking Ffion just accept what I say? Theo thinks he did it. I've convinced him, and he didn't even bother to argue. I just told him he was off his head and he didn't ask questions. He actually said sorry.

Sandra's face softened. She thought, I'm going to miss Theo. We had good times. But he's too young, he's got no staying power.

186

Sandra didn't need to be told that Theo was getting bored with her. She'd seen him watching young girls. She asked herself, What's a girl to do? She's got to live. A woman's got to look after her own interests by any means she can. That's what I'm doing; what's wrong with that?

She heard someone come in and came out of the cubicle. Ffion was there.

Sandra sounded aggressive. 'What do you want?' Then her voice took on a pleading note as she said, 'Ellie and the others believe me; why can't you? Or if they don't they won't admit it. They know women can't afford not to support each other when it comes to men. At least why can't you mind your own fecking business.'

Ffion said, 'Oh, screw that. This is serious.'

'Why? Theo's father can afford it.'

'Not that.' Ffion didn't attempt to hide how much she felt like slapping the stupid little slut. 'I don't give a damn if you take him for every penny you can get. This is about Hilary.'

The focus of Sandra's one visible eye seemed to click into place. The whining note in her voice was gone. 'What about Hilary?'

'Are you in touch with her? Look, I'm serious, can't you warn her off this Irish business?'

Sandra was concentrating now. 'What's happened?'

'She's not in Ireland, she's back here and she's trying to stir up trouble.'

'Oh, come on, Ffion, what trouble? This is Hilary we're talking about?'

'I hear things in my job. I think she's getting in over her head.'

'Over her head? What are you talking about?'

'From what I gather she stumbled on a bad situation and she's trying to blow the lid on something the government and the Army have to cover up. If it came out it would be a political disaster, but I don't think she's any idea of the damage it would cause if the truth got out. Most of all to the people she thinks she's defending.'

'Christ, what's she done?'

'There's a D-notice being issued which will stop the newspapers investigating, but Hilary is making a nuisance of herself, she doesn't understand what she's dealing with; and she's been noticed.'

'Hilary? What could she possibly know which could ruffle anybody's feathers?'

Ffion shook her head. 'I don't know. I overheard something, that's all. The government's running shit-scared anyway, with all these inner city riots going on. There have already been calls in Cabinet for the Army to go into Liverpool…'

'You're joking?'

'That's not going to happen, but there's talk of arming the police.'

'Fecking shit!'

'We'd better get back.'

As Ffion followed her across the bar back to the party, Sandra turned and said over her shoulder, 'You'd better not be having me on.'

She thought, but couldn't be sure, that she heard Ffion say, 'If anyone knew what I've just told you, I'm dead meat. Even a hint of a leak and I'll lose my job. We're going to have to trust each other on this.'

As they came back to the table, Andy was telling a story. He had everyone's attention and he was enjoying himself.

'And then,' he said, his voice dropping to melodrama, 'I went into the b-b-bar and there was this awful smell. I asked the b-b-bartender what it was and quick as a flash he said, "Failure".'

There was a brief pause before the others laughed.

'It amused me, anyway,' Andy said.

21

Howard telephoned Ffion to thank her for coming to his party. It was a trumped up excuse to call her, and he could tell from her tone that she thought so too.

'Why are you ringing me? To make me feel bad because if I weren't a rude cow, and very busy, I would've rung you to thank you for a lovely time?' Then she said, 'What's on your mind, Howard? Out with it.'

'I want to apologize for what Ellie said.'

She didn't ask what he was talking about. So she is upset, Howard thought. And I don't blame her. Finding her lover in bed with her mother is something most people would prefer to keep to themselves, however laid back Ffion pretended to be about it. He thought, I wonder how Ellie knew about it?

Ffion said, 'Why should you apologize? She's the one who said it, not you.'

'I want you to know I'm sorry it happened; it must've been horrible for you. Ellie was awfully insensitive. Particularly after going through what she did over Matt, you'd think she'd be more careful.'

'Ellie's an emotional bulldozer, that's what made her want to be a social worker. She thinks all unhappiness is either economic or criminal, and can be solved by following her advice.'

Oh, God, Howard thought, she has been brooding about it. She must blame me for not defending her and shutting Ellie up.

Assuming that Ffion knew what he was thinking, he said, 'If I'd challenged her at the party there'd have been a full-blown row. It seemed best to drop it. Nobody takes any notice of anything Ellie says anyway. And she was drunk.'

'Shut up, Howard. Methinks thou dost protest too much; if you go on any more about it, I'll suspect you of deliberately trying to stir things up.'

'That went well,' Andy said when Howard put the phone down. 'Why didn't you t-t-tell her what else Ellie said?'

'What?'

'When Ffion was in the loo with Sandra. Didn't you hear Ellie saying that she thought B-B-Beverly must've seduced Ffion's lover deliberately to get back at the b-b-bitch for being the daughter from Hell? She said if she had a d-d-daughter like Ffion, she'd do exactly the same thing.'

Howard burst out laughing at the look on Andy's face as he tried to imagine Ellie as any kind of a femme fatale.

'Did she really say that?'

'Oh yes. Patrick was trying to shut her up and Ellie let fly.'

'What else did she say?'

'That Ffion is evil and manipulating and would b-b-betray her own child, if she had one, to get ahead in her career. She said that b-b-basically Ffion isn't all that bright and she's only got into a position of power because men want to screw her. And then she said Ffion's terrified of getting old because she's got no inner resources and once her looks have gone – which won't be long now, Ellie said, – then people will see she's no g-g-good at her job and that'll be the end of her.'

'She really said all that? Wow! Quite a speech she made. I'm glad you didn't tell me that before I rang, I'd never have dared say a word.'

Howard added, after a moment, 'I wonder why Ellie hates Ffion so much?'

Andy shrugged. 'Oh, who cares about those silly bitches, Howie? I want to go shopping.'

Ffion put down the receiver on Howard and frowned. His call had set her thinking. What he said, and also the way he said it, in that *faux*-solicitous way he had, suddenly made her realize that Ellie had made a public mockery of her deepest feelings.

And I didn't even notice it at the time, she said to herself; but Ellie obviously did a good job of humiliating me.

It still hurt Ffion to think of Vaclav. She'd never felt so deeply about anything or anyone as she did about Vaclav. It wasn't just sex. I've had plenty of good sex, but with Vaclav the way he made me feel loved was something else. When I was with him I'd feel I'd willingly have given up everything I care about to prolong that moment by a few minutes.

That was real love, Ffion thought; and Ellie made a public joke of it. I trusted Ellie with my secret and she betrayed me.

Ffion told herself, It was my fault, telling her. But the way I felt that day, finding Vaclav like that, it just swamped me. I couldn't contain it, I had to tell someone. And there was Ellie.

The phone rang.

She answered it expecting to hear Howard, apologizing for his apology which might seem to have made too much of Ellie's remarks. Silly man, shall I laugh or tell him where to go?

It wasn't Howard; it was her secretary telling her that the Ministry driver was on his way to pick her up. There was a busy day ahead.

Before going out Ffion studied herself in the bedroom mirror. She put her hand up to her face and touched the taut skin over the cheekbones. Were those fine lines about to become full-blown wrinkles? My God, she thought, we're all getting old. We're certainly not young any more. That party was Howard's fortieth. The rest of us are only a few years behind. Matt would be already middle-aged by now.

Compared to the others, she thought, I'm not that bad. I still weigh the same as I did at twenty-one. Ellie must be three stone heavier than she was at Trinity; I heard her tell Sandra at Howard's party that her spare tyres were the honourable trophies of a woman who lived a fruitful, fulfilling family life. Yuck!

Good God, the woman got a First. She had a good brain and she's just let it go to waste. She thinks I'm selfish and antisocial to want to get somewhere in the world. And Ellie's not alone. Imagine aspiring to the lowest common denominator!

All the same, Ffion was shocked to discover Ellie's ill-will towards her. She was hurt. I tried to help her after Matt was killed, she told herself. Doesn't she remember how I trekked out to that suburban dump and brought her back to live with me in Chelsea; and then put up with her all that time before I fixed her up with Patrick!

I really was her best friend, and she repays what I did for her by going out of her way to make me a public laughing stock. Well, to Hell with her.

The doorbell rang, the driver had arrived. Ffion grabbed her handbag and ran down the stairs. OK, Ellie Bassett, she said to herself, I'm going to make you sorry.

She rang Patrick at City University that evening. 'I really want to talk to you,' she said. 'To ask your advice, really.'

'Well, of course, if you think I can help. It's only…'

He's afraid of what Ellie would say if she knew, Ffion thought, and smiled to herself.

'I'd be most terrifically grateful. But I know it's difficult for you, students being the dirty-minded little beasts they are. Do you remember that time at Trinity when that handsome law lecturer … oh, I forget his name, but he was married with small kids. He was in Searsons with a young woman and someone told his wife and she'd almost divorced him before she realized it was her sister he was with…?'

Patrick laughed. 'Yes, now you mention it, I do remember something. He was arranging for the sister to look after the kids while he took the wife on an anniversary cruise. It was a major scandal at the time. He could have lost his job.'

'I wouldn't want for you to risk the ire of Ellie. I don't think we should risk meeting anywhere you might be recognized.'

'You're right. Have you any ideas?' He sounded relieved, she thought.

'I live in Cloudesley Road now. I couldn't stay on in Wandsworth after Vaclav and I split...'

'I was sorry to hear about that. Bad business.'

Ffion thought, If he heard about it from Ellie, he's probably thinking Vaclav had a lucky escape. Best not say anything, though, I don't want to remind him of her.

She said, 'Anyway, my flat's less than a mile from Northampton Square. Do you still cycle to work? You could nip up to see me for half an hour.'

'I'll try,' he said. 'What number Cloudesley Road?'

He came at about seven, wheeling his bike into her hall and shutting the front door with his foot before taking off his helmet.

Once in the sitting-room, she offered him a drink. He said he'd better not, not cycling in London on 'an empty tummy'. But then he said perhaps a little one... God Almighty, she thought.

She offered him sandwiches she'd prepared for her own supper after he'd gone.

'Well,' he said, 'perhaps we could eat together. Ellie's out at a Women's Group meeting tonight.'

'Good, then we can share a bottle of wine. When you cycle home, it won't be on an empty...ah...tummy.'

He seemed to have forgotten why he'd come, but finally he asked, 'What did you want to ask me? You know I'll help you if I can.'

'Yes, it's probably nothing much, it's about Ellie,' she said. 'Paddy, why does Ellie hate me so much? What does she think I've done to her?'

He looked concerned. 'Why would you think such a thing? You've done so much for her, she's so grateful to you.'

'It's what she said at Howard's party. About me and Vaclav…'

'I'm sure she doesn't hate you. She was drunk, that's all. And she does get het up about these women's rights issues. Ellie tends to see most women as victims of something, mostly men. She can relate to them then.'

'My mother ran off with my fiancé. Doesn't that make me a victim?

'No, I think she thinks you're laughing at her. She's a bit scared of you…you do rather give the impression that you don't need anyone's help.'

Ffion looked at him piteously. 'But I do. I miss Vaclav terribly.'

Her eyes filled with tears.

'Don't cry,' he said, and gave her his handkerchief.

She dabbed her eyes and tried to smile. 'Thank you for coming, Paddy. I feel so much better now. I should have known Ellie wouldn't have meant to hurt me by what she said.'

She stood up as though accepting it was time for him to go. 'I wonder if she knows how lucky she is to have a man like you. You're so understanding.'

'Any time,' he said, following her into the narrow hall.

'Will you give me a quick hug? For old time's sake.'

'Sure I will,' he said, taking her in his arms.

'Oh, God,' she whispered, 'I've missed having a man hold me.' She pressed against him.

'Careful,' he said, 'Ellie and I haven't made love for months. It feels like years. I don't want to get carried away…'

'Don't you?' She kissed him.

'Oh my God,' he said, 'At Trinity I used to fantasize about doing this to you…'

'Like this?' she said.

Is that all there is to it? she asked herself. He's hooked. But what's the point? Sure, it may make Ellie feel bad when she finds out, but Patrick's so bloody boring, is it worth it? And she thought, Oh, Yuck! Yuck to the whole thing.

22

On a raw cold Sunday afternoon in April Hilary, dressed in an unflattering grey polyester track suit and an old duffle coat, came out of Archway tube station and started to walk towards the entrance to Highgate Cemetery in Swain's Lane.

Hilary knew she looked as though she was dressed for an Arctic expedition, but she'd rather be comfortable than fashionable. If Sandra's embarrassed to be seen with me, she thought, that's just too damn bad.

Sandra was waiting for her at the gate to the Cemetery. She wore a fur hat and dark glasses, the lower part of her face muffled in a trailing woollen scarf.

Hilary said, 'My God, you look like an undercover agent. Are you avoiding a private investigator or something?'

Sandra took her arm and hurried her away from the entrance down one of the walks among the graves. 'I've got to talk to you.'

'Why here, for God's sake?'

'We can talk here without being overheard.'

'Couldn't you come to my flat?'

'No, that's the last place.'

'Sandra, you own it. You know no one would overhear us there.'

'I can't be seen there.'

Really, Hilary thought, Sandra's paranoia's getting to be more than a joke.

She said, 'Is something wrong?'

Funny, she thought, my first reaction is always to think something's wrong. Something about being a parson's daughter, perhaps. A self-fulfilling expectation. She probably wants to tell me she's getting married again, this time to a Mafioso. She asked, 'When's the wedding?'

But Sandra didn't laugh.

'Shut up and listen.'

They walked for some time. The winter afternoon faded and then went dark. Hilary started off dismissing what Sandra was saying as absurd.

'You're talking about Britain in the late 20th century,' she kept saying. 'This is a civilized country, with civilized people.'

'It's a *post*-civilised country,' Sandra said. 'Haven't you heard about what happened to the fecking Roman Empire when their society began to unravel?'

When Sandra had finished saying what she had come to say, she said, 'Wait here for five minutes and then go back to the main gate. That'll give me time to get away without us being seen together.

She's totally paranoid, Hilary told herself. But then she thought, But suppose she isn't?

She wasn't sure what to do. The street lamps shining through the Spring leaves on the trees cast moving shadows on the pavement. The street was very quiet; the odd car passed, moving slowly. Don't these people have pets, she asked herself, no one's even walking a dog.

Am I being followed? she thought; is someone watching me?

At the entrance to the Tube station, she picked up a taxi. She felt safer then. And ridiculous. Sandra always has been a drama queen, she thinks it makes her interesting. The psychologists probably have a name for it; the Cassandra Syndrome or something.

She went home to ring her father. I must talk to the Rev Dad, Hilary kept telling herself, he'll make sense of this for me. Sandra herself had said she was probably safe in London, because as Sandra's friend, Sandra's Loyalist connections would give her some protection.

But Sandra had been very clear, 'Return to Ulster and you'll disappear. You're on your own if you do.'

Hilary paid off the taxi in Hemingford Road. As she walked down the familiar street, she became calmer. Through lighted windows in the imposing gentrified houses she could see children playing, or sitting round watching television. In one elegant living-room, a small boy was even sitting at a piano; she could hear the music, Mozart distorted by the ebb and flow of the wind.

It's ridiculous, she thought. People like these...

The phone was ringing as she let herself into the flat.

Her mother on the line sounded distressed. 'I've been trying to get hold of you,' she said. 'Please come home. There's very bad news. Your father is dead.'

The Rev Dad collapsed and died as he recited the Nunc dimittis at the close of Sunday Evening Service.

It was a lovely way for him to go: everybody said so. Even Mum. He was surrounded by his most loyal parishioners; he'd been looking forward to going home to his favourite cold cuts for supper, and then watching something undemanding on television.

And as far as anybody could tell he didn't suffer at all. One moment he was there at the altar in his beloved church, bathed in the gold light of a resplendent Spring sunset streaming through the stained glass window with its centrepiece of kindly St Peter welcoming the souls of the worthy at the Gates of Heaven, and the next he was lying dead and he exhaled those lovely words from the Song of Simeon as his last breath.

Sue came to the funeral. Without Duncan. They'd talked it over together and decided he should keep the children at home, that's what Sue said.

'We haven't quite decided how to deal with this one,' Hilary overheard Sue tell her mother. 'I mean, how do you explain death to children that age without scaring them and possibly damaging them for life?'

Now for the first time Hilary thought she was going to cry. It was funny how weeping crept up on you at a time like this. She hadn't shed a single tear at the funeral service, nor when she took the phone call from her mother telling her of the Rev Dad's death. She'd been so desperate to talk to him after what Sandra had said, but now that he was dead she thought, I suppose I'll miss him, but how? We hardly saw each other, our lives didn't connect any more. What mattered was knowing he was there.

But there'd be no more memories of good times she shared with him. And all the past memories that they'd treasured together, they'd gone too. Without him there to participate in them, they'd lost their two dimensional reality and become as flat as old photographs.

And yet, she told herself, of course I loved my Dad. But what does that mean? I knew he was on my side; he cared for me and hoped I would be happy and tried to protect me. But those were his duties as a father; they weren't specific to me, Hilary. Only to his daughters; me and Sue, he loved us the same way.

But I was special to him, she told herself, he felt different about me than he did about Sue.

Hilary thought she knew why that was. He was frightened for her. He knew she would not find it easy to fulfil herself as wife and mother because she did not have the looks or the social skills to attract love to her. He didn't have to worry about Sue that way; she'd acquired what was necessary for happy family life; at least he thought she had. As a family they all hid anything bad in their lives from each other. Think happy, be happy; it was as simple as that.

I didn't know him as a man, only as the Rev Dad, so how could I love him? Hilary thought. I know he voted Liberal; he didn't like broccoli or the smell of onions or horror movies, but as to what moved him to passion or hate or even anger, I don't know.

With shame and sorrow she told herself, I loved him because he loved me, that's what it amounts to.

She heard Sue ask, 'How are you going to cope, Mum? Have you thought about that?'

Her mother said, 'Being married to a vicar all those years amounts to a degree course in dealing with people dying. I suppose it's a relief this is the last time I'll have to do it.'

Susan said, 'Don't tempt Fate, darling, you may marry again. There's probably a C of E dating agency fixing up elderly widowers with highly qualified church ladies like you.'

Hilary refused to pretend to be amused.

'It isn't fair,' she said. 'You've dedicated your life to the job just as much as the Rev did, but now you're out on your ear. And presumably you'll lose the roof over your head, too. They'll want this house for the new vicar.'

'It's far too big, anyway,' Mum said. 'I wouldn't want to go on living here alone. But I'll miss the garden-'

Her lip trembled and her eyes filled with tears.

I've never seen Mum cry, Hilary thought. She was shocked, actually frightened at the sight of an older woman's tears. And, shamingly, she was ashamed at her mother's show of weakness.

Susan said quickly, 'Don't worry, Mum, we'll sort something out between us. There's no point deciding anything now. You must be exhausted.'

You could get an allotment, Hilary thought. And then, feeling guilty, she asked herself, why am I being like this to Mum, so harsh and almost … almost dismissive?

They heard the telephone ringing from the house.

Sue took it as a personal affront. 'Who'd be ringing you at this hour? And on a day like today! Don't answer it.'

Hilary went to answer it. She heard her mother telling her, 'Tell whoever it is to ring back tomorrow. It's much too late to be telephoning respectable people now.'

'Howard?' Hilary pressed the phone to her ear, trying to hear.

Howard's voice sounded thin, as though he were straining to speak at all. 'Hilary, it's Howard. I'm sorry to disturb you but... we are friends, aren't we?'

'You're my best friend, or course you are. What's wrong, Howard?

'I really need to talk to you. There's something ... I can't say any of this on the telephone.'

'I'll be back in London tomorrow.'

'Somewhere in the open, with lots of people.'

Oh, God, first Sandra, now Howard. What's got into everyone? Was Howard, too, going to warn her that she was in imminent danger?

She said, 'What about the south end of Waterloo Bridge. My train comes in to Waterloo. Then we can walk along the river if you want to talk.'

The next morning Susan drove her to Guildford to catch the train. Her mother and Sue were both resentful that Hilary was leaving.

Mum had perfected the stricken look of one who feels she has a right to expect better treatment.

'But darling,' she said, 'I thought you'd want to be at my side now. Surely it's not so important that you go back to London. I was hoping you might give up living in that filthy city and move nearer me. You could get yourself a little job in Guildford or Woking and-'

Hilary was firm. 'I like living in London, and the work I do is important...'

201

'Your writing? But that's only a hobby, surely. You could do it from here.'

'You and the Rev Dad didn't make the sacrifices you did to send me to university for me to waste it on a little job in Guildford.'

In the car on the way to the station, Susan didn't say much; but Hilary could feel her sister's exasperation.

Sue burst out with it as they approached the station.

'I must say I think you're being very selfish leaving Mum alone like this.'

'She's not alone. You're there.'

'For goodness sake, Hilary, you know I've got to get back to Duncan and the kids. They need me and Mum needs you.'

'I'm leaving because someone needs me much more than Mum does right now.'

'You're lying. You're just trying to get out of your obligations.'

This was really too much, Hilary thought.

Sue stopped the car outside the station.

Hilary opened the door preparing to get out. She said, 'We're not living in the old days when unmarried women stayed at home to look after their parents. Mum's perfectly capable of looking after herself. I've worked hard for what I've got and I'm not going to give it up to turn Mum into some kind of surrogate child.'

God, she thought, I sound like Ffion Finlay. What's the matter with me?

She said more quietly to Sue, 'I like my life; I've chosen it. I can't give it up now.'

'But what about me?'

'What about you?'

'I can't look after her.'

'Sue, nobody's asking you to. She's the grown-up, she'll decide for herself. She's not too old, she's got a life ahead of her. Let her get on with it. She's very far from helpless.'

She got out of the car and turned to thank her sister for the lift, but Susan, stony-faced, drove off before she could even slam the door shut.

In the train, Hilary worried about Howard. He'd sounded so helpless on the phone, so lonely. What sort of help was he looking for from her? Was he unhappily in love, or was it something to do with the hospital? Whatever it was, she would be there for him. Hadn't he done as much for her?

He was waiting for her on the bridge. It was a drizzly, cold, depressing day, the cloud seeming clamped to the sulky river. The way he was leaning on the balustrade and staring into the water as it sucked at the base of the arches reminded her of old black and white films where the mere sight of a bridge meant someone was going to jump off it. She began to run towards him.

'Howard,' she called, 'here I am.'

He turned and saw her. Smiling, he said, 'Great to see you.'

She thought, It's OK, I panicked, that's all. I was scared. I don't know how I could bear a world with no Howard in it.

They walked down the steps by the National Theatre on to the Embankment.

She smiled up at him and it felt as though her heart had turned to ice inside her. He was weeping.

She said, and her voice trembled, 'Is it as bad as that? It's all right, Howard, I'm going to help you. Whatever it is, we'll find a way through it.'

She led him to a seat and they sat beside the river, their backs turned to the Theatre and the people around it.

'Now,' she said.

He shook his head. 'I can't, not here.' He smiled weakly and added, 'It's all this concrete made to look like wood, it's so soulless.'

She stood up and, taking his hand, pulled him to his feet. 'Come on,' she said, 'let's take the tube to Hampstead and walk on the Heath. We can pick up something for a picnic on the way.'

'Darling Hilary,' he said, 'we'll still be in the same country. It's not the weather for a picnic.'

'The weather is partly a state of mind, I'm quite sure the sun will be shining when we get to Hampstead, and we can look down at the cloud hiding the city.'

So they found themselves walking in the dripping woods behind the old *Spaniards Inn*, the clean smell of wet leaves underfoot.

He stopped and leaned against the trunk of a tree, slightly breathless.

Hilary thought, He doesn't look well.

Howard said, 'I didn't know anyone I could talk to except you. I'm sorry if I interrupted your holiday.'

She didn't want to tell him it wasn't a holiday. The Rev's death seemed to belong to another world entirely. Looking at Howard's face, she was afraid.

'Tell me now,' she said.

He took a deep breath. Then he said, in a curious flat voice, 'They've done tests. I got the diagnosis yesterday. I've got AIDS.'

Hilary grabbed him and they clung together.

At last he pulled gently away and cupped his hands round her face. They were both weeping.

Howard tried to smile at her. She heard him whisper, 'It's all right, we can cry all over each other and you'll be quite safe. Tears are one of the bodily fluids that can't transmit the bloody HIV virus.'

Somehow, they both managed to laugh.

23

Ellie walked slowly home along Dalston Lane. She found no pleasure in the walk; she felt crushed by the pressure of houses and traffic. At least in Shoreditch there'd been the canal where she could wander and let her thoughts roam free.

She was dragging her feet because she didn't want to get home.

Patrick was the one who'd wanted to move. They needed somewhere bigger, he said, the children were growing up, they needed a proper family home. And it made economic sense. Shoreditch was fast becoming a fashionable area, they could get a good price for the house, move somewhere with more space which hadn't been gentrified, and still have money over for renovation. It'll be fun, he said, a real family project.

She hated the house they bought, a grim-faced Victorian terrace property in a street full of bedsits where, Ellie was convinced, innumerable alcoholic squatters and drug addicts over the years had died without anyone noticing. She also hated Hackney. Her social worker's soul rebelled against the hopelessness around her.

This place wasn't meant for people like her. She was intimidated by the lurking violence on the streets, an undercurrent of threat from the gangs of youths who fought at night in the alleys. All sense of shared humanity seemed to have been banished from the streets; her own need to care for others had become a handicap making her as vulnerable as physical disability. She thought, I don't have any control over what happens to me here.

Is this what feminism was all about? It's not what I went on marches for, or sat for hours on cold pavements getting trampled on by hostile cops, singing *We Shall Overcome Some Day*. We hoped to change our lives for the better, but what have we done with equality?

I wanted respect, I suppose, respect and recognition as a woman. What feminism's done for me is make me lose confidence in womanhood. And, she thought, confidence in society itself.

Ellie remembered a conversation with her mother she'd had years ago. It stuck in her mind because it was the first time she'd they'd ever talked that way to Mum, seriously as woman to woman. She was home in Wembley Park for the Easter vacation. They were sitting on the patio to get away from the clamour of the children in the house.

Mum said, 'Are you one of these Women's Libbers, Ellie?'

Ellie was embarrassed that her mother was so out of touch. 'Oh, Mum, we're feminists now. A serious political force to be reckoned with. We've had it with being treated as second-class citizens. You must agree with that.'

'Be careful what you wish for, it might come true.'

Ellie hadn't said so, but she knew that she did not want her life to be like her mother's. 'It's a question of terms, isn't it?' she said. 'I want the things most women have always wanted, like a husband and family, but not on the same terms as you. I want a life of my own as well, my own identity.'

Rather to Ellie's surprise, her mother said, 'Of course you do. Do you think I didn't? But there are sacrifices to be made. I opted for security and, I suppose, the protection of conforming to society's expectations for a woman's role.'

'But I have the strength of feminism behind me. That gives us all the strength to take what we want.'

And Mum smiled, Ellie remembered. She smiled a sort of proud but pitying smile and said, 'Do you feel safe trusting other women that far? I hope you're right.'

Ellie, dragging her heels now in Dalston Road, recalled clearly how she had dismissed her mother's fears. She's too old to learn; she has nothing useful to say to us, she thought. So why do I feel sad thinking of that conversation?

She thought, Women like Ffion may have wanted to reject womanhood, but in doing so they've lost touch with other women. How can they face being isolated like that? No, she told herself, that's not the question. Why can't I face it; why am I afraid of being like that? Does having children make it impossible for a woman to be a true feminist?

What's happened to the hope and faith in society we once had? Ellie asked herself. Feminism was part of that. But as post-feminists we've become afraid of other people. Is that what Mum foresaw?

Ellie shook her head; she didn't want to accept that. She thought, And what about men? Patrick, for instance? Could the long hair and the stubble and the pseudo ethnic clothes and his annoying tendency to raise a hand in a kind of blessing and intone to a gang of thugs 'Love and Peace, Brothers' be his way of dealing with the same fear of the streets?

His students think he's insane; that or temporarily off his head with drugs. Ellie couldn't help smiling at the idea. She thought, Oh, my poor Patrick, perhaps I should have tried to understand. But then she told herself, It's his fault. He should've listened to me in the first place

When Ellie got home, the children were out. Dylan was probably with his mates. Ellie hardly saw him these days. Saffron wouldn't be back for another hour or so. At some point, Ellie thought, I've got to nag her to do some studying. But not tonight. Tonight I'll just be grateful for one peaceful evening.

Ellie hoped that by the time Saffron came home Patrick would be back from college. She felt guilty about it, but she hated being alone with Saffron. They had nothing to say to each other. Ellie would try to ask non-provoking questions about how the girl's day had gone, what she'd had had for lunch – the usual mother things – but Saffron would like as not ignore her. The best Ellie could get out of her was a grumpy 'Oh, Mum, you don't understand'.

Why are things so difficult between us? Ellie wondered. Saffron's so like me at her age, how can I not understand her. She looks like me – same mousy hair and heavy eyebrows, same heavy build. I could tell her how to learn to live with it, if she let me. The other kids used to try to make fun of me. They called me Ellie-Belly.

Ellie remembered how she used to beat them up. It helped to come from a big family. Does Saffron get bullied? She thought, she'd never tell me if she did.

At least Saffron can talk to Patrick, Ellie said to herself. She chats easily to him, telling him about her life and doings as she can never talk to me. Patrick took Saffron's closeness to him very much for granted. When Ellie said something about it to him, he laughed and said surely she wasn't telling him she was jealous of her own daughter.

It was true, or sort-of true. Ellie found herself thinking that she would find it easier to share her husband with another woman than with her own daughter. I don't feel guilty about that, Ellie thought, I blame Saffron for it.

A car backfired. Ellie almost threw herself to the ground. Not so ridiculous, she thought, a few streets away a young black girl had been killed the other day, caught in the crossfire between gangs.

Ellie looked around, embarrassed that someone might have seen her reaction. Not cool, not cool at all. Saffron would've been furious with her if she'd been there.

She looked at her watch. She must hurry. Tonight was the twenty-fifth anniversary of leaving Trinity. Old friends were coming round for supper and a nostalgia-fest.

Oh, God, she thought, I wish they weren't coming. Twenty-five years! There's nothing much to celebrate.

Will any of them remember? she asked herself. Twenty-five years since Matt was killed. A car crash – what a stupid way to die and ruin my life.

Why did you leave me, Matt? she thought. I've never stopped needing you.

Patrick hadn't said anything that morning, only that he'd try to be home early for the party. He'd had to work a lot of late nights lately. It crossed her mind that maybe he wasn't quite up to the job. Ellie did feel guilty, thinking that. Patrick had always trailed rather in Matt's wake. She wondered if he still missed Matt. It was funny, with Matt meaning so much in different ways to both of them, that they never mentioned him between them.

Even after the guests arrived, she wasn't enjoying the evening. She'd made lasagne for old times' sake. It was her speciality, in those days; she used to make it in the flat in Raglan Road on a Friday and take it down to the beach cottage to feed whatever friends turned up over the weekend.

Tonight the old crowd was there; her room-mates, several of Patrick's rugby friends, and several of his colleagues at City University. Ffion phoned that she might be late, and Howard hadn't replied to the invitation. Patrick was going to try to contact him.

Patrick had made a tape of some of the old songs. *How Sweet it is to be Loved by You.* He used to love Marvin Gaye's voice. Another of his favourites followed – Marianne Faithfull singing *As Tears Go By.*

Oh, Ellie thought, I wish I could get back the way that music made me feel then, as if I were on the brink of something about to explode. Oh, yes, I'd forgotten, that's The Animals. How I loved Eric Burdon.

Don't Let Me Be Misunderstood ended and Hilary began to tap her foot to *You Were Made For Me*. She laughed and said, 'I adored Freddie, I really did. I'd have married him if he asked me.'

Sandra said, 'You can't be serious.'

They were silent as the singer changed. It was Barry Maguire singing *Eve of Destruction*.

'My God, I'd forgotten that,' Ellie said.

'How was it that we scarcely noticed the Vietnam War while we were at TCD?'

'Most students were scarcely aware of what was going on in our own fecking backyard,' Sandra said.

Ellie was silently mouthing the words of the refrain: *But you tell me over and over again my friend, Ah you don't believe we're on the eve of destruction...'*

'Someone was singing that on the beach that last night...' Hilary said.

Ellie turned away, thinking, If we'd only known, that song was prophetic but we didn't listen.

'I'll get another bottle of wine,' she said, mumbling, and moved away from the other two.

Sandra and Hilary watched her walk away. Sandra said, 'Do you think she knows?'

'She has to. Except she's probably in denial.'

'The wife's often the last to fecking know. That's what they say.'

'Who's they?'

'Well, you know—'

'Do I? I'm not sure I do.'

'Maybe you should tell her.'

'Me? Not me. I'm not going to tell her. She'll hate me.'

'She'll hate us when she finds out we knew and didn't fecking well tell her.'

'We could be wrong.'

'Of course we're not wrong.'

'I think she must know. She rules him with a rod of iron.'

Hilary pondered the oddly stilted vocabulary associated with the clichés surrounding adultery. The words seemed to distance themselves from real life.

Nor could she stir up strong feelings over this alleged affair between Ellie's husband and Ffion.

But Sandra was eager to enjoy the tribulations of others. She said, 'Patrick's been building up for some kind of crisis for months. What else was that business about, calling himself Paddy and wearing leather jackets and trainers? He's going through some sort of male menopause, that's all.'

She sounds like she's licking her lips, Hilary thought.

Sandra had been drinking heavily. She said to Hilary, 'Well, you've made a right balls-up of the last twenty years.' She paused and added, 'So have I. What a joke, the way we were and what we hoped for and how we've fecking ended up.'

'Not ended,' Hilary said, 'we're not finished yet.'

'Don't say you still hope to get pregnant? You're cutting it fecking fine, if so.'

Sandra pulled up a visible bra strap and adjusted the aim of her aggressive bosom. She said, 'Wouldn't one of our gentleman friends rise to the occasion and do the necessary? That'd be better than a test tube, wouldn't it?'

Her voice was suddenly very loud in the room.

Hilary blushed and was speechless. There was an awkward silence.

Sandra, embarrassed by the effect of what had been a light-hearted suggestion, made matters worse.

'Howard would do it, I'm sure he would,' she said. 'He's always liked you and he's quite good-looking, why don't you try him?' Then she asked the room at large, 'Where is Howard, by the way?'

Ellie came back into the room as Sandra said this. Ellie looked at Patrick. 'Didn't you get hold of him?' she asked.

Patrick suddenly seemed very tense. 'I did,' he said, 'but he said he couldn't come.'

'Why on earth?'

Patrick said, he almost hissed, 'It's no good, Ellie. Howard's got AIDS. That's why he didn't think he should come.'

There was a long silence. Then someone said, 'How awful. Did he get it from one of his patients?'

Patrick said, 'I don't know how he got it.'

Then Sandra said, 'But he can't. He can't have it. He played rugby. He can't be gay.'

The way she said 'gay' made Patrick say in protest, 'Homosexuality isn't a disease, Sandra. And straight guys get AIDs too.'

'Oh, God, how awful,' Ellie said. 'My poor Howard, of course he should have come. He needn't have gone too close to the children. Didn't you tell him?'

'I didn't know what to say,' Patrick said.

Sandra said to Hilary, 'Well, I suppose that rules him out as a potential sperm donor, Hilly?'

Hilary looked appalled. 'I can't believe you said that,' she said.

They couldn't pretend to be celebrating after that. One by one they made a move to leave.

'Don't go,' Ellie said, 'Patrick asked Ffion to come. She'll be here soon.'

'Fecking Ffion?' Sandra said. 'Why did you ask her?'

'She's one of us,' Ellie said.

'Don't you know your husband's screwing her fecking arse off?'

Everyone fell silent.

'Of course I do,' Ellie said.

Before Sandra could say any more, Hilary took her arm and tried to pull her away. 'It's time we went, Sandra. What's happened to Howard is too awful.'

Hilary steered Sandra across the open-plan basement towards the stairs to the hallway where they'd left their coats. She turned back to Ellie, who hadn't moved.

'Thanks for the party,' she said. 'Say goodbye to Patrick, will you?'

Left alone, Ellie sat down at the table. Patrick had disappeared. He's probably gone to his den to try to contact Howard, Ellie told herself. Or maybe he's ringing Ffion to tell her not to come.

She thought, what made me say that to Sandra? If Patrick is screwing the arse off Ffion, it's the first I knew of it. But the way that Ulster bitch said it, wanting to score over me, I couldn't give her the satisfaction.

And after all, she said to herself, I'm not surprised he's having an affair. We haven't made love for ages, it was always a bit of a bore between us. He has to be getting sex from someone. I suppose I thought that's what the hippy revival nonsense was all about, he was making a fool of himself over some of the female students. Our sex life's never been much to write home about, but at least he gave me my children. That's the strong bond between us. It didn't seem that important if he was having it off with other women.

She asked herself, So what's making me so pissed off? To be honest, if it was Sandra Patrick was having an affair with, I wouldn't mind. At least I could despise him that that's the best he could get. Or Hilary, I'd be glad if it was her; he'd be doing her a favour, I'd almost like him for it. I wouldn't begrudge Hilly that, I really wouldn't

But, she thought, it being Ffion really pisses me off. What can she get out of him that I couldn't that she'd want to make love to him? How could my boring old Patrick get it on with someone like Ffion. She wouldn't look twice at him.

Unless she did it to spite me, Ellie told herself, she's getting back at me for something. God, what a bitch.

There was a sudden commotion in the hall. Ellie looked up to see Ffion coming down the stairs into the basement.

'Where's the party?' she said.

'It broke up early. We found out that Howard's got AIDS. Nobody felt much like carrying on after that.'

Ffion found an opened bottle of wine and a glass and poured herself a drink. She lit a cigarette and inhaled deeply, watching Ellie curiously.

'I know,' she said. 'It's terrible, isn't it?'

Ellie's voice was flat as she said, 'And then Sandra blurted out that you are having an affair with my husband.'

'Did she really?'

Ffion blew a series of those damned smoke rings of hers.

'Is it true?'

'Hardly an affair. We slept together.'

'Why?'

'You know, that's the whole difference between you and me, Ellie. You want to know why; I prefer to ask why not.'

'You sound like an American. Why don't you bloody well go and live there?'

Ffion grinned. 'I tried, they won't let me in. Just before we went up to Trinity, I was cautioned by the cops for possessing dope. That's it, as far as getting a US visa goes. You won't get rid of me that easy.'

Patrick suddenly appeared on the stairs. 'I thought I heard voices,' he said. 'Hallo, Ffion, I'm afraid you're too late, the party broke up.'

'Because Sandra told everybody that you two are having an affair,' Ellie said. Her voice was shrill now.

Patrick looked at Ffion. She shrugged.

Patrick started to bluster. 'Please, Ellie, listen, it isn't how it sounds. I didn't mean it to happen…'

Ellie ignored him and turned to confront Ffion. 'We want an explanation,' she said. 'We want to know why you did this to us?'

Ffion looked slowly from Ellie to Patrick. Then she said, 'You've a very bad habit, Ellie, of assuming you're speaking for Patrick. Try asking him how he feels, and don't say I didn't warn you. Go on, ask him.'

Patrick braced himself for the question, but it was as though Ellie had lost interest. She said to Ffion, 'I want to know. Did you ever love him?'

Ffion said, 'No, of course I didn't.'

'And he didn't love you, so why did you do something so cruel...?'

Patrick shook his head. 'I do love her,' he said. 'I can't get her out of my mind, I don't want to live without her. Ellie, I'm so sorry, but in a way I'm glad it's out in the open. Now there's nothing to stop me leaving you and the children to be with her.'

He stopped as if expecting Ellie to protest, then went on, 'I didn't mean this to happen but I can't fight against it any more. I'm so sorry, Ellie...'

Ffion said, sounding annoyed, 'Is this some sort of joke?'

Ellie shrieked, 'Patrick, do you know what you're saying? Have you gone completely mad?'

'I'd like to know the same thing,' Ffion said.

Patrick said, 'Oh, let's face it, Ellie, it's been over between us for ages. You treat me more like a child than a husband. All that matters to you are the kids and your friends and the unfortunates you help at work. It's as though I'm just something else for you to look after.'

Ellie looked shocked. She said to Ffion, 'You lied to me. You must've known how he felt.'

'No,' said Ffion. 'This isn't what I want at all, it's got absurd.' She turned to Patrick and addressed him as though

215

he were mentally retarded, slowly and distinctly, 'I don't love you, Patrick, I never did. There's nothing between us and as far as I'm concerned, there never will be.'

He smiled at her, as though he thought she was putting on a good show and it wasn't necessary to say any more.

Ellie said, her voice full of pity, 'Patrick, Ffion doesn't love you. She's been playing with you.'

'Of course she does,' he said, 'she does love me.'

'No,' Ellie's voice was firm, 'she never loved you. She's done this to get back at me; it's nothing to do with you.

Ffion smiled. Ellie, meeting those inscrutable violet eyes, knew all at once that this was something she and Ffion had to work out between them.

Patrick would not be the prize. He was in the way.

'You'd better go,' Ellie told Patrick. 'Ring me tomorrow and we'll talk about what's to be done.'

Patrick said to Ffion, 'I love you. Will you come with me? Please.'

'Love, Yuck!' Ffion said. She didn't look at him. She turned her head as if seeking something interesting in the room.

Without another word, Patrick left. They heard him in the hallway, then the sound of the front door shutting behind him.

Ellie said, 'I suppose you think I deserve this?'

'He's a moron,' Ffion said. 'What are you going to do?'

'I don't know. What would you do?'

'Nothing. Nothing at all.

Ellie stood up, rather stiffly. 'I'll get a bottle and you unplug the phone. You'd better stay here tonight. If I know Patrick he'll wait on your doorstep for you to come home, it's too pathetic....'

Ffion said, 'Really, why are men so utterly absurd?'

'They take themselves seriously,' Ellie said. She paused, then asked, 'Why did you do it?'

Ffion stubbed her cigarette out on a dirty plate on the table and then lit another. Without a word Ellie got up, fetched an ashtray and put it in front of Ffion. Ffion pushed her pack of Sweet Aftons across the table towards Ellie.

'Help yourself. Or don't you still smoke?'

'No, I gave up. But I'll have one now.' Ellie picked up the cigarette pack and looked at the image of Robert Burns and the river on the front. 'Sweet Aftons,' she said, 'God, this takes me back. Matt smoked these all the time at Trinity.'

'Didn't we all? Did you ever wonder why Irish cigarettes made in Dundalk had a Scottish poet on the front of the pack?'

'No, but I expect you're going to tell me. Why?'

'Burns's sister Agnes lived in Dundalk.'

'That's not even interesting.' Then Ellie said, 'Do you know today is the anniversary of the day Matt was killed?'

Ffion nodded. 'He was a life force. Something was missing in most of our lives after he went.'

Ellie's eyes filled with tears. She clenched her fists, desperate not to cry. We're on our own, she told herself, we've got to have this out.

She said again, 'Why did you do it?'

Ffion said, 'You betrayed me. At Howard's fortieth. Ellie, Vaclav was the only time I've ever felt at one with other women. Loving him made me a different person and it was wonderful. And you mocked that.'

'I don't understand.'

'I confided in you about Vaclav because I trusted you. And you offered the deepest emotion I'd ever felt to all those no-marks at Howard's party as a cheap joke. I wanted to pay you back.'

Ellie tried to remember. I must've been drunk, she thought, I was angry – something about Sandra. She said, 'It was just something to say, I didn't think.'

217

'Ellie, you got a First, you could have done anything. You had choices and you made your choice. You haven't any excuse for saying stupid things off the top of your head to betray other people's trust. You're not stupid. If you pretend you don't know what you're doing, I'd say you're malicious; and cowardly…'

Ellie burst out, 'OK, I was jealous.'

She was astonished at what she'd heard herself say. Me, jealous of that Teflon Jezebel? That's rubbish, she thought. But she didn't seem to be able to stop herself.

'As I saw it, those people at the party were my witnesses,' she said. 'I wanted to destroy what you had with Vaclav because that kind of love was mine, it's all I had. Since I lost Matt, my life has been a series of compromises.'

'That's not my fault.' Ffion ground out her stub in the ashtray and lit yet another cigarette.

Ellie scowled at her. 'You had everything else – success, looks, everything offered you on a plate. Why should you have that too?'

'Ask God, or genetics; or even the laws of probability. I don't know. We're all responsible for our actions. It's a post-feminist world, Ellie, none of us can sit back and leave men to deal the cards for us; women hold the bank now.'

Ellie took another of Ffion's Sweet Aftons. 'Does that have to mean that society won't be divided into men and women, but into women like you and women like me fighting it out?'

'Can't we co-exist? No, I don't think we can.' Ffion didn't seem alarmed at the prospect.

'Oh, come on,' Ellie said, smiling, 'if a group of women can bring about peace between Loyalists and Republicans in Northern Ireland, we'll surely find a way.'

Ffion shrugged. 'We'll have to have a war first; then, if we want to enough, perhaps we could find a way. But do we want to?'

Ellie went to put the kettle on for coffee. She was thinking, Nothing has changed. Patrick will come back, we'll go on as we were. I don't even really care if Ffion slept with him or not. She tried to do me harm. That I can't forgive. I can't let her get away with that.

'No,' she said, answering Ffion's question. 'I don't suppose we do.'

24

Was it really as long ago as that? Hilary thought. Can it really be five years since the Rev Dad died? His death seemed to Hilary nearer in terms of time, but he also felt like a distant memory. Or, rather, she remembered him still as though she was herself a much younger person, still almost a child. A long time ago. She missed her father; she missed her younger self. Especially over the Christmas break.

Her mother had moved into a bungalow on a new estate on the edge of the village; her life now seemed to consist of reminding herself of happier days.

Hilary made a point of spending Christmas with her; at least, she thought, we can be miserable together. This year, thank heavens, Susan and the kids stayed at home in Edinburgh, so Hilary and her displaced Mum spent the time alone together.

They grieved for the rambling old Vicarage; they couldn't bear to go to Church because Mum couldn't stand the new vicar's accent, which was positively Liverpudlian; worse still he used the Alternative Prayer Book and invited the members of the congregation to hug their neighbours at the end of the service.

Hilary and her mother were unwilling even to hug each other.

When New Year's Eve at last arrived, Hilary said, 'Well, we had a good wallow, Mum, didn't we?'

She was mightily glad that she was returning to London the next day. 'I've got to get back to work,' she said, though she was pretty sure that her mother didn't believe her.

I'll go to Ireland next year, whatever happens, she told herself, I'll go back and try to find that boy from the group of musicians who'd survived the soldiers' ambush. I owe him an apology.

She had failed to get any public notice taken of the outrage. Even the newspapers and magazines that published her previous work severed all connection with her when she approached them with the story. I let that be an excuse for not carrying on with the story regardless, she thought now, still ashamed. But those were different days. She'd been scared.

That was years ago, back in the mid Seventies. Sandra's Dark Forces can't still be after me, she thought. And then she wondered, Were they ever? It was Ffion told Sandra to warn me off; perhaps she just wanted to shut me up for some political agenda of her own.

Mum was giving Hilary one of her put-upon looks, sort of long-suffering and brave, as though to say Hilary was letting her down by not staying at home to look after her mother. But old and frail as she was, the look concluded, she wouldn't complain at the selfishness of the younger generation. They had their own lives to lead, and they'd know soon enough how it felt to be sad and alone, and old.

Younger generation my backside, Hilary thought, I haven't been young for years; decades, even. Was I ever?

She said, 'Why don't you go to Susan next year, Mum? I hate to think of what the Rev Dad would've thought of spending a Christmas like we've just had?'

Hilary was surprised to see her mother look positively relieved. 'Do you mean that, dear?' she said.

Hilary looked apologetic. She said, 'Oh, of course it's been great being here with you, but it doesn't do either of us much good sitting here being miserable and trying to bring back the past.'

221

'Oh,' her mother said, 'you've taken a weight off my mind, darling. I thought you'd hate the idea of abandoning the past, that's why I've stayed on here.'

'And I thought-'

'I've spent the whole of the time you've been here worrying about how to tell you.'

God, is she going to tell me she's got a terminal illness. Or it could be she wants to marry again.

'Tell me what?'

'I'd thought that next year I might go away for Christmas. Duncan's mother wants me to go with her on a cruise to Madeira. What do you think?'

'Mum, I think it's a great idea.'

Her face says it all, Hilary thought. I got it all wrong. She hated our Christmases as much as I did.'

'Actually, dear, I've been thinking I'd like to move nearer to Sue. I really don't want to stay in the village without your father. Things are so different now, with all the new housing estates. I'd feel useful again with Sue.'

Hilary thought, All those wasted years we've been at cross-purposes. We might've had so much more fun together. She said, 'Is Dad's crate of Communion Wine still in the garage? It's probably drinkable by now – genuine vintage.'

'I'd forgotten all about that. Let's drink a toast – Happy New Year, darling.'

Hilary felt her mother's papery lips against her cheek.

Travelling to London in the train next day, Hilary felt that she'd reached the end of a term of imprisonment in a well-meaning but restrictive institution. The Family Life Clinic, she thought, a place of correction and rehabilitation, a bit like boarding school.

For a long time, before university even, Hilary had been burdened by the assumption that her life would be shaped by a duty to her parents. It was old-fashioned, she knew, and her parents had never actually said anything, but once Sue married and she didn't, Hilary took it for granted that she was expected to be a dutiful daughter.

But here was her mother confessing that she was as unaccepting of her self-prescribed role as was Hilary; Mum wasn't anywhere near ready to become an aged parent. In fact, Hilary thought, maybe she never welcomed her role as the vicar's wife and mother of children. Thinking back now, Hilary had never seen her mother as a happy person; except, perhaps, when she was working on her garden.

Hilary stared out of the train window at the sprawling terraces of Wandsworth and Clapham; the Christmas decorations on the houses and in the streets were now a bit the worse for wear after a stormy New Year. All those families, Hilary thought, all bound together by a perceived duty to love, trying to get on together. And it can work, Hilary told herself; at least they could all be glad they weren't alone.

I wish I could tell Ffion that, Hilary said to herself, Ffion has always said the family is such a harmful, destructive thing. I wonder what kind of Christmas Ffion had; probably it wasn't much better than mine. Only different.

As she unlocked the front door of her flat she thought, Perhaps I'll call Ffion and ask her to come round for a drink. Full of New Yearish zeal, she dumped her case in the hall and went through to the kitchen to telephone Ffion before she changed her mind.

Her elderly tabby cat, which had been fed by a neighbour over Christmas, jumped in through the cat-flap in the back door and rubbed himself against her legs, purring loudly. Hilary leaned down to stroke him before putting the kettle on to boil; it was good to be home.

The message light on the telephone was flashing. She was about to ignore it and telephone Ffion without checking it, but old habits die hard. The Rev Dad drummed it into her since she could remember that people left messages in an emergency and they could be important; they must never be ignored.

The message was from Howard. His voice was weak and he seemed to be struggling to make himself heard.

'Ring me,' he said, 'please.'

The message had been left two days ago. There were no further calls from anyone else; and Howard hadn't tried to ring her again. He must've realized I was going to be away until after New Year, she told herself.

But she had a bad feeling. She dialled his number and got the engaged tone. Perhaps he'd left the phone off the hook. He was a doctor; a ringing telephone was more threatening to him than to other people. Not that he had been able to work for some time, of course, but doctors were born, not made; someone might need him.

Hilary thought, He's out, or he's gone to the pub, he could've been drunk and not put the receiver down right. There's no need to panic.

But something felt not right.

She called a minicab to take her to Howard's flat in Fulham.

As she waited for it to arrive, she tried to tell herself that over the years she'd had many calls like this from Howard. He'd be feeling grim, or he'd want company, or just a chat; there'd be no more to it than that. She thought, why do I feel like this now, as though there's something really wrong?

Most of the residents of the street where Howard lived seemed to be away. Many of the rather twee houses (twee to Hilary's eyes, anyway) were shuttered, and the curtains in the upstairs windows were closed. A pall of thick mist blurred the outlines of the buildings and drenched everything so that all Hilary could hear was the sound of persistent dripping from leafless trees, television aerials and telephone cables.

She walked up the steps to Howard's front door feeling very alone. She banged on the knocker and bent down to shout through the letter-box, 'Howard, it's Hilary.'

There was no answer. But she thought she heard a radio playing inside. She banged again; nothing happened.

I'm being a fool, she told herself; he's gone shopping or out to the cinema.

She walked round to the street that backed on Howard's. The house that she calculated was directly behind his had an alley at the side with a door leading to the back yard.

Hilary knocked on the front door.

After a delay, an elderly woman opened it.

She seemed reluctant to be polite. 'What do you want?' she said.

She thinks I'm selling something, Hilary thought; or maybe a Jehovah's Witness. Are Mormons ever women? But I think they go around in twos.

Hilary tried to explain to the woman. She felt ridiculous; there was so little to go on to justify the fuss she was making.

'I'm worried he may have had a fall or something,' she said. 'Could you let me through your side door so I can climb the wall into his garden and try his back door?'

Amazingly, Hilary thought, the woman seemed to believe her.

'Do you want me to call the police?' she said.

Hilary hesitated. She was beginning to panic, even as she was telling herself she'd no cause to be so scared. The woman accepting her story so easily made her feel worse.

Then she shook her head. 'He'd never forgive me if he's just popped down the road and comes back to find policemen all over the house. I'd rather try on my own first.'

The elderly woman, now trying to be helpful, found a stepladder to help Hilary clamber over the wall into Howard's garden.

As she climbed the few stone steps to Howard's patio and reached the back door, Hilary wished she'd let the neighbour phone the police. The patio was so neglected; there was grass growing between the paving stones, so unlike Howard. He used to be proud of his pot plants. Now they'd been reduced to dank stalks. She was full of foreboding.

The back door wasn't locked. She turned to wave at the old woman and, taking a deep breath, walked into the house.

She found Howard in the bedroom. He was in bed and looked asleep. But the phone on the bedside table was off the hook, and a bottle of pills was overturned. There was also a faint odour in the room which did not smell to Hilary like anything associated with the living.

She could see that he was dead. She didn't touch him.

The bedroom window overlooked the garden. Hilary threw up the sash and leaned out, trying to get fresh air into her lungs. The neighbour was waiting in her garden, waiting to see what happened.

Hilary called out to her. 'I think you'd better call the police.'

In her head she heard the warnings of hundreds of characters in detective stories: Don't move the body; don't move anything in case of disturbing forensic evidence.

So she did not replace the telephone receiver, or pick up the spilled pills, or turn off the radio still playing by the bed. It was Radio Three playing Rimsky Korsakov's *The Czar's Bride*; much too cheerful to accompany death.

She sat beside the body trying to take it in that Howard was dead. He'd tried to call her to help him; there was no one else for him to call.

She whispered to him, 'I'm so sorry, Howard. You risked everything to help me, and I've let you down.'

When the police banged on the front door, she went down to let them in.

'Is this the house with the suspicious death?' the first policeman said.

Hilary pointed up the stairs. 'He's in the bedroom. But don't get excited, it's not that kind of suspicious death. He had AIDs.'

She was ashamed of her satisfaction at the look of fear that crossed the cop's face. And she felt worse when he asked her gently, 'Did you find the body, Miss?'

She nodded. She was afraid she would burst into tears if she spoke aloud.

He said, 'We have to bring in a special unit in a case like this. It won't be long. Why don't you go round to the lady who called us and let her make you a cup of tea? We'll come and talk to you there later.'

Hilary nodded and left. Something even jollier was playing on the radio: Percy Grainger's *Country Gardens*. It was Howard's kind of music, she thought

Then it was turned off.

25

Sandra remembered someone telling her once that if she could only get over her inferiority complex about being neither flesh nor fowl nor good red herring when it came to being Irish, she had it in her to be a businesswoman to be reckoned with.

That was a long time ago, probably at the end of their last Trinity term before they dispersed for the summer vacation with their Finals in October. As far as Sandra remembered the four of them – Ffion, Hilary, Ellie and herself – were in the flat in Raglan Road, panicking about the amount of study they had to do if they were going to get their degrees.

They never really doubted that they would pass their Final exams, Sandra thought. They'd come to Trinity to get degrees, of course they would. For them it was simply going to be tough to get back into the routine of study after the social whirl of the events of Trinity Week and the Ball.

But that didn't include me, Sandra told herself. I wasn't like the others – the English and the Protestant Ascendency Irish. From the beginning my grating accent, my Belfast background, and my strident religion had marked me out in their eyes for failure.

Ellie (she thought it was Ellie) said, 'What about you, Sandra. What'll you do if you don't pass?

And Ffion said, 'Don't worry, Sandra will never starve. She'll make money and it'll have nothing to do with education. Betty Grable insured her legs for a million bucks, but that's small beer compared to what some of the richest men in the world will be prepared to lay out for temporary tenure of Sandra's fabulous breasts.'

Well, that wasn't quite as Sandra remembered it; perhaps the bit about the business brain was something she'd added afterwards to make her feel good. But Ffion had been right.

I showed them, Sandra thought, looking round the lavish opulence of her bedroom with satisfaction. She knew exactly how vulgar and ostentatious her boudoir was and that's the way she liked it. You've got it, flaunt it.

She'd made a fortune. The rich old men looked after her; they gave her real estate, and racehorses with purer bloodlines than any royal family, and yachts, and cars; there was even a railroad in the United States she owned.

But she was the one who had converted the property into luxury apartments and offices; she had made sure the cars she was given were rare vintage models which would accrue steadily in value. They had.

True, it always felt like a lifestyle made of ice and liable to melt if emotional warmth crept in. Her one fear was that she would fall in love for real.

And now she had. And she was happier than she had ever thought possible.

Derek Briggs opened her eyes to what commitment and real love could mean. And the best of it is, Sandra thought, that he isn't far behind the rest in the material provision department. Not that she cared about that anymore.

When one morning the telephone started to ring very early, while it was still dark, Sandra, fuddled with sleep, thought it was the alarm going off. She reached over to turn it off. The phone continued to ring. She checked the clock. Six o'clock in the morning was a ridiculous time for anyone to telephone. It must be a wrong number.

The phone stopped, and then at once started to ring again. Sandra, suddenly fully awake, jumped out of bed, pulling on her dressing gown and grabbing the receiver.

It's got to be Derek ringing from fecking Australia, she thought. Thank God, at last.

It was weeks since he'd been in touch. She'd expected him home months ago, but she knew well enough there was always some last-minute business to be done, so she didn't worry too much.

And then he stopped ringing at all.

She grabbed the phone. Her pent-up anxiety exploded in expletives. 'Dek! Feck it, Dek, is that fecking you?'

No one answered. Sandra could feel someone was on the line, but no one spoke.

'Derek…'

The phone went dead.

Now she was sure there was something wrong. She had no way to contact him. Derek had told her never to contact him on his business trips. 'Can't have that, doll,' he said. 'For one thing, you wouldn't know the time where I am. It might be the middle of the night.'

And calling his mobile phone just for a chat cost far too much. He had made a joke of that, he'd said he wasn't going to pay through the nose to hear a string of obscenities from her; if he needed to talk to her he'd ring her.

Of course she'd tried to ring him in the first month he went away. His mobile number had been discontinued. Bastard, he gave me a wrong number, he knew I wouldn't leave him alone, she told herself. She thought it was quite funny. At first.

Was he trying to get in touch now? Sandra went back to bed, but she couldn't sleep. She was anxious now.

Perhaps it was a wrong number, she thought again, someone's illicit lover expecting the loved one to be there and instead getting an earful of my choice language. That was funny, too, maybe.

Sandra thought she'd died and gone to Heaven when she first started living with Derek in this house in Romford. It was her dream home. He'd been very generous, she'd spent a fortune getting the place just as she wanted it, which was as unlike the poky two up and two down hovel in Belfast she'd been brought up in as she could make it.

Derek had a swimming pool built, an only slightly smaller replica of the virtual lake of a pool at the Hotel Fontainebleau on Miami Beach. Derek was very proud of that; he pronounced it as two separate English words: Fountain Blue. The first time they'd stayed there he'd said to her over *pina coladas* served in coconut shells, 'That's for me, doll. This is the way to live.'

Of course Sandra wouldn't dream of asking anyone from her TCD phase to visit; they were all snobs, they'd think it was tremendously vulgar. Ellie in particular would probably think it an affront to political decency. But here in this house Sandra at last felt at home. She felt safe.

Derek wasn't like her other men, he wasn't born to money like her previous protectors. He'd worked for his wealth, and was still working to increase it for a future she hoped very much to share with him. He wasn't old. And he was fecking English. She smiled to herself, thinking that their accents - his South London and her Belfast Shankill – were one as uncompromising as the other.

Derek made her feel more secure, and happier, than anyone else ever had.

Sandra gave up trying to sleep, swinging her feet off the bed and wriggling her toes in the thick white pile carpet. This is the life, she said to herself.

She was on her way down to the kitchen to make coffee when there was a tremendous hammering on the front door.

A man started shouting. 'Open up, Police!'

There was a loud bang and a panel on the front door splintered. A second impact broke the locks and the door swung open.

Policemen swarmed into the house. A woman officer who seemed to be in charge held up a document, poking it in Sandra's face. She said, 'We have a warrant to search the premises, please stand aside.'

Sandra tried to grapple with her, shouting, 'What the feck do you think you're doing.'

A police constable held her back, twisting her arm behind her back when she tried to bite him.

'Where's your husband?' the policewoman asked.

'I'm not fecking married,' Sandra said. 'Who are you looking for?'

'Are you denying that Derek Briggs lives here?'

Sandra was angry, and she was scared. 'What right have you to barge into my home like this?' she said. 'I'm going to ring my lawyer.'

'Arrest her.'

'On what charge, you fecking fascist cunt?' Sandra said.

'Abusive behaviour, obstructing the police, and resisting arrest for starters.'

Sandra tried to keep calm. She found any contact with the police disquieting. She always had done, but her paranoia about the Force had got worse since she lived with Derek. In the back of her mind she was always afraid that something like what was happening now might spoil her idyll.

I know so little about Derek, she thought, I was always afraid of asking questions. I don't know the people he works with or even where he works except he spends a lot of time in expensive international hotels. And what about that oily little man in his pin-striped suits and what look like patent leather dancing pumps who comes to the house at night and goes straight into Derek's study without saying a word to me. Derek said he was his lawyer but he looked to me more like an actor playing a Mafia boss on TV.

Sandra said to the policewoman, 'You'd better let me get dressed first. And then perhaps you'll tell me what this is all about.'

Policemen were all over the house. Sandra went into her bedroom and found her drawers opened and her underwear scattered all over the floor.

'Is this the Vice Squad?' she said to the policewoman, who had followed her into the room. 'Do you think Derek's a pornographer, is that it?'

The police officer pointed to her computer. 'Is this the only computer in the house? We'll need to take away all computers and the contents of the filing cabinets in your husband's office.'

'How often do I need to tell you, Derek Briggs is not my fecking husband.'

'Does your name appear on the deeds of the house?'

Sandra began to be really worried then. She'd asked Derek so many times to put the house into both their names and he'd always promised, but he never had. On the other hand, there were other documents she had signed for him. He'd told her as she wrote her signature that these were assets he was putting in her name because that was the most tax efficient way of transferring money to her and making her secure. And she had put everything she had into his name. He said it would be safer out of the reach of the British tax authorities. Abroad. Safe. She'd be secure.

Secure? I trusted him, Sandra thought, how could I be such a bloody fool.

The woman officer looked at her with contempt, but she was less aggressive now.

'Do you know where Derek is?' she said.

'Mr Briggs is in Australia,' Sandra said. 'He's been there for months.'

'When did he last get in touch?'

233

Sandra was afraid she might faint. She staggered a bit. She said, 'He's left me, hasn't he?'

The policewoman sent a uniformed constable to fetch a glass of water. She didn't answer the question. She didn't answer any questions, she just kept on asking them.

'How do you know he's in Australia?'

'He told me he was going there.' Sandra paused and looked at the woman's scornful expression. 'I don't know, do I? He could be anywhere.'

The policewoman decided not to take Sandra to the police station. They had reached some sort of tacit compromise; Sandra could stay in the house to point out documents and files and records which might have some bearing on Derek's business dealings.

Sandra rang Ffion.

'I need help,' she said. 'It's Sandra.'

'Who?'

'Sandra, for feck's sake.'

'Oh, *fecking* Sandra.'

There was a pause. Then Sandra said, 'You did law at TCD, didn't you? You're the only person I can think to ask.'

Sandra tried to explain what had happened.

Ffion said, 'I've never practised law, you know. It sounds to me as though you need the real thing.'

Ffion was trying to think of anything she'd learned at Trinity which might be relevant now.

Sandra was obviously panicking. She said, 'I don't know any lawyers. Derek had a man who came here sometimes who he said was his lawyer, but he never told me his name.'

'Even if you did know his name, don't for God's sake contact anyone associated with Derek. Trust me, you've got to distance yourself from Derek Briggs and it's best you play dumb.' Ffion hesitated and then she said, 'Just act natural.'

Ffion hoped Sandra wasn't going to start weeping. She said, 'I'll ring your policewoman and come the heavy legal rep and try to find out what they're investigating Derek for. What's her name?'

Ffion heard Sandra gulp; she was going to cry. 'Oh, for God's sake, leave it to me. I'll ring you back.'

Sandra said, with feeling, 'Thanks, Ffion.'

Ffion did ring back later. Sandra's police officer turned out to be the sister of a junior Home Office minister Ffion had done work for. The police had traced Derek to Brazil; he'd never been in Australia. Nor had he ever had any intention of returning to Romford.

'He's been running some sort of money-laundering scam, and any assets left in this country are now forfeit,' Ffion told Sandra.

'My house?'

'Is not your house. It's being seized as we speak. You're very lucky they're not interested in pursuing you. Apparently you signed documents you shouldn't have. But I think they'll drop any possible charges against you because you're not worth it; they can't get blood out of a stone. You're penniless.'

'Am I?'

'Yes.'

'What am I going to do?'

'Sorry, I can't help you there, it's not one of my areas of expertise. Try getting a job.'

'What kind of a job? I haven't any skill or qualifications. I did a general studies degree, which doesn't count for much these days.'

Sandra thought for a moment, then she said, 'Couldn't you introduce me to someone? You must know lots of rich old men.'

'If I did, I wouldn't dream of introducing them to you.'

'I don't suppose I could stay with you for a few days?'

'No way.'

'What the feck am I going to do?'

'You're still nominally a Proddy, aren't you? You'd best pray for divine intervention. You might win the Lottery.'

When Sandra heard the word "Proddy" she felt as though Ffion had hit her over the head with a wet sandbag. Oh my God, she thought, please not that. Please don't force me to go back there.

Sandra shuddered. Just the thought of it, and the tentacles of her heritage seemed to be closing around her, squeezing the life out of her.

Then Ffion said, 'Failing all else, I suggest you try Ellie Grant, she's paid to help the destitute, isn't she?'

Yes, Sandra thought, yes, that's what I'll do. Ellie will help me; we were at Trinity together, there's a bond. I'm not alone after all; I have connections.

26

Ffion stared out of the plate glass window of her office – well, it was a glass wall rather than a window, really – at the Thames three hundred feet below. A string of barges were making their way downstream. She thought, I wish I was there on board one of them, one of those miniature marionette-like figures leaping from vessel to vessel wielding their barge poles in an elaborate slow dance on that stage of floating coffins.

It was months now since Howard died. Ffion was surprised how much she missed him. So much of the time when he was alive she'd been angry with him for his attitude, treating her as some kind of sub-species of homo sapiens similar in significance – or lack of it – to drones in the world of bees.

And then she laughed, seeing her own absurd egomania revealed in what she was thinking. She thought, At least he showed me what I was up against; most men aren't so open about their contempt for females. They can't even be bothered to express it, she thought, but in my experience it's something they all share.

Ffion had heard about Howard's death from Hilary. Thank God it was Hilary found him, Ffion thought. If it had been anyone else, even Ellie or Sandra, they probably wouldn't have thought to let me know. Hilary is the only person I know who understands that antagonism can be a closer bond between people than liking. She knew how I felt about him.

Ffion was the one who had tried to find out after Howard's death when and where he was to be buried. She took it for granted that the Trinity contingent would want to go to his funeral. She and Hilary would, anyway.

But Howard's body had been collected and removed from London at the first opportunity. It was released to a member of the family, that was all the police would say.

'Someone said that none of his TCD friends would be welcome at the funeral,' Ffion told Hilary. 'The family seems to think we're in some way responsible for him being infected with AIDS. As if.'

Hilary, too, had been shocked after Howard's death to find how little she knew about the man she thought of as her best friend. Even his family's name; she'd had trouble remembering his surname when the police first questioned her. He was always just Howard to her.

He changed my life, she thought. How different it might've been if I'd had the baby. I'd have kept it somehow. I suppose I'd have got a job. Mum would have helped, but I didn't know that then. I thought it was the end of the world, and none of the family would speak to me again. That's what I told Howard and he believed me. I might see it differently now, but in the light of what we knew at the time, and what I thought I wanted, he risked losing everything for me.

God, she thought, if there's an afterlife he may know what I'm thinking, that I wish he hadn't. I'd be happier and a better person if he hadn't. But I don't blame you, Howard, it wasn't your fault. It was mine.

Ffion said, 'Howard's family wanted it kept quiet because of him having AIDS. They were furious when I rang.'

'How did you find them?'

'Howard told me once he was a real son of the Shires. I asked about. And Trinity helped too, putting alumni back in touch.'

Hilary decided to leave it at that. She said, 'Perhaps his family was thinking of him, that he'd want the AIDS kept secret.'

'It wasn't a secret. The bloody hospital knew when he had to stop working because of his health. Howard didn't try to keep it quiet.'

'If we can't go to the funeral, let's us all meet and have a few drinks – a kind of wake for him. OK?'

But it wasn't possible to organize it. Ellie preferred to remember Howard BC. 'Before Contamination', she said. It would be too sad. How could she say such a thing, Hilary thought, being flippant like that?

'Yuck!' Ffion said. 'What a bloody hypocrite Ellie is.'

Ffion, though, was too busy to spare the time. She didn't say but the way she remembered Howard wasn't as a friend. Simply, she trusted him. But she didn't want anyone to know that; it was too pathetic.

Sandra refused to consider the idea of the wake. She'd wanted nothing to do with Howard from the moment she knew he was homosexual; and once he had contracted that repellent disease, she was terrified that she might even now be incubating the infection from eating and drinking with him when he'd visited the flat in Raglan Road. He hadn't come there often, but he must've used the bathroom when he did. She said to Ffion, when she asked her about the wake, 'Frankly, I believe these perverts bring their filthy diseases on themselves.'

'So die all evil-doers, as your Christian connections might put it?' Ffion had said, and added, 'But don't forget you're living in a glass palace now, Sandra, and people in glass houses shouldn't throw stones.

Now Ffion asked herself, Why did I say that to her? What am I, Cassandra? How was I to know she was living with a South London wide boy.

She went back to her desk and sat down. Now she could see only sky, and the sight of it caught her by surprise. After looking down at the river, and the traffic massed on

Battersea Bridge, with all those scurrying people, the sky had something significant to say. It struck her like seeing a Brigid Riley painting after hours of studying Monet; it had an existence of its own, disconnected from human life. She'd never realized, or even thought about it. Day after day, the sky was just there, meaning nothing, simply a blank canvas that was outside. But it reflects human reality, she thought, it's the expression of what is true.

But it's more than that, she told herself. She watched dark clouds chasing each other across the white light of the obscured sun. God, she thought, that must be what happens to the poisonous fumes, those clouds are the pollution filling up the atmosphere.

Perhaps Ellie handing out her leaflets telling people to Save the Planet had a point, but so what? It was all far too late, thanks to woolly-minded do-gooders like Ellie herself, people who thought all human life was sacred; Ellie was adamant we needed to increase the stock of people, no matter how dangerously over-populated the planet was. They were our future, Ellie said.

If so, why doesn't she try to change it? Ffion thought. The woman needs shooting. Watching the drama unfolding in the sky, she said to herself, We're doomed, we're all doomed.

And then Kate, her secretary, knocked and came into the room.

'There's someone to see you,' she said.

'Who? There aren't any appointments, are there?'

Kate looked awkward. 'No. But she's a schoolgirl.'

'A what? What does a schoolgirl have to do with me?'

'She says you know her mother. Her name is Saffron Grant.'

Saffron was waiting in the doorway. She was wearing school uniform.

Ffion nodded at Kate. 'It's OK,' she said.

Saffron came across the room towards the desk. Ffion waited, thinking, I didn't realize till I see what a meal she's making of walking across the space what a big room this is.

Saffron said, 'I'm sorry to come here like this. I didn't know what else to do.'

Yuck, Ffion thought, she doesn't just look like Ellie, she sounds like her too.

'Why have you come? Presumably Ellie doesn't know you're here?'

'No, she'd have a fit. I've bunked off school.'

'Should I be flattered? What do you think I can do for you?'

'My Mum's doing everything she can to force me to do something I desperately don't want to do.'

Ffion thought, that sounds like Ellie. She said, 'And that concerns me how?'

'I thought you might help me take a stand against her bullying,' this replica Ellie said.

She's very sure of herself, just like Ellie, Ffion thought.

'Are you pregnant?'

That was the first question that occurred to Ffion. At fifteen, or whatever age this girl was, Ellie might well have been pregnant.

Saffron started. 'Did she tell you that?'

'No.'

'How did you know, then?'

'Why else would a girl your age want to talk to me? She wants help, that's why. And what's the most likely reason she wants help, she's pregnant. It's elementary, kid.'

'Well, it was when I...'

Ffion put up her hand to stop her. 'I'm not interested in the sordid details of your sex life. The last thing I want to know is how it happened and what he did and how you felt and crap like that. I don't give a damn. You're going to have a baby. What's Ellie trying to make you do you don't want to?'

Saffron began to look upset. 'She's taking over. She doesn't take any notice of me or what I want, it's as though it's got nothing to do with me. I've no say at all.'

Ffion almost laughed at that. My God, she thought, Ellie's gone into the breeding game, as though her best bitch is going to have puppies.

Saffron looked at Ffion, expecting sympathy. When none was forthcoming, she went on, 'She and Dad have already put our house on the market. They're going to move to somewhere deadly in the sticks and then I'll have the baby and she'll bring it up as if it was hers and I can still go to school so I'll have a future. They've got it all worked out.'

'Yuck.'

'I told Mum I want an abortion. I've told her that from the start. But it's no good, she doesn't listen, she just takes over.'

Ffion thought, She may look and talk like Ellie, but she's not Ellie; I mustn't forget that.

She asked, 'Why me?'

'I need someone to help me. I'm so angry Mum won't listen to me, I thought who I could go to who would annoy her most and it was you. If she thinks I'm that desperate, she might listen.'

'You'd better sit down.'

Saffron sat down opposite Ffion at the desk. 'I'm under age, Mum says I can't try to get an abortion without her permission and she's not going to agree to it. And our family doctor would tell her if I try to go behind her back. And time's getting on, soon it'll be too late…'

'I expect you've had all the counselling you can take from Ellie already.'

'She thinks I'll love it when it's born and then everything will be all right. I won't, I know I won't. It's quite simple, I've made a horrible mistake and I want to put it right and get over it. But Mum's doing her best to make me ruin my life because of it. I won't even be able to get it adopted because of her. She wants it. I may only be fifteen, but I've got plans for my life ...I've made up my mind, but she thinks I'm too young to have a right to decide. I hate her.'

Ffion remembered a far-off day when she had said she never wanted children and Howard hadn't believed her. She thought, I always knew my own mind even when I was younger than this girl, and all my life since has proved I was right.

She was disconcerted at what she thought then, she tried to suppress it. That's the main reason I miss Howard, he never admitted he was wrong. He never knew what makes me tick.

She'd almost forgotten Saffron. She said, 'Ellie thinks she's doing her best for you. It's too simple, when people try to force their opinions on you, to say you hate them. No one will take you seriously when you say childish things like that.'

She thought, What am I doing, defending Ellie when everything this wretched girl says about her is true.

'Mum's a fascist, it's a simple as that. She's never had any kind of life and she want to stop me...'

'I'll tell you something about Ellie you may not know...'

'What's to know?' Saffron plainly resented all this talk of her mother.

Ffion thought, She doesn't just look and sound like Ellie, she's a bully like her.

'Ellie was a very brilliant student, did you know that? She was the top student at University and she could have had a really amazing career. But she chose to marry and have you and your brother because she thought she played a more valuable role in society by doing that... I think she made a stupid decision, but it was her choice and I don't suppose she's ever regretted it. She doesn't want you to make a wrong step you'll regret later.'

243

'I don't need protecting. I know how to look after myself.'

'There's not much evidence of that, though, is there?'

'I wouldn't have got pregnant if Mum hadn't been telling me for years that it was the most wonderful thing to have sex with the special man you loved and wanted to be with for the rest of your life. She said that's why I shouldn't sleep around, because it was worth waiting for…'

Ffion was exasperated. This girl was a bore.

She said, 'Oh, don't tell me, you're an innocent who got carried away by lust the first time a boy kissed you and thought this was what your mother meant and that was it? You can't be that silly.'

Saffron quailed at Ffion's contemptuous sarcasm. 'It felt like it was the real thing.'

'But stupid or not, you still have the right to decide what you want. I'm just not sure what you think I can do.'

'Oh, I've worked out how we can sort that. There's a doctor I've been to near where my Gran lives. He doesn't know Mum, and when Gran went into the Home she changed from having him as her GP. I can go to him. You can come with me and say you're my mother, and sign the consent form. And then when it's fixed up, I'll tell Mum I'm staying over with a friend.'

Self-dramatizing little beast, Ffion thought. Why would any woman want to saddle herself with this?

She said, 'I don't think that's the best way to go about it. It's bound to be a crime, impersonating a mother or something. I'd never get away with it. Anyway it's not necessary. Time to grow up, kid. There isn't a problem. There are specialist clinics you can go to who won't tell your mother. They're not allowed to, even if you are under age.'

'She doesn't have to consent?'

'No.'

Ffion thought, Ellie must know that, she must have come across cases like this in her work. It's a common problem.

Ffion sat down at her computer. 'I'm putting in "termination of pregnancy". If I just put "abortion" the system would probably give me a list of government cock-ups.'

She could tell that Saffron disapproved of being made fun of.

'Mum must know this stuff better than you,' she said. 'She must've being lying to me deliberately about needing her consent.'

Ffion paused, waiting for the computer to respond. 'Possibly,' she said, 'but it's quite likely she's in denial, and refused to take the information in.'

'No, she wanted me to think I didn't have the choice. I'll never forgive her for this.' Saffron sounded as though she might get hysterical.

Ffion was watching the screen. 'The important thing is to concentrate on getting this sorted,' she said. 'Forget your mother for a moment. Once you let emotion get the better of you, you're done for.

There was a brief silence. Then Ffion switched off the computer. 'Here's the telephone number of the nearest clinic to where I live. You can't go to one near you because you might be very unlucky and someone you know might see you.'

'Oh, God, if Mum ever finds out...'

'Ring them now and make an appointment. Dial nine to get an outside line.'

Saffron lifted the receiver. 'Will you come with me?' she said.

'No, thanks. Take one of your own friends, someone more ...' Ffion was going to say sympathetic, but she said... 'closer to your own age.'

'I need you to come. Please...'

Ffion frowned, staring at the girl. It wasn't what she said, but something in her voice stirred a far-off, elusive memory of her own distant childhood. Times she'd wanted her mother and Beverly wasn't there.

Saffron was saying, 'Sometimes I look at my hands and I see them there at the end of my arms, but it's as though they belong to someone else…'

Ffion smiled. 'You think this pregnancy isn't real…that someone else is having this baby? Believe me, kid, it's real all right.'

Saffron looked sharply at Ffion to make sure she wasn't mocking her. 'It's in my body, but it isn't anything to do with me, it belongs to someone else…'

'That's the Ellie effect,' Ffion said. She was surprised at the gentleness of her tone. 'Well, you're the one who's going to have to deal with it.'

'It's all mixed up in my head with being obsessed by the idea of Mum dying.' Saffron sounded as though she might start to cry.

Ffion said, 'Yes, I know that feeling. I used to imagine my mother being dead. Most of the time I believed I'd killed her. I wish.'

Saffron suddenly looked hopeful. 'Will you come with me? Then I'd be sure it was real. There's no one I'd trust more than my mother's enemy,' she said.

Horrid little bitch, Ffion thought. When I think what Ellie's given up for her… 'I'm not your mother's enemy,' she said. 'I don't know what gave you that idea. You should think about this carefully. I'm told a girl often finds she wants her mother to be with her, even if she doesn't think she will.'

'No fear,' Saffron said. She was vehement. Then she seemed to think this needed further explanation. She said, 'She'd take over. This is about me. It's my feelings that matter now, not hers. If she even knew about this, it would be all about her feelings. Her loss, her suffering, my betrayal of her. She wouldn't even think of what I might be going through.'

'OK, you've made your point. You won't get any commiseration from me.'

Ffion asked herself, Could Ellie really care so much about this arrogant little cow? Hasn't she any idea what this girl of hers is really like? And then she thought, But Ellie thinks Saffron is a reincarnation of herself; she's supposed to make Ellie immortal.

Selfish cow, she thought. But she wasn't sure herself which one of them she was talking about

'You could've done all this for yourself, you know. I'm sure you know you can type "abortion" into Google and all this would have come up.'

Saffron grinned at her, Ellie's crooked grin. 'I guess you're right,' she said, 'I'm nowhere near as brilliant as my mother was.'

'No,' Ffion said.

Saffron made the phone call. It was done, the initial appointment made.

'Will Ellie find out you're playing truant?' Ffion asked. She wanted to get rid of Saffron now; she disliked prolonged involvement in someone else's life.

'Not likely,' Saffron said. 'She thinks I like school because I get away from her.'

Saffron seemed unsure whether she should give Ffion a hug.

'Thank you,' she said. 'You've saved my life.'

That phrase again, Ffion thought. What made Howard do what he did for Hilary? She'd seen it with her own eyes and she still didn't believe it had happened. Compared with that, what she was doing for Saffron didn't seem extraordinary. But then Saffron wanting an abortion wasn't surprising. It was beyond belief that Hilary could consider such a thing.

Ffion opened a drawer in her desk and took out a pack of cigarettes. She didn't offer one to Saffron. 'It's easy for me to help you, Saffron. I don't love you.'

'I never asked to be loved. It seems to me it's just an excuse for people to rule your life.'

Ffion thought, How children do make monsters of us all.

27

On a cold night in December 1990, Hilary went to answer loud knocking on her front door.

She shouted through the door, 'Who is it? Who's there?'

Old habits die hard, she told herself. Would she ever get over her fear that unexpected visitors were out to get her?

A woman's voice said, 'For Christ's sake, it's me. I'm freezing my tits off out here, let me in.'

'Ffion?'

Hilary opened the door. If Ffion weren't Ffion, Hilary would have said that she fell into the house. But Ffion didn't do things like that.

'You're pissed.'

'Ratarsed. I've been celebrating.'

Ffion took a deep breath and walked carefully into Hilary's living-room like someone in deportment class balancing a book on her head. There she threw herself down on the sofa.

Hilary had never seen Ffion like this. She felt very prim and proper in comparison. But even drunk, Ffion was still glamorous.

Ffion rummaged in her handbag and took out a Havana cigar in a metal tube with a screw top.

She also brought out a half bottle of whisky.

'Come on, bring out the glasses, we've got to drink her health.'

'Who's health?'

'Mary Robinson, of course. Keep up, Hilly. She's been elected President of Ireland.'

Hilary had spent the day working on an article she was writing for *Wives and Mothers* magazine. That was her main source of work these days. They wanted a piece about clever ways to adapt outgrown clothes so the younger sibling didn't feel they were hand-me-downs. Hilary had done her best, but she'd struggled to think of anything to say. She hadn't had a chance to watch the News.

'The Mary Robinson who was at Trinity?' she asked.

Ffion was fiddling with the cigar, which she had taken out of its metal tube and was trimming with a small gold and onyx cutter like a miniature guillotine.

'Of course that Mary Robinson. An inspiration to us all. She let all those eejit men from the big political parties flounder around like shadow boxers trying to knock each other out, and then she sneaks in and pulverizes the lot of them. For God's sake, what are you waiting for, get some glasses and bring me an ashtray.'

Hilary was impressed. Ireland's first woman President, and not even a candidate from one of the big parties. And this was a woman who'd been at Trinity with her; she'd spent hours drinking coffee in the Buttery; she must've waxed indignant at the curfews and curtailments forced on women students; she, too, must've joined the crush in the Ladies Room in No.6, and sat dry-mouthed in the Exam Hall with her future at stake and her mind gone blank. But perhaps Mary didn't, she thought, she must have known she wouldn't fail.

Ffion was saying, 'Do you know, RTE broadcast her victory speech live rather than the Angelus. Another first. I tell you, Hills, this is the start of a new era in Ireland.'

Even given that Ffion was intoxicated, Hilary was astounded that she should wax so lyrical about another woman's egregious achievement.

Ffion went on, 'Don't you see, she did it on her merits. Not because she was or wasn't a woman, but because the public saw her as the best person for the job.'

250

Hilary brought glasses and the ashtray. Ffion poured whisky, and they both toasted the new President; and Ireland; and then Trinity and an Irish political system that didn't drive people into rigid pens of thought like cattle in a market.

'Imagination lives!' Hilary said, and took a puff at Ffion's cigar.

'Yuck,' Ffion said, 'don't Bogart that stogie, my friend, sucking on it like that. Christ Almighty, you're ruining it.'

Hilary was wondering why Ffion had come to share Mary Robinson's triumph with her. It was some years now since Ffion had got Sandra to warn her off going back to Ireland because of what she'd tried to make public about that awful night when the British soldiers had killed the group of folk-singers. But perhaps that was it; Ffion would know that neither Ellie nor Sandra would feel particularly involved in what had happened; but Hilary would.

But that was then, Hilary told herself, and she felt sad. I want to be, I wish I were part of it, but I've been left behind. Ireland has a great new young future, it has no use for me.

And she thought, I'm like England, a backward-looking, outdated land deluding itself that it still has a day to have. Ireland grew out of England years ago; and its grown out of people like me.

Ffion said, 'I can't blow rings with cigar smoke, it's not the same as cigarettes. That can't be right, can it?

She puffed for a bit. It was true.

'You're out of practice,' Hilary said.

They were silent for a while.

This is nice, Hilary thought, being here like this with her; companionable. I can't remember being so at ease with anyone, not even family.

Ffion was saying, 'Do you ever think that what mattered so much to us all at Trinity felt kind of doomed? You know, that the Ireland and Trinity we experienced was like that dead coral reef in Australia, beautiful but losing the energy to sustain life?'

Hilary laughed at Ffion's hyperbole. 'No,' she lied.

She was afraid that if she told the truth and said 'Yes' she would weep with self-pity.

Ffion ignored her denial. 'Don't you think that what we felt is vindicated by one of us becoming President now, and with an overwhelming popular vote? We're not just part of some tourist nostalgia trip through the mists of a Celtic twilight. This gives us all a role in Ireland's future.'

'A supportive role perhaps, I suppose,' Hilary said. She added, 'I never knew you felt this way.'

The excitement died in Ffion's eyes. She seemed suddenly depressed.

'I need to cling on to any kind of future today. That's why I went on the piss. And probably went overboard about Mary Robinson.'

Hilary waited, almost afraid of what was coming.

Ffion drew deeply on the cigar. 'I've lost my job.'

Her voice as she announced this was so dispassionate that Hilary couldn't believe she had heard right. For God's sake, she thought, Ffion *is* her job, what's she going to do?

'You've what?'

'I've been fired. I was told to clear my desk and they said if I didn't leave the premises at once, they'd call security and have me removed.'

'Who did? They can't just fire you, you're privy to too much.'

'Oh, some prick in the Cabinet Office. But if you mean who's behind it, it's Ellie Grant.'

'How could Ellie do that?'

'How did she persuade them to sack me, or how could she do such a vicious thing to her former landlady?'

'But what reason did they have to sack you?'

252

'Ellie gave it to them. And I gave it to Ellie. I told her once, apropos of something else. When I was seventeen, I was cautioned for possessing drugs.'

'So? That's it?'

'It's called a "police record". In my case an undisclosed police record, which makes it worse. Drugs, you only have to mention drugs and you're done for in my kind of job. Worse than being found insane.'

Hilary got up then and went to fill the coffee percolator in the kitchen. We'd better sober up, she thought, this is serious.

When she came back she said, 'Tell me what happened?'

'Oh, I once mentioned to Ellie that I'd been refused a visa to the United States because of this drugs caution. I was planning to go to America with Vaclav. It was nothing. Years before I was at a party in a country house somewhere with some pop musicians and the police raided the place. They were out to get the lead singer, I think.'

'And that's it?'

'It's enough. Ellie wrote to a Minister in the Home Office who knows Patrick, using her office notepaper. She said she knew through a drugs dealer several of her clients mentioned as a pusher, and she didn't think it would look good if the public knew I was a convicted addict.'

'You mean she lied?'

'Well, the police record's true enough. It's so long ago I forgot all about it.'

'But why?'

'She told me she'd make me pay. After I slept with Patrick. It's a bit disproportionate, but she's always been out to get me.'

Hilary frowned. 'But is that it? Can't you appeal?'

'I signed the Official Secrets Act. Ellie's not the only one, there are a lot of people who wanted me out of their way.'

Ffion seemed to take that for granted. How can she be so calm, Hilary asked herself, I couldn't bear to know I was hated that much.

Ffion tossed her dark hair back from the violet eyes and grinned, 'That's the price of success, darling,' she said. 'If they all liked me, I'd have been a failure.'

'And Ellie?'

'She did this to force me back into line among the monstrous regiment of women like her. She thinks she's left me for dead. That's what those stupid male politicians in Ireland thought about Mary Robinson. There's only one way to deal with Ellie. I'm going to prove I'm very much alive and kicking.'

'So what are you going to do?'

'I'm going to use what I've got. I'm going to write my memoirs.'

'But you can't. Can you? They'll stop you with the Official Secrets Act.'

Ffion suddenly looked positively gloating. Hilary was disconcerted.

'It'll be fiction. Everything will be true, but names and positions will be changed.'

'But who'd want to read that?'

'Oh,' Ffion said, 'it'll have everything: sex, corruption, the lot. I'm going to call it The Sordid Secrets of the Great and Good. Everyone likes a good crime story set in high places.'

'But...'

'Don't worry, Hilary, no one will dare sue. That would be as good as admitting their guilt.'

Hilary went to make the coffee. It's the drink talking, she thought, she's just lashing out. She'll never write a book like that.

Part Three

28

There was terrible news. As soon as she heard, Sandra rang Hilary.

Her voice was full of suppressed excitement. 'Have you heard?'

Hilary looked at the clock on the bedside table. It was seven o'clock in the morning. No one made phone calls at seven o'clock in the morning.

'Heard what?'

'Saffron's dead.' Sandra said.

Hilary was impatient. 'What are you talking about? What Saffron?'

'What the feck's the matter with you? Saffron, Ellie's daughter Saffron. Spoiled brat Saffron. The one who got pregnant at about twelve and had a miscarriage, as in Ellie's round robin at Christmas that year saying the whole family was in mourning for the girl's little baby – can you imagine? That Saffron.'

Hilary's brain actually felt bruised.

'She wasn't twelve; she was fifteen,' she said.

'Whatever, that Saffron. She's been fecking murdered.'

Hilary felt sick.

What must Ellie be feeling? she thought. But she knew what Ellie must be going through. Hadn't she lost her child, and in the worst way. Nothing could be worse than having your child's life deliberately taken by a stranger.

And then she said to herself, Yes, there's something worse, if you deliberately murdered your own child.

Hilary tried to pull herself together. She could hear Sandra sounding exasperated on the line. There was music in the background – *We Didn't Start the Fire*, a moronic accompaniment.

She said, 'How do you know?'

Sandra sounded relieved. It seemed to Hilary that by telling the news, her friend was trying to make sense of what had happened.

'I know someone in the Met, in CID. He told me. He said Saffron was reported missing on Sunday by her room-mate at the university. She started at Bournemouth this year, apparently. Dorset police got in touch with the Met because they needed someone to go round and talk to the parents.'

'Why? They don't think they had anything to do with it, do they?'

'Once they found the body they had to question Ellie and Patrick. Finding out what sort of girl she was, I suppose. You know, was she the sort to go off with strange men, that sort of fecking thing. And there was the rigmarole of identification, of course.'

Oh, God, Hilary thought. 'What do they think happened?'

'Oh, you know, the usual thing. Saffron was with a group of students in a pub. The others wanted to go on to a club. Saffron didn't want to, and she said she'd walk back to the Hall of Residence.'

'Didn't somebody go with her?'

'She wouldn't hear of it; she said she wanted to be on her own. Of course now the police think that may be significant. They're trying to find out if she'd arranged to meet someone.'

'What kind of world is it when a girl can't walk home alone at night in a crowded city? Who'd be expecting an awful thing like this to happen?'

'Anyone who reads the fecking newspapers, I suppose. They found her body in the New Forest yesterday evening; it'll be all over the papers today. I thought you ought to know.'

Sandra, having dropped her bombshell, was now at a loss as to what to say. It was as though the drama had crashed like a wave and moved on, leaving her behind. She had a distinct feeling of anti-climax.

She thought, I can only make myself care about her death by telling everyone how awful it is. It's all I can do. I can't help Ellie or Patrick.

Hilary seemed to be thinking the same thing. She said, 'It seems so inadequate, but wouldn't Ellie want to know we're here for her?'

'But we're not, are we? How can we be? All we can offer are empty gestures.'

Hilary asked herself, If I ring Ellie, what could I say? There's nothing to say that she could bear to talk about. 'Perhaps a note saying we're there if she needs us?'

'I think there are cards for this sort of thing you can buy now,' Sandra said. 'I'll get a really nice one and send it from both of us, shall I?'

When Ellie received this card she wondered at first who had sent it. Hilary and Sandra sounded to her like cold callers, or members of the customer services team of some corporate enterprise.

Even when she remembered her flatmates from Trinity, she was offended by the intrusion. Her whole existence was reduced to Saffron's murder.

She was obsessed with Saffron's unknown killer.

The nature of her obsession changed as time passed and she grew ever more convinced that the murderer would never be found. At first, she tried to imagine what had motivated this man; why had he wanted to hurt Saffron? And, horror of horrors, did she, as a mother, have any part in starting the process which led to rape and murder? Had the decisions she'd taken for Saffron – right down to sending her to study in Bournemouth instead of somewhere quite

259

different where a murderer didn't lurk – contributed to her death?

The police investigation was intense for a while, but then it got overtaken by more immediate atrocities. Media interest dwindled for lack of new departures in the story. And as Saffron's murder faded from people's minds, Ellie lost interest in the killer as an individual. She turned her anger against those who had failed to discover who he was, including the general public who might, knowingly or unknowingly, be shielding him. Society, she told herself, fostered the violence and distrust and lack of care which let these things to happen to innocent children.

A hard core of anger burned inside her. All the time, whatever she was doing. The physical pain was much, much, worse than heartburn but that's the sort of agony it was. It filled her body with burning acid. And her mind, too, was in pain, particularly when she lay in bed at night with her head pounding, afraid to fall asleep to dream of herself awake and Saffron alive and happy, as though the dream were the reality and the nightmare something she would wake from. At this stage, she often got carried away imagining ways in which she could take violent physical revenge on anyone and everyone because her child had been hurt.

But Ellie's worst moments were the times, usually during sleepless nights, when she almost hated Saffron for getting herself killed and bringing this misery down on her mother.

And then Ellie loathed herself for such thoughts.

All this time, she could not cry.

Patrick tried to help her. He was unusually tender in his patience and his attempts to understand what she was feeling. He missed Saffron desperately, but, Ellie told herself, he didn't feel, as Ellie did, that part of her had been ripped from her body. He went back to work as soon as the funeral was out of the way, trying to bury himself in work to take his mind off Saffron.

He kept saying, to anyone who would listen, 'She was my pride and joy.'

And then came a time when Ellie felt an overwhelming need to talk about Saffron. To remember incidents and occasions the two of them had shared, jokes they had found funny, people they had liked and laughed with.

She had had no contact for months with the ordinary life other people had been living all this time parallel to her own half-life as the mother of a murder victim. People she knew had e-mailed or written, and then withdrawn, leaving her to lick her own wounds. Sandra and Hilary had not telephoned, secretly afraid that they could not cope with raw emotion Ellie might not be able to suppress.

In the end all she could do was to go back to work.

The first day back, she knew this was a mistake. But there was nothing else to do.

For months, even before Saffron left home to go to Bournemouth, Ellie had been feeling more and more alienated from her job. Actually alienated too from the social services system she had once believed would create a truly inclusive society which would deliver on Utopia.

She'd been feeling that she no longer had anything in common with her colleagues. Or even with the clients. I'm too old, she told herself, all these younger people have a different agenda entirely. They understand the world in terms of rights and entitlements and fulfilling targets, not love.

She asked herself, What do I mean by love?

The best she could do was work out that she wanted to help people do what's best for them. She'd studied and practised and passed exams to qualify her to be able to decide for them what that was. Ellie couldn't work out why her colleagues didn't understand her methods.

261

It was all much worse when she returned to work after Saffron's murder. Her workmates didn't seem to know how to talk to her anymore. They treated her as though it was bad manners that she'd come back at all to involve them in her personal tragedy.

Worse still, she found it hard to apply her former standards of love and sympathy to her clients. Their troubles were eclipsed by hers; she was beginning to think that too often they brought their troubles on themselves.

Oh God, she thought, I'm beginning to sound as brutal and insensitive as Ffion.

And that, in a way, was the worst thing of all for Ellie. She started to be tortured by guilt for what she'd done to Ffion. She thought, The woman has nothing else to live for except her job; I've destroyed her life.

In the back of Ellie's mind, the idea began to grow that this was why Saffron had been murdered. God was punishing her for an evil deed.

Should I tell her I'm sorry? Ellie asked herself. Even if she doesn't forgive me, she'd know I regret it. And then she told herself, It won't bring Saffron back.

Ellie took to going home at lunchtime rather than eat in the canteen at the council offices. She became a bit obsessive about it, cutting corners on casework and pretending she had appointments with imaginary clients so that she could get home in time.

It was bizarre, she knew that. The Australian soap opera *Neighbours* became the most important thing in her life. From day to day, personal, family or emotional dilemmas were solved by characters motivated by enlightened...well, there was no other word for it, love.

Neighbours would have her apologize to Ffion, no doubt about it; and Ffion would forgive her. But then Ffion wasn't the sort of character the programme would tolerate living for a single moment in Ramsay Street.

Then one day, just as the programme was starting, a taxi drew up outside the house. The front door bell rang, and kept ringing. Exasperated, Ellie opened the door.

Ffion was on the doorstep.

Ellie felt herself shrink inside her skin. For a moment, the intruder seemed like an apparition of the old Ffion before she, Ellie, destroyed her.

Ellie actually put up her hands in front of her face to ward Ffion off. For Ffion was unchanged. Still darkly beautiful; still compelling attention just by being there; still triumphant. I left you for dead, Ellie thought, how can you look unharmed?

'What do you want with me?' Ellie said, Hamlet-like.

'For God's sake turn that bloody television off.'

'But...'

Ffion did not wait to be asked inside, but pushed her way into the house. She felt she had to get Ellie out of the outdoor light and under cover.

She looks ghastly, Ffion thought. She's still wearing the same clothes she used to wear in the Chelsea flat. Her skin's grey, a lighter shade of her grubby clothes; it must be months since she washed those clothes.

They sat facing each other across the kitchen table. Ellie noticed that something was different about Ffion. She looks like an axe blade someone's sharpened, lethal and ready for action.

'You've cut your hair,' Ellie said.

'I have,' Ffion said, 'and so should you.'

'What do you want?' Ellie sounded petrified.

'I'm sorry about what happened to Saffron.'

Then Ellie's eyes filled with tears. 'You're the only person who's come out and spoken about her,' Ellie said. 'No one seems to know she's dead. Sometimes I think I've gone mad and it hasn't happened, she isn't dead; she just hates me.'

263

'She didn't hate you. She just wanted you to stop forcing her to live her life your way.'

Ellie's lifeless eyes – like a fish, without expression or colour, Ffion thought, suddenly came to life.

'Why do you say that? You didn't know her.'

'She came to see me once and asked me how she could get an abortion.'

Ffion took out a packet of cigarettes and lit one. She offered it to Ellie, who took it with trembling fingers.

Ffion went on, 'I told her that if that was what she wanted, it was possible. I showed her she had the choice.'

'How could you do that?'

'Why hadn't you?'

Ellie banged her fist on the table, making their mugs of coffee jump and spill over.

'How could you? How could you do that to me?'

'I didn't do it to you. I did it for her. If I hadn't, you'd have lost her. All I did was listen to her and hear what she said.

There was a long silence. Ffion's perfect smoke rings seemed to hover like slipping haloes in the air above Ellie's muddy hair.

She said, 'You know what I did, don't you? About your job?'

Ffion nodded, watching Ellie's face.

Ffion said, 'Did you know? About the abortion? Did you get me sacked to punish me for that?'

'Saffron told me. When it was all over. She said you'd told her that she'd want to tell me, and she did, she said. But I couldn't forgive you.' Ellie paused, then asked, 'You know why?'

Ffion shrugged.

'I couldn't bear it that she went to you and not to me.'

'But she did go to you. At the start. You wouldn't listen.'

'I know. That's why I hated you.' Ellie shook her head. 'I don't know. I'm sorry I did what I did to you. I've wanted to tell you that. I regret it very much.'

'Oh,' Ffion said, 'you don't have to worry about that now. It's all worked out for the best. I'm glad you did. I'm writing a book, and it's going to be published and the publishers think it's bound to be a best-seller. I'm having the time of my life. And I owe it all to you.'

Ellie was startled. It was disconcerting to find Ffion had come back to life so decisively. 'What book?'

'It's called *The Sordid Secrets of the Great and Good*. But that's not what I came to tell you.'

'What's that?'

'It may not be what you intended, and I'd never have done it if you hadn't forced it on me, but changing career has made me much happier.'

'Well, I'm glad. But why tell me?'

'Because you should do the same. It's the perfect time for you to do something for yourself.'

Ellie hesitated, expecting herself to tell Ffion to go to hell.

'How can I? You're talking rubbish. I'm a trained counsellor, I know about the phases of grief. I'm not ready.'

Ffion ploughed on regardless, doing her human icebreaker at the North Pole act. 'You've always been so smug about helping other people and caring about them, well start thinking about doing something for Ellie,' she said. 'Do you remember Ellie Bassett, a woman with a first class brain? Resuscitate her from a thirty year coma, why don't you? You've got to help yourself. Do anything you can—'

'I can't. It's too late to change now. I'm only qualified to do the job I do.'

My God, she's right, Ellie thought, I want a different life. But it's too difficult.

'Bollocks. You could set up an organisation to help the relatives of murder victims, you could do that. Campaign for something, to focus your anger. It doesn't matter what it is, just do something.'

'Oh, Ffion, go away,' Ellie said, sounding weary. 'Leave me alone.'

Ffion stubbed out her cigarette and closed the pack. 'You're probably right,' she said. 'I'm wasting my time. Saffron was murdered, Ellie, not you. You could help yourself, but you're not going to try, are you? God, that taxi cost me twenty quid to get here just for this.'

Ffion got up to go, but Ellie stopped her.

'You might as well have lunch now you're here,' she said. 'Recoup your losses, at least.' Then she added, 'Please stay, Ffion. I could do with the company. And another of your fags. Those Sweet Afton really take me back.'

'Any port in a storm, I suppose,' Ffion said, and sat down again.

29

On a foggy weekday morning in January, Hilary was standing alone in the graveyard of the small Catholic church in Dorchester-on-Thames, an ancient village near Oxford where the River Thame meets the Thames.

She was there to mark the anniversary of Howard's death.

The pretty village, with coaching inn and glorious Abbey, had not prepared Hilary for the desolation she felt at the sight of Howard's lonely grave.

The Thame had flooded after one of the wettest Decembers on record, and had not fully receded. Hilary had worn her stout walking shoes to visit the country, but she could feel the cold slimy water round her toes. Everything seemed bleak; the dripping trees, the yellowish mist clinging to the dying grass, the locked and unlit church.

She thought, I miss you so much, Howard. Nothing has gone right for any of us since you left us.

Howard's grave was not exactly neglected – if it had been, Hilary would undoubtedly have been in tears. The grass had been mown regularly, and there were no dying flowers in a pot full of foetid water left at the foot of the plain headstone. It was simply part of the faceless community of the dead in this discreet little cemetery close to the river, overhung by an ancient yew which dropped berries like drops of blood on the unpretentious graves beneath.

Someone might have come, Hilary told herself, Howard was our friend, they can't have forgotten. How quickly we lose sight of one another.

I can't blame them, she told herself. They had other things to do, moving on with their lives. Ffion was in America promoting that wretched book of hers. She was getting a lot of attention for it, in the newspapers and on television.

She'd probably forgotten Howard altogether, unless occasionally she put two fingers up at his memory and hoped that there was an afterlife so he could see how wrong he'd been about women, and her in particular.

Hilary even smiled to herself. Whoever said revenge is a dish best served cold couldn't possibly have meant as cold as Ffion's on Howard in this freezing graveyard.

Hilary hadn't expected Sandra to come. Even when they were at TCD she'd never come to terms with Howard's sexuality. She had never altogether escaped those old Paisleyite rantings about the works of the Anti-Christ.

Unless. Something momentous was happening to Sandra, Hilary knew that. A few months ago, when they'd shared one of their intermittent reunions under the clock at Waterloo Station, Hilary hadn't recognized her.

She still dyed her hair, but no longer platinum blonde. Now it was light brown, which looked like her natural colour. And she'd grown it longer, into a shoulder-length bob. She'd also moderated the eye makeup.

'What do you think?' she'd asked Hilary.

'Great. What happened to the teenage tearaway?'

'She grew up, I suppose. Aged forty-five. The truth is, I've met someone.'

'Sandra, you've never stopped meeting someones.'

'This is different. This one digs with the left foot. We're in love.'

People on the crowded station turned and stared as Hilary shrieked, 'You're going out with a Roman Catholic?'

Sandra took Hilary's arm and pulled her towards the Snack Bar. 'Shut the feck up, you'll get us arrested.'

Hilary smiled at the memory. No longer able to feel her feet in her sodden shoes, she looked at Howard's grave and thought, Unbelievable.

Hilary tried to remember the Papist Pal's name – that's what Sandra called him. She'd met him on the Shuttle flight to Belfast when she went back for her mother's funeral. The plane was crowded. They sat together and got into conversation when he offered her his newspaper to read.

The Papist's Pal had a small hotel and bar in Derry. Sandra pretended Derry was her destination too, and they travelled there together.

She missed her mother's funeral. 'Meeting him like that on the plane was a sign from her,' Sandra said. 'She saw the light on the other side, and she wanted me to leave the past behind and be happy.' She didn't say anything to Hilary, but she liked to imagine her father's face when she didn't turn up to lay her mother to rest. He may have been preparing to kill the fatted calf and welcome me back into the fold, she thought. And he couldn't even tell me never to darken his door again because I wasn't there.

To Hilary, for Sandra to date an RC was about as unlikely as Ian Paisley becoming a man of peace. At Howard's desolate grave, she thought it was a pity that Sandra's sudden enlightenment didn't cover her attitude to homosexuality; but, she thought, one step at a time. Which reminded her of her frozen feet.

She had brought a pot of pansies to plant on the grave. At least they would have a chance to survive in the ground. Loose flowers looked so dreadful when they died and no one came to take them away. The pansies with roots were an act of defiance against the acceptance of decay.

She knelt down and tried to loosen the soil with her hands so that she could press the plants into the soil, pulling the loose earth up round them.

It was harder than she'd expected and her fingers made no impression on the ground. Oh, God, she thought, I'll have to leave the pot as it is, I can't bury it.

Behind her, making her jump, a man said, 'Perhaps I can help you?'

Hilary got quickly to her feet. On her knees she felt at a distinct disadvantage in the presence of a stranger.

'Oh,' she said, 'I didn't know you were there.'

A well-dressed young man, good-looking - almost pretty - and giving an impression of gentleness, said, 'Your pansies are lovely. They were Howard's favourite flower. You are here for Howard, aren't you? Are we the only two who...?'

'Yes,' she said, 'yes I am.' She hesitated and then said quietly, 'I can't believe he's not alive anymore. Even after all this time, I can't believe that.'

The young man who, when she looked at him closely, was not as young as she'd first thought, nodded in agreement. 'I remember you,' he said. 'You're Hilary, aren't you? I'm sorry, I can't remember your surname.'

'Were you one of Howard's friends?'

'I hope so,' he said, 'I loved him.'

Hilary looked at him more closely. 'You were Andy, weren't you? I mean, you are Andy. Of course I remember you.'

He smiled and said, 'What's left of Andy, anyway.'

Hilary smiled. 'I'm sorry,' she said. 'You were with him for ages, weren't you, and then you disappeared. We thought you'd probably left him.' Too late, she tried to take back these words, with their insulting inference that he'd deserted Howard in his time of need. 'I didn't mean that how it sounded,' she said. 'We thought one of you had met someone else.'

Andy shook his head. 'You mean like Ellie's Patrick did? I remember how angry you and your friend Sandra were when I said I thought an affair would make Patrick more interesting – something like that, anyway.'

Hilary laughed, thrusting a wet strand of hair back inside her hood. 'I'll tell you a secret. I think with hindsight we were probably angry because we thought you just might have a point. What did happen to you and Howard?'

'He told me to go,' Andy said. 'He insisted. He said he'd fallen in love with someone else and, in the time left to him, he wanted to be with him. Not me. He told me to get out of his way.'

'So you left him?'

'I believed that's what he wanted. And I was terribly hurt, you know? I'd thought we'd be together to the end. It's not as though I didn't know what was involved. We all knew that. Everyone who was gay knew what to expect.'

The desolation in his voice made Hilary want to put her arms round him to comfort him, but she was afraid he might not like that.

He went on, 'I know now it wasn't true. He explained in a note they gave me after he died. He'd left it with his solicitor. He said he'd wanted me to get on with my life, not hang around nursing him for as long as it took. He wanted me to know he sent me away out of love.'

'Oh, I'm so sorry. For you both...' She tried to imagine what Andy must have felt. 'You'd have wanted to stay, wouldn't you? If he hadn't sent you away?'

'I thought that by being with him till the end I could show how much he meant to me. Why do people find it so hard to trust love?'

'I think because they don't see themselves as worthy of it.'

'You don't think the grand gesture of self-sacrifice is usually selfish?'

'He'd have been afraid of tying you down and spoiling your future. He must have known you loved him; don't you see that he showed that by sending you away. He wanted to prevent you devoting your life to him, but he knew you wanted to or he wouldn't have done it so -- so brutally.'

'He only had a few months; we could have been happy together.'

'It's so hard, making decisions based on the way you think other people feel.'

'Funny, that's what that woman Ffion said. The one none of you liked.'

'Ffion said that?'

'That's what Howard wrote in his note to me. He said Ffion went to see him and told him that he was a bloody fool to stop me doing what I really wanted to. She said he was a control freak and she should know what harm that could do after all the years she'd known Ellie.'

'Ellie? She made out Ellie of all people was a control freak? Honestly, that must be one of Ffion's weird jokes. Ellie's so not a control freak…'

Or is she? Hilary thought. She was with Patrick, perhaps, but somebody had to decide what he wanted for him. But then there was Dylan. Dylan who wanted more than anything to be a pop star. He had married an Australian girl and gone to live there with her to escape Ellie's pressure on him to get a regular job with a pension.

And Saffron? Saffron didn't get herself murdered to escape Ellie, it was ridiculous to think any such thing…

Andy was saying, 'It's academic now. But it did help that Howard told me. It made me think that he thought Ffion had a point, and he might've been wrong to turn me away. I hated the thought that he really believed I would thank him for "setting me free", as he put it.'

Hilary nodded. 'I feel close to him here. I'm glad he wasn't cremated. He will be at peace here.'

'Yes.' Then he added, 'I'm glad you came. Talking to you about this has made me feel so much better. Almost as if he's talking to me through you. Silly, isn't it, the way we clutch at straws?'

'I feel I've settled some unfinished business with him too. Now my memories of him can be happy. He risked a lot to help me once.'

They left the pansies in their pot at the foot of the headstone. Andy cleared out the rotting leaves that choked the vase and filled it with a bunch of white roses he'd brought with him. The smell of the roses was strong and sweet and filled Hilary with a sense of ease.

They walked out of the churchyard together. The church cat walked towards them purring a greeting.

'It's a peaceful place,' Andy said. 'I'm glad he's buried here.'

'Is it where his family come from? Is that why he's here.'

'It's near where his parents lived. It was their church. They were Catholics and I know his being gay made things difficult.'

Hilary caught her breath. She hadn't known that Howard was brought up Catholic. She was suddenly aware of what that meant, of the enormity of what he'd done for her; he risked his immortal soul by what he did. And in her head she begged God, Please forgive him, he was a good man.

Andy was saying, 'Howard always said he wanted to be buried in the country, where he could breathe pure air.'

'Oh,' she said, catching sight of her watch, 'I've got to go. I'm going to miss my train. I think we passed a hotel in the High Street. I can ring from there for a cab to take me to Didcot station.'

'No,' he said, 'please don't. I've got a car, I'm driving back to London alone. I'd be glad of your company. Please come to the hotel and we'll have a drink and something to eat and then we can wander around this historic village to say our goodbyes to Howard before we go back together to our daily lives.'

She smiled shyly at him. 'Yes, I'd like that,' she said. 'I think that's what Howard would like, too. He wouldn't want either of us to be left alone today.'

'Howard's wish is a great basis for making us friends, don't you think? We'll drink a toast to that.'

'That's nice,' Hilary said, 'one lost friendship leading to the birth of a new one. I'll be glad to drink to that.'

They went together through the arch where the stagecoaches used to go into the Inn to pick up passengers and change the horses.

As they went up the steps to the side door to the bar she thought, How charming it is. Just the sort of local for Howard.

Andy said, 'It's an interesting old place, this. Said to be haunted. But I don't know why.'

Hilary smiled and said, 'Well if it is, I'm sure he's a happy ghost, don't you think?'

30

Ffion walked out of Broadcasting House and stood for a moment on the pavement in Langham Place looking for a taxi.

The traffic was blocked solid in Portland Place and as far as she could see all the cabs waiting to move forward a few feet were taken.

Why do I do it? Ffion asked herself. All this effort for a few minutes making bright remarks on the bloody radio for practically no money. And for Radio Four, for God's sake! How many Radio Four listeners are going to buy *Sordid Secrets of the Great and Good* because of a few bright remarks at this hour of the morning?

The traffic lights went green, then red, then green again, and still the jammed vehicles did not move. She crossed the street and walked towards Oxford Street, turning often to check if there was a taxi in sight.

And then she was brought up short.

Coming towards her on the crowded pavement, Beverly's expression was as shocked as her own.

Ffion gasped and said, 'What are you doing here?'

She heard her own voice and immediately felt mortified. Of course it wasn't Beverly. What she'd seen was her own reflection in the plate glass shop window. The pedestrians she'd seen surrounding Beverly were actually reflections too, now looking askance at her and moving away from the madwoman amongst them.

Ffion was suddenly afraid to walk further. It might happen again; she couldn't bear to see herself as an exact replica of her mother, hard-faced, untouchable, and above all – old! My God, she thought, why didn't anyone tell me?

She went into a coffee bar and ordered an espresso. She sat on a stool in the window and fumbled for a cigarette. Smoking is ageing, she thought, and now I know it's true.

She lit it all the same. Her hands trembled. It's too late now, she told herself.

The coffee tasted disgusting. She couldn't drink it. But it was an excuse to sit unnoticed and pull herself together. What had happened had been a real shock to her.

My God, she thought, am I turning into her? I didn't recognize anything of myself in that woman in the bloody window, it was her in every detail. Do I really look like that? Even the way I walk, it looked like Beverly's walk.

Outside in the street, the traffic had begun to move freely at last. Ffion told herself, I must get home. I must change the way I look, have my hair cut, dye it even. I can't go anywhere or be seen by anyone till I've got some new clothes. I can't risk this ever happening to me again; I just can't.

Once home, she poured herself a stiff whisky. Once she'd drunk that, she'd get started on her rejuvenation.

The message light on the telephone was flashing when she went to start making calls. Impatient she pressed the play button.

The message asked her to contact the Australian Embassy. A Mr Holder, and an extension number.

Perhaps they want me to do a book tour over there, she thought. Though it did seem a bit odd. Usually the publisher arranged that sort of thing.

Mr Holder, when he answered his phone, didn't sound like the type who would be interested in *The Sordid Secrets of the Great and Good*. He sounded like the sort of man who might have gone to Geelong Grammar School with Prince Charles. Or maybe Rupert Murdoch.

Mr Holder had to tell her that her mother, Beverly Finlay, the famous dress designer, had died in Sydney, Australia. In view of her celebrity status, what did Ffion want done about releasing the news to the media?

Ffion, when she got her breath back, said, 'You'll have to give me a bit more information than that. How do I know this isn't a hoax? How did she die?'

Mr Holder didn't like giving her the details. He didn't sound like a man who dealt easily with emotional things. It seemed that Beverly had been strangled in a hotel bedroom in the second best hotel in Sydney.

'Do they know who did it?'

'It seems she had a male companion, a musician called Vaclav Novak. It's thought he killed her after a quarrel.'

Mr Holder added, 'He went straight out and threw himself off an approach span of the Sydney Harbour Bridge. That's why the police think he did it.'

'I know perfectly well why he did it. If I'd been shut in a hotel room with Beverly for any period of time, I'd have throttled her, too.'

Ffion thought Mr Holder's tone became rather vindictive as he said, 'When Novak jumped, he took a Stradivarius violin with him. That was smashed, I'm afraid.'

Ffion was shocked. She said, 'That violin is irreplaceable. Vaclav wasn't; there are plenty of musicians who play as well as he did. His Stradivarius? What a terrible thing to do. Also, that instrument was worth well over a million pounds, it was made in 1690 or something. Not that Vaclav could ever have afforded to buy it, some maestro who trained him as a kid left it to him in his will years ago.'

Mr Holder finished the call. He said, 'I'm sorry for your loss.' He sounded terribly insincere.

Ffion sat for some time looking out of the window at a patch of daffodil bulbs thrusting through the grass close to her garden wall. And the blossom was starting to come on an ornamental cherry. It would soon be Spring.

She thought, Imagine, I once thought I was in love with Vaclav. I must've been mad. She felt nothing. Not even curiosity.

Ffion didn't give Beverly a thought. She felt as though she'd just heard that a troublesome stalker who'd been a pest in the past had been put in jail for some other offence and would now be out of her life.

When Beverly's lawyer rang her later to tell her that she was her mother's sole beneficiary and asking how he should proceed, she said, 'What do you mean, proceed? Do what you usually do.'

The lawyer said, 'I mean about the body. Do you want her brought home? And will you be going to the funeral? There are arrangements to be made.'

'Then make them there, in Sydney,' she said. 'It's unhygienic to think of bringing a body all that way; and for why? Have her cremated.' She said as an afterthought, 'I shan't be going to the funeral.'

Then she said, 'Didn't she leave Vaclav anything?'

'Vaclav? Oh, her gentleman friend? No, she didn't mention him.'

'He should have stuck with me,' Ffion said, and she smiled; but of course the lawyer didn't know that.

A few days later Ellie rang up. She was nervous, not sure how Ffion was going to respond to commiserations.

'I read about your mother in the paper. I'm sorry,' Ellie said quickly, before Ffion had the chance to be off-putting.

Ellie could almost hear the shrug in Ffion's voice. 'She got what she deserved. And talking of that, have you thought any more about what I said to you the other day?'

Ellie would much rather have kept the plans she'd been making to herself. They might never happen. They probably never would. After that day when Ffion caught her watching *Neighbours* at home when she should have been at work, Ellie had let herself dream of things she would have liked to have done with her life.

She told herself, But it wouldn't be so different from what I did. I've done my best to help people, and I've had a good marriage. She stopped herself thinking the next thought, about her children, because she was afraid to ask herself the inevitable question, Had she loved them too much and driven them away from her? Why had they left her alone? Alone with only Patrick to care for.

She thought, I can almost hear Ffion telling me, 'It's a natural process. All children have to "kill" their parents if the kids are going to grow up and learn to live on their own. It's part of growing up.'

But Ellie couldn't see that. It's not true, she told herself, you reach a compromise, OK, and then you co-exist with them. And then you find a way of loving them in a slightly different way - almost as equals, if you like. You don't have to destroy them.

She thought, Can you love too much? Did I love Matt too much? For my own good, no; but for his good? I suppose I did; my love irritated him. If so, I was the one who got hurt. I've made a mess of my life so far, I've wasted so much.

But then Ffion made her realize she'd been given a second chance. And then she'd started to think what she would like to do with the rest of her life. If I ever find the courage to do anything different, she thought.

So now, on the telephone, she blurted out in answer to Ffion's question, 'Yes, I thought about what you said. I've got a plan.'

'You have? Seriously? What is it?'

Ellie was sure Ffion didn't believe her. Because she didn't quite believe it herself, she was defiant. 'It's something I'd be proud of. But it's not just me, Patrick would have to agree.'

'Don't be absurd, Ellie. Patrick's never stood in the way of anything you want to do.'

'Yes, he did. He wouldn't stop being in love with you.'

'That's because he never was in love with me; he only thought he was. You can't put a stop to a delusion, because it doesn't exist.'

'You're such a sea lawyer, Ffion. Do you want to hear my plan or not?'

'Go ahead, I'm all ears.'

'I want to open up this big old house of ours to as many young homeless girls in Hackney as we can pack in. They'll have a room they can make into a home and live here with us until they're ready to move on. Between us, Patrick and I can use our expertise to help them get on their feet.'

'Do you really think it'd work? What about funding it? You'll need a bit more than jumble sales and sponsored runs.'

So Ffion took her seriously, Ellie thought. She's interested. Ellie was encouraged.

'This house should be a family home, we'll all muck in together. When the girls get jobs I'm sure they'll contribute to the costs. We want to give them a new start in life. We'll all the part of a family.'

'What'll you do to bring them in, search the streets nights and go up to them and invite them back to yours?'

'I'm not worrying about that.'

'But Ellie, couldn't they be dangerous?'

'Of course not, they're children. They can only come here if they can show us they really want to try to change.'

'Why should they trust you? They'll think you're loonies, and a soft touch. And why do you think it's worth it? The world's falling apart, with the Gulf War and the collapse of the Soviet Union, and God knows what's going to happen… I mean, how can you believe you're going to make a positive difference by giving a few delinquent teenage tarts a place to stay?'

Ellie said, 'I think the only way forward is if individuals do what they can. That's what's happening in Ireland. Think what Mairead Maguire and Betty Williams and the other peace women have achieved there. There's no other way when the problems are so massive. We'll bring in as many girls of as many different ethnicities as possible...'

'Is there really such a word?'

Ellie hesitated. She could tell that Ffion was laughing at her, but she was too serious about this to give up. 'This is what I want to do,' she said. 'I believe that together Patrick and I can make it work. I really believe that.'

There was a pause. Then Ffion laughed. She said, 'Well, this is your lucky day. My mother left me money. Lots of it. I'll fund your project, as long as you call it something with her name in it – you know, something like the *Beverly Finlay Home for the Hopeless*. I'll set up a Trust and you can do what you want.'

Ellie's first thought was that Ffion was joking. It was cruel, but that was Ffion. She's probably more upset by her mother's death than she's letting on and she's taking out her grief on someone she knows is soft enough to forgive her, Ellie thought. And I do, in spite of myself.

Ellie said, sounding amused, 'Wouldn't that be wonderful. But why would you do a thing like that?'

'Why? Because of all the projects in the world Beverly would most hate her money to go to, it would be something like this. It's so not what Beverly would do and I'll enjoy thinking about that. You'd bloody well better make it work.'

And then Ellie believed her. She was overwhelmed; and also grateful that Ffion had made it possible for her to accept. She's made it seem as if I'm doing her the favour, she thought.

'You mean it, you'd really do this?'

'I don't want her dirty money. She never loved me, and that's fair enough. I knew where I stood with her. But having her money would humiliate me.'

'But…' Ellie started to say. Ffion ignored her.

She said, trying to explain, 'It's more than that. Beverly took it for granted that even long after I was on my own she had rights over me. Anything I achieved was her achievement too; anything I built– a career, a position; even my relationship with Vaclav – she took it as hers by right because she happened to be my mother. In spite of never delivering on being my mother.'

Ellie wanted to try to tell Ffion that her own mother had been the same, taking pleasure in Ellie's high spots, participating in her achievements through her pride in Ellie. But that didn't mean she was claiming them as though they were her own. And hadn't Mum always been there to listen, to advise, to guide? That wasn't possession, it was part of love. She wanted to say to Ffion, 'Perhaps you misunderstood'.

'I'm sorry,' Ellie said.

'Why?' Ffion frowned, and then she said, Your project will commemorate her as she would least want to be remembered, as a mother figure. What do you think?'

'We'll be grateful for the money, whatever the motive.'

Ffion laughed. She said, 'You know, it's weird, but people who've done me harm have come to bad ends. Is it some sort of divine retribution, do you think?'

'What on earth are you talking about?'

'Well, first Howard tried to mock what was important to me, and he dies of AIDS. And you tried to harm me and Saffron is killed. And then this happens to Beverly, who stole the only man I ever loved. And Vaclav, who betrayed me, he kills himself. Do you really think all those things can be coincidence? All my enemies punished…'

If this was Ffion's idea of a joke, Ellie felt like crying. She couldn't even say, 'I'm not your enemy,' because in a way she knew that she and Ffion could never be on the same side. But could Ffion really be so hard; surely she must be using flippant remarks to hide her true feelings?

'You know,' Ffion was saying, 'I can't help feeling that at the end Vaclav killed Beverly out of love for me. He must've read about my book in the papers, and it must have been overwhelming to realize that he'd made a terrible mistake all that time ago.'

Ellie thought, Or is the shock of grief making her temporarily insane?

Ellie said, 'Surely there could never have been anything between you and Vaclav after you found him in bed with Beverly and you broke his hand...'

'No, you're right, no one could forgive what he did.'

'Doesn't it occur to you that it'd be hard to forgive you for what you did? He never made it as a soloist; you probably ruined his career.'

From the sound of her voice, Ffion plainly thought Ellie was teasing. 'You're just jealous,' she said, 'no great musician is ever going to kill himself for love of you, never in a million years.'

Ellie dared to laugh then. 'So that's one thing we have in common then,' she said.

31

Ellie's voice was doing funny things on the phone, defying her efforts to sound calm. It was thin and wobbly and struggled to make any sound at all.

'Ffion, can you come? Patrick's in intensive care in Bart's, he's had a heart attack.'

Ffion did not bother to ask questions. She was sure Ellie wouldn't be able to tell her what had happened. Where was Patrick when he was struck down, what was his prognosis? Only those sort of details could tell her if Patrick was dying. But Ellie was beyond making that sort of judgement. As far as she was concerned, Patrick was about to be taken away from her, all hope for him was lost and she didn't know how to face the worst.

'Ellie, keep calm,' Ffion said. 'I'll come. Have you told Dylan?'

She thought, Why did she ring me? What's it got to do with me?

Ellie spoke in that thin, hoarse little voice of hers, 'I don't want Dylan. Please come, Ffion, please…'

Ffion swore under her breath. It had taken her over a week to work out what she wanted to say in the next section of the new book she was writing, and it was all there in her head, urgently needing to be written down. Any distraction and it would be gone.

'Bart's, you said? Where in Bart's?'

'The visitors' room for intensive care.'

'Wait there till I come. I'll be as quick as I can.'

Ffion put the phone down. The roof of her mouth was dry and her hands shook as she saved what she'd been writing on the computer screen and turned it off. Then she put on her coat, locked the door behind her, and flagged down a taxi.

In the back of the taxi, passing through familiar streets which had been the background to most of the significant events of the self-governing part of her life after Trinity, she knew without any doubt that Patrick was going to die. She was quite sure of it. Poor Patrick, he'd never had much luck. Between Ellie and herself he'd had a raw deal in life. She thought, I never tried to get to know him as a person; he came in useful from time to time, that's all.

She stared at the notice stuck to the partition between her and the driver: Thank You For Not Smoking.

She lit a cigarette. She smoked Gauloises now, it was getting harder to find Sweet Afton in London.

The driver slid back the glass.

'Can't you read?'

'So don't bloody thank me.'

'I've a good mind to turn you out.'

'Then you won't get a tip. For God's sake, man, my friend's dying in Bart's, stop wasting time.'

Grumbling under his breath, he drove on.

She thought, Patrick's the last of the men who've been part of all our lives since we left Trinity. First Matt, then Howard, and now him.'

And then she told herself, We'll scarcely notice, not even Ellie. Men don't count much anymore, they're more like a habit, really.

She said aloud, 'Not as bad as smoking, though.' But it's only what old women do, talking aloud to themselves, she added to herself.

The driver scowled at her in the rear view mirror.

She said, 'I'm getting old. Don't they say talking to yourself is the first sign of madness?'

At Bart's, on her way to intensive care, she thought, How ridiculous, what difference does it make in the scheme of things? But all the same, she couldn't believe what was happening. My God, she thought, can Patrick really die? Did he ever really live?

It had never occurred to her that such a thing could happen. Well, it could happen of course; in theory, it could. But not now, not yet, not to me, not in a tangible, foreseeable future, it was something to be dealt with when I reached that vague, unreal state of half-being called old age. Not even then to me. Matt's death had been an accident, or human error; Howard had died because he had a terminal disease; he had a terminal disease because he had put himself in the way of infection. It wasn't exactly his fault, but it was a predictable consequence of a decision of his. This was something unpredictable, a whim of Fate. There was no logical reason why Patrick should die now, against his will.

And then Ffion thought, Perhaps it isn't against his will. Perhaps he's had enough.

It's going to happen to me, she told herself. One day it will, but why not now? Why Patrick and not me? There'll be no one waiting for me in the intensive care waiting room; no one hurrying along the corridor to be a comforting presence in defiance of impersonal death.

Not that it'll make any difference to me, she thought. It doesn't change anything for Patrick that part of Ellie will die with him. The same with Hilary when Howard died. It's people who love the dying who suffer death.

She hurried along corridors where the staff had not yet taken down the Christmas decorations. The sight of the faces of the nurses frightened her as they passed, self-absorbed, concentrated, as though she, an outsider, did not exist. She glared at them in angry frustration, but they did not notice.

Ellie was sitting in the corner of the visitor's waiting room. She was alone, though the occasional tables in the room were littered with empty plastic coffee cups and polystyrene food cartons.

She looked up as Ffion came in. 'So you're here at last,' she said.

'Is there any news?'

'No, no one's come near me since before I rang you.'

'Do you want some coffee?'

'No, I don't want any bloody coffee.' Then she said, 'Oh, Ffion…'

'Don't start crying now, that's not going to help anybody.'

'I can't bear it, if I lose Patrick I don't know how to bear it.'

'You will. Men die before women because they can't survive without them. Women survive because they can. You've still got things to do.'

She looked at Ellie, who was blotchy-faced, her watery eyes brightly red-rimmed. The thought occurred to Ffion that it was a mercy Patrick could not see Ellie now, he would find no comfort in the sight of her.

'He may be all right. You shouldn't think the worst.'

'I can't help it. I've got to prepare myself.'

Ffion knew that this was the moment when she should take Ellie by the shoulders, pull her towards her, and give her a hug.

No. She didn't do it.

Ellie, watching Ffion struggling to find something to do to help her, knew what she was thinking. With something between a sob and a giggle, she stepped forward and clasped Ffion in her arms. She said, 'It's bad. It's very bad.'

'I'll get us coffee,' Ffion stepped back from Ellie's embrace.

'It's terrible stuff,' Ellie said. 'Perhaps we could go out and find a pub. They told me there won't be any news till he comes out of theatre. They're operating now.'

'What exactly has happened?'

'They've got my mobile number, they'll ring if they need me. I've got to get out of this place. The moment I came in here, I felt stripped of all my personality and identity. Everybody treats me as if I'm Greyfriars Bobby, a faithful little dog who wouldn't understand if they explained what's happening.'

'Just another non-person,' Ffion said. 'I know what you mean. The System Triumphant. Let's go.'

They fled like schoolgirls playing truant.

In a pub in Spitalfields, Ffion ordered Irish coffees and brought them over to the table where Ellie had sat down. Ellie had put her mobile phone on the table in front of her and stared at it as though daring it to ring.

'Now,' Ffion said, 'tell me.'

'There's not much to tell, except that he was at work and he had a heart attack and someone called an ambulance. I can't believe it, Patrick's never had anything wrong with him.'

She drank the Irish coffee, which left a creamy moustache on her top lip.

'All I can get out of the people at the hospital is po-faced stuff about years of smoking and drinking... honestly, the way the nurses treat me you'd think they were accusing me of deliberately poisoning him.'

'Had he been working too hard, anything like that?'

'No. Not really. He'd sort of buried himself in work a bit after Saffron. That upset him terribly. He's been busy with the Beverly project, of course. But Patrick and I didn't really talk much about that sort of thing. I suppose it might have helped if we'd been able to.'

'But that used to be the special thing about you and Patrick, you could tell each other anything.'

Including, she thought, about his 'affair' with me.

Ellie shrugged. 'Anyway, he'd got a bit silly with some of the students, you know, trying to prove he isn't past it, that sort of thing. One of the girls complained. 'What an idiot! Patrick, I mean, not the girl. But it was probably because he missed Saffron, you know, the father-daughter thing. He'd lost out on that.' Then Ffion added, 'That's pathetic.'

Ffion hadn't noticed the moment when Ellie began to cry. She didn't make a sound, or move, but suddenly as she sat there the tears started to trickle down her cheeks and drip off the point of her chin.

'Do you know what I think?' Ellie said. 'I think after that girl complained he was afraid that there was something wrong with him. You know, that he was a bad man.'

Ffion wanted to laugh, then stopped herself. Good God, a bad man! 'That's absurd, my God, how our stupid delusions make us suffer. Especially men.'

'If only he'd had mates to talk to. Men don't seem to have friends like we do, do they?' They've no one to tell them what they're doing to themselves. Patrick hadn't, anyway. Not like we have Sandra and Hilary – and each other.'

'Speak for yourself.'

But Ellie wasn't listening. She was still thinking of Patrick. She sounded very sad. She said, 'He lost confidence in himself. That was the trouble. And he didn't know how to deal with that. That's why he had the heart attack. I couldn't do anything to help him, I didn't know how to reach him anymore.'

Ffion wondered, Does she realize we're both talking about Patrick in the past tense?

Ellie stared at the Irish coffee, which was getting cold. Ffion tried not to look at her. She couldn't say what she was thinking, that that's where all Ellie's touchy-feely claptrap about love and caring got you, when it came down to it people weren't straight with each other.

The mobile phone started to ring and Ellie snatched it up to answer it.

'Yes,' she said, 'yes, I'll be there.'

She turned to Ffion, her face white as stone. 'The consultant wants to see me. We've got to get back at once.'

The urgent paraphernalia of death took over after that, but Ffion knew that at some point Ellie would have to come back to that conversation in the hospital.

That's good, Ffion thought, then it will be over between us. She's told me too much now about Patrick – and her – she's bound to hate me for it. We won't have to see each other again, ever. That's a relief.

But curiously she wasn't relieved. God knows why, she thought, but I'm going to miss Ellie.

It was a blustery April day, but not cold. Ffion stopped her taxi and decided to walk up Dalston Lane. She felt herself suddenly at one with the city. She sensed something fresh and invigorating in the air; something that had nothing to do with stale humanity.

The place suddenly had a life of its own. Everything seemed to be in motion; litter swirled across the pavement, and the surface of the puddles in the street rippled. An old billboard on an empty house waved in the gusts, desperately trying to draw attention to its tattered message: GOD IS LOVE. At the edge of cemented front gardens, defying overturned refuse bins and rusted pram and bicycle frames, bulbs were beginning to break through the crumbling surfaces. It's spring, she thought.

Ellie's house looked just the same. Ffion had expected something would have changed. How could the cataclysmic events in the life of that family home have happened and had no effect at least on the appearance of the building. Surely there should be some outward sign that Patrick was dead. But the St George's flag still hung in the window of one of the homeless girls; in another upstairs window a young woman sat at a computer in a purple bedroom; yet another, with her back to the open window, was following an exercise class on the television screen to Helen Reddy's *I Am Woman*.

God, Ffion thought, is that record still going strong? I remember doing exercises to that to flatten my stomach at Lotte Berk's Studio in the 1970s. I even remember the words.

She found herself singing along...*I am strong, I am invincible, I am woman...* And it seemed ironic that what had once been thought of as the anthem of liberated womanhood had ended up as a shortcut to the female body beautiful. There must be a moral in that sometime, Ffion told herself, but God knows what it is. I'll ask Ellie sometime, she'll work it out.

Ffion knocked at the front door and Ellie, looking just the same as she always had, give or take a stone or two, opened the door.

Ellie said, 'Oh, it's you. Come in.'

'I was passing.'

Ellie didn't pretend to believe her.

Following Ellie down the steps to the basement kitchen, Ffion was conscious that she was looking for signs of Patrick's absence. There were none.

Ellie opened a drawer in the big family table. Ffion couldn't help remembering Patrick's face when Ellie once said, "Saffion was conceived on that table."

'Here,' Ellie said, holding out a package wrapped in brown paper. 'I thought you'd like to have something of Patrick's. It's the watch his father gave him. It meant a lot to him.'

'I can't accept that, you know I can't. It's too personal, you should keep it. Dylan might want it one day.'

'I want you to have it.'

Ellie put out two mugs and started to make coffee. She said, 'It's all right, I've been thinking a lot about this. I want you to know. If Patrick hadn't fallen genuinely in love with you, and been rejected, he'd have started to have silly flings with students and young women way back. They wouldn't have meant anything much to him and that would have got me down, I know it would. What I'm trying to say is our marriage would've broken up years ago. So I'm grateful.'

'That doesn't sound like Patrick to me. He wasn't that stupid.'

Ellie finished making the coffee and they sat down opposite each other at the table. 'He'd have done it to prove he still could. It wouldn't have been much to do with me. But you've always said I'm a control freak, and I couldn't have borne the humiliation. Patrick's father made his mother's life a misery putting it about once he passed forty, that's why I don't want the watch.'

Ffion asked, 'Are you still going to take in those homeless girls?'

'Oh, yes, of course. As long as there's a need. That's what I do, fill a need. It's my purpose in life. Things will go on the same as before. That way I feel I'm still in charge of my life.'

She paused and then said, 'It's funny, isn't it? You and me, I mean. We both did what we set out to do, quite different things, and our starting points were poles apart, but we end up in more or less the same place.'

Ffion didn't like that. 'How do you mean?'

'We're both alone. I never dreamed I'd be alone, without a big family. Without any family at all…'

'And I always intended to be alone. But in a way I'm not. There's Vaclav's son…'

'Who's Vaclav's son? Nothing to do with you, I presume?'

Ffion laughed. 'No fear. His mother is some American bitch Vaclav went with when he was with Beverly. I liked that about the boy, he's solid proof Vaclav didn't love Beverly. Vaclav told him to come to see me.'

'Wow! What did he want?'

'What he could get, I suppose. I paid him to go away.'

'And did he?'

'Well, I thought he had. But he took it as a sort of challenge. When he earned enough to pay me back, he got in touch again. He's a theatre director in New Mexico or somewhere. I didn't take his money, but I liked him for offering. He rings me up sometimes to see if I'm still alive.'

'That's nice.'

'It is, actually. Surprisingly.'

'I wonder what he'll do when one day he rings and finds out you're dead?'

'Get in touch with my solicitor, I expect. Or I'll leave a note telling the solicitor to get in touch with him. He must hope I'll leave my money to him. Why else would he want to keep in touch?'

Ellie, Ffion noticed, didn't take issue with that. She thought, Do I really think that? It's never occurred to me before. Are people beginning to think of me in terms of death?

To her surprise, Ellie seemed to understand. She said, 'It's a chilling thought, isn't it?'

Ffion sighed. 'Do you remember, when we were young, how it seemed positively outlandish the way grown-ups planned their lives as a preparation for old age?'

'My parents did that. I think that's why they had so many kids, so they'd be sure to be looked after when they were past it.'

Ffion laughed. 'It was probably why culling girl babies at birth never caught on in this country; at least they'd come in useful as carers one day.'

'Honestly, Ffion…'

'Well our liberated generation visualizes men doing much the same for us. The ultimate function of kids and marriage is a protected old age. Yuck!'

'You made the right choice; you chose to stick to money.'

293

Ffion made a face. 'Of course we could always turn to religion.'

'That's one of the lessons Trinity taught me,' Ellie said. 'Everything I learned from living in Ireland told me to distrust God.'

Ffion's smouldering violet eyes lit up. 'That's it,' she cried.

'What's what?'

'That's the subject of my next book. Religion. Don't you see, Ellie, it's the challenge I've been waiting for all my life? I'm going to take on God!'

There was a pause as Ellie took this in. Then she said, 'Well, I guess the reports of our imminent superannuation have been exaggerated. There's life in us old bitches yet.'

And the rest of the morons out there had better not forget it, Ffion told herself. This is a fight to the death. Literally.

32

Hilary, in the train from Guildford to Waterloo, was wishing she hadn't agreed to go to what would be the final reunion of the 20th century for the former TCD flatmates.

Andy told her to go and enjoy herself. 'You'll regret it if you chicken out. It's kind of a day of reckoning.'

'It's different for you,' she said. 'You're too young to know what I'm talking about.'

'Poor old thing,' he said.

Outside Woking she caught a glimpse of gold through the trees lining the railway line. The minarets of the mosque always surprised her and made her happy that this so English suburban commuter town in Surrey so surprisingly contained the first such symbol of a much wider connection to other continents and cultures in the world.

Her whole life she'd been looking out of trains leaving Woking station, and the mosque had been there. It was the oldest in England, opened in the last decade of Victoria's reign. And yet, she thought, I never even noticed it until I went to Trinity. Perhaps they took some of the trees down. The first time I saw it, I thought it was a marquee for some sort of exotic exhibition. God, how blinkered we all were then.

Her uneasy feelings of shame for her former self fitted in now with her feelings about this Millennium reunion. It seemed to her to mark the start of old age. She thought, the Millennium isn't about a new century to me. It's the year I'll get to be sixty and an OAP, which means the end of life as I know it. Or rather, I and the people from Trinity who've been fellow-travellers will lose our life force.

She'd tried to explain to Andy. They were having breakfast together in the kitchen, as they did most days. Andy looked at her over the top of the *Guardian*. He said, 'It's just one day to another. You've still got your job and this house and your friends and family. Nothing will change. What's to be scared of?'

'The 21st century will be a new world where I won't feel I belong. From now on the only certain prospect I have is that I'll die in 2000 and something.'

She smiled, indicating she was having a senior moment and he wasn't to take any notice. She didn't want to talk about it. But, she told herself, he doesn't understand. The new Millennium can still be the start of something for him. For me it means becoming invisible.

Fundamentally optimistic, however, kind-hearted Hilary, by the time she got off the train at Waterloo and marched down the crowded platform to a Souza march over the tannoy, decided that it could be worse. She enjoyed her job as home editor of Wives and Mothers. She loved the cute cottage near Guildford that she shared with Andy – each with their own room, of course, like brother and sister. And she hadn't given up hope of catching up with Ireland now that Ireland had caught up with the modern world. She imagined it as being a bit like bringing up a child, nurturing it till adulthood and then visiting the adult and being proud of the job she'd done.

She told herself, Perhaps I will go back to Ireland, which defined my youth. It would be an act of defiance against the 21st century. Memory is an act of defiance.

But too many people had warned her she wouldn't know the place anymore; she wouldn't feel at home. She thought, first they warned me not to go because I was some sort of security risk, and now it's because Ireland might have changed so much it would be a risk to my sense of security.

It was a blustery day. On Waterloo Bridge she saw a young man in a long old-fashioned tweed coat leaning on the wall above the steps leading down to the Embankment. He reminded her of Howard, who had waited for her there the day he told her he had AIDS.

As she walked across the bridge, the wind whipped up miniature white horses on the river and set the string of barges moored close to the shore dancing like Michael Flatley's River Dancers. She would catch a bus to Islington from the Aldwych. She'd sit at the top of the bus; it would be fun to catch a glimpse of Fleet Street before the bus turned down Chancery Lane.

I wonder if I'll recognize it, she thought. The iconic national newspapers are all gone; the *Daily Telegraph* building and the *Express*'s Black Lubianka and all the other testimonials to our glory days have been abandoned to financial wide boys from the City. Only Reuters is still there at 85 Fleet Street; but for how long?

Hilary smiled to herself. I once dreamed of being London Editor of the *Irish Times*, she thought. As if, I was never even a real journalist; let alone a real Irishwoman. But I did meet an American girl from TCD who was in the London office; as Ffion used to say, nothing's impossible.

And then she thought, I hope she still does say things like that. If the old Ffion has changed that much the rest of us might as well give up.

She began to wonder if she would recognize her three flatmates from the Trinity years. She hadn't seen any of the others since she and Andy pooled their resources and bought the cottage. That was more than three years ago now.

She'd heard that Sandra and her Papist Pal had gone to live in America. Hilary presumed they wanted to escape the religious and political divide they'd never be allowed to forget in Belfast or Derry.

Hilary thought, But they won't escape; it's not the prejudice of the people round them, it's inside them both. Theirs was always a doomed love. Poor Sandra, she tried so hard to get free. And she thought she had when she broke away from her family. And then that boy, William Something or other, killed himself.

She told herself, It'll be good to see Sandra again, if she's back in England. And Ellie, of course. God knows, she's had the hell of a time the last few years, but I bet she hasn't changed. Hilary smiled. Ellie's probably still wearing the same clothes in the same mud colours as when I last saw her.

And Ffion?

When Ellie had rung Hilary to tell her about the reunion, she'd said something like 'she's still the same old Ffion, still going strong'. Hilary had been amazed to hear that for the first time Ffion would host the reunion.

'But why aren't you doing it. You always do,' she said.

'Ffion offered, and I said yes. I always had Patrick in the past. And I can't really explain, but I feel we're on the brink of something different… a new era.'

'You too?'

'Ffion herself wanted to acknowledge some sort of new departure. She said there are so few of us left we need to combine forces to face the feelings of uncertainty we must all be feeling as we're being swept aside by the young.'

'You don't have to explain. It'll be different, anyway. Should we bring anything – food or wine?'

'She said she'd get it off tax as part of publicity for *The Bully in the Playground*, which is the working title of her next book.'

'What's that about? Is she lifting the lid on the teaching profession?'

'No, I think she's cutting God down to size.'

Hilary laughed. 'Heavens, is she crazy?'

'Well, I suppose God can't sue.'

'He could hit her with lightning.'

Hilary smiled as she walked along Cloudesley Road towards Thornhill Square. She began to be glad that she had made the effort to come. London was so beautiful in October. Fallen red and gold leaves underfoot, and the roofs of parked cars wore them like jewels where they'd dropped spinning from the plane trees.

The three of them arrived at Ffion's flat together; Hilary on foot; Sandra in a black cab; Ellie by bicycle. It was only after the fuss of taking off their coats, and Ffion asking what they wanted to drink, that they had time to take each other in.

Ffion said, 'Do you remember that very first night in Trinity Hall we played the Truth Game? We don't have to play it now. The truth's only too obvious on all our faces.'

'We all still look like the same people,' Ellie said.

Do we? Hilary wondered. She didn't look like the Rev Dad's daughter now; she looked like her own mother.

And Sandra now looked like a drag queen, part clown, part showgirl, and too mature to convince as either. Hilary thought, Poor Sandra, she believed in forever love, and she took a punt on being happy and lost. That's what happens to gamblers.

'Where are you living now?' Sandra asked Hilary. 'When I came back from the States last year I tried to get hold of you at the flat but you'd moved on.

'I live near Guildford now. With Howard's Andy. You remember him, don't you? We've bought a cottage together with two cats called His and Hers.'

'But...'

'No, there's nothing like that. We're very happy the way we are.'

'Companions of the bosom,' Ellie said. 'Didn't someone say that about someone or other in your situation?'

Hilary asked Sandra, 'What's been happening to you?'

'I've given up on fecking men. At least I had one good one, that's some consolation.'

'I'm sorry.'

'Thanks. Anyway, I've been doing a computer course and I'm good at it. The world of work is opening up to me, what do you think of that?'

Ffion said, 'About time too.'

'What about you, Ellie?' Sandra sounded as though she only asked out of politeness, she already knew the answer – more of the same.

'Oh, I'm still scraping stray girls off the streets of Hackney and bringing them home with me to sort themselves out. I love it; I think I was born to care for troubled people.'

Ffion said under her breath, 'And if they weren't troubled, you treated them as though they were.'

Then realizing that they had heard her, she looked stricken. She said quickly, 'I expect you're wondering why you're here and not at Ellie's?'

They all watched her, expectant.

Hilary thought, The Truth Game would never even start to tell us what's gone on in her life. She's still beautiful, more beautiful really, with those cheekbones like Marlene Dietrich and those eyes; she's more striking because she's older and that kind of beauty is unexpected when youth's gone.

Sandra told herself, she's got the fecking money, of course Ffion can afford to look that good. It's a very good dye job, but you can tell she touches up her hair, and she must have a personal trainer to keep herself that fit-looking.

And Ellie wondered, what's gone wrong? She seems haunted. And her skin looks like she's holding a death mask in front of her face.

Ffion said, 'I'm not sure I know why myself. I think I want to reaffirm us as a group. I want to feel some of the old strength and support we used to get from each other. We were young together, and no one else we've ever known since has been young in quite the same way we were.'

Sandra said, 'What's brought this on? You never saw yourself as one of us, did you?'

Ffion said, 'Sod you, I'm not apologizing for anything.'

She went out to check on the food.

While she was out of the room, Hilary, sitting beside Sandra on the chain store sofa, looked around and said, 'This is the first time I've seen where Ffion lives.'

Sandra said, 'Does she really? Live here, I mean?'

Literal as ever, Hilary said, 'Of course she does. This is her address, I write it on a Christmas card every year.' Then she added, 'I must admit this place looks as though she's permanently thinking of putting it up for sale.'

Sandra looked around, judging the bland decor. 'You know, she could be working for the security services. This place is like a fecking safe house for a spy. There's no evidence of her, is there? Nothing personal at all; no Ffion fingerprints.'

Ellie said, 'But that's very her. It's everything I've always found rather frightening about Ffion: impersonal, clinical, a bit inhuman…alligatorish…'

'Whatever that fecking means,' Sandra said.

Hilary was relieved to hear that sign that the old Sandra had not quite disappeared under disappointed love.

Ffion came back into the room and sat down at the table set ready for the meal. She looked white and shaken, as though she'd had a shock.

Ellie said, 'What's happened, Ffion? Something got burned? Can we help?'

'No, no one can help.' Then she took a deep breath and said, 'I'm very sorry, I forgot to put the bloody food in the oven. I've put it on to cook now, but it won't be ready for at least an hour.'

There was a short silence and then Hilary said, 'Well, we all do things like that. I was talking about "senior moments" to Andy this very morning.'

'No, it's not that.' Ffion's violet eyes gazed at them as though she wasn't sure whether to trust them. Then she took out a blue pack of French cigarettes and lit one. 'I know what's wrong,' she said. 'I've been diagnosed with early onset Alzheimer's.'

There was a stunned silence.

Sandra broke it. 'So God's won,' she said. She sounded impressed at this evidence of the Power of The Lord. 'You announced you were going to challenge God in that fecking book of yours and this is His fecking answer.'

But Sandra was fighting back tears. She thought of Ffion, years ago now, coming to protect her from the dreadful woman policeman who wanted to put her in jail when the cops raided her lovely home in Romford and told her Derek Briggs was a big time crook.

I didn't even have to ask her, Sandra thought, I told her what was happening and she just automatically came and saved my life. Coming to think of it, she's the best fecking friend I've ever had.

Hilary was remembering how Ffion had gone round to see the terminally-ill Howard when, out of love, he'd told Andy to get out of his life. She was the one who made Howard believe how much Andy loved him.

I'm sure he died easier knowing that, Hilary told herself. No one asked her to do that, but underneath that hard veneer she's sensitive.

She thought, funny, even when we thought we didn't like her, we all relied on her.

Ellie was thinking of Saffron; and of the day of Patrick's death in Bart's when Ffion came to support her. And the money that kept her project with the wayward girls going to spite Beverly.

Ffion said, 'God hasn't won yet. I'll write the book.'

Ellie hesitated; then she got up and went to Ffion and sat down next to her at the table.

'When the time comes when you feel you don't want to be alone, you will come to live with me. There's plenty of room in my part of the house. I can look after you, and so will the girls.'

Ffion shook her head. 'I couldn't let you do that.'

'You must. That's how it has to end between us, in some sort of showdown. That's always been what women do, in the end their best achievement is to care for those they…'

She'd been going to say 'love', but looking at Ffion's face she didn't dare. 'For those who need them.'

'You can keep trying to convince me, but I won't change my view that that stuff is a weakness which turns women into victims of their own sentimental nature. I couldn't let that happen, even to you.'

Sandra went to Ffion and then thought better of hugging her. She said, 'There's plenty of time for you to finish your book, if that's what you want. If your hands are affected, you can write direct on to the computer. And if you can't, I can. You can dictate it to me.'

She added, 'You can pay me, then you won't feel guilty.'

Hilary said, 'We can't abandon you, we're part of each other's lives. You may not like it, but you're definitely a defining part of my past. Quite an important part, actually. That means we're part of each other for life, whatever happens.'

Hilary paused. That time in Howard's flat in Merrion Square was too important – she didn't dare think about it now.

She went on, You've always been what holds us together, Ffion. You were a defining part of our lives and we can't let you take that away from us.'

'Hey,' Ellie said, 'the food must be ready by now. Can I help you with the food, Ffion?'

Ffion looked from one to the other. Then she got up and said, 'It's lasagne. Don't dare anyone say I don't keep up the traditions of our past.'

There, I've said it, Ffion told herself. Our past indeed. Yuck!

But both Ellie and Hilary thought they saw tears in the violet eyes.

'Did you make it yourself?' Sandra sounded amazed, and a little wary.

Ffion laughed and said, 'Don't expect miracles. It's lasagne, isn't that enough for now?'

Senior moments, Hilary thought. Weren't they all thinking the same thought? We are, all of us, at last almost completely grownup.

At the table Ffion, tasting the lasagne, said, 'Yuck!'